THE
HOLLOW
WOMAN

THE HOLLOW WOMAN

Simon Ritchie

CHARLES SCRIBNER'S SONS

New York

Library of Congress Cataloging-in-Publication Data
Ritchie, Simon.
  The hollow woman.
  I. Title.
PR9199.3.R524H65   1986   813'.54   86-15479
ISBN 0-684-18702-7

Published simultaneously in Canada by Collier Macmillan
Canada, Inc.
Composition by Westchester Book Composition, Inc., Yorktown
Heights, New York
Manufactured by The Haddon Craftsmen, Inc., Scranton,
Pennsylvania
Designed by Jack Harrison
First Edition

For Rebecca and Jennifer

I should like to thank Michael Gilbert
for his support and encouragement,
Paula Diamond for her advice and enthusiasm,
and Betsy Rapoport for her careful help.

1

PAIN. I knew all about pain. I learned about pain when I lost my arm and found that monster clinging to the ends of my torn nerves instead. They had taught me that there is no choice and so there is no point in moaning and cowering. You can live with pain or you can die with pain; if you want to live, you must bear it.

I remembered I was Sisyphus, and once more at the bottom of the hill I put my shoulder to the oppressor and began the climb to the top. I had always done it. I would do it tomorrow, too.

When I opened my eyes I saw a yellow brick wall just outside the window. For a second I wished it had been the sky or a tree, not a wall, and the rock slipped against my skin making me gasp. I grimaced at the wall. It was a lovely wall. It was there. A fact. Someone coughed gently behind me, and I brought my head around too quickly. I thought I would vomit, so I closed my eyes tight. "Nausea?" inquired a man's soft voice.

"Mmmph," was all I could manage. I didn't dare nod.

"Tell me when it passes." There was time, his voice said; he could wait.

"—kay," I agreed. I heard the distant clatter of healing work in the corridor outside my room, and in the faraway halls a tinny voice broadcast the need for Dr. Simboy, or so it seemed. The sharpness and clarity of the sounds surprised me, but none of them had any real meaning.

I peeped, and the bedside table didn't move very much.

"Gone?"

"Almost," I said, and carefully walked my eyes over to where he sat. He was a large, round and doughy doctor. A white coat vainly tried to cover him, succeeding only along his arms and at the back of his neck. But he looked just right, as if none of his bulk was excess. You would never have called him a fat man, even though he was fat.

He smiled at me. "That's the concussion," he said. His face fell into prepared folds, and all of them turned up at the corners like happy mouths. He radiated plump contentment with an intensity that bordered on the fatuous, and I thought of Buddha. "I'm Levine," he said, and his dark eyebrows moved together in a quizzical frown. "And you are...?" He was a man gone fishing, as happy to wait as to catch.

"This is a test, isn't it?" I asked him. He increased the wattage in his beam and nodded. If it would make him even happier to know the answer, I wanted to tell him. For the smallest fraction of a second, I was terrified that I didn't know who I was; but when I spoke I said, "Jantarro. John Kenneth Galbraith Jantarro." With relief I realized that part of me, at least, knew. It sounded right, so I didn't think I was wrong.

"And now, Mr. Jantarro, do you know where you are?"

"Yes," I said and then immediately understood that that was not enough. "Hospital," I told him and was rewarded again with a blast of comforting warmth. "I've forgotten something," I declared, and I couldn't tell why I was suddenly concerned.

He nodded his head as smoothly as a buoy bobbing in a gentle swell. "You probably have. It will come back." He studied me for a bit and then said, "Would you like to try to remember?"

My heart was beating wildly and my mouth had gone dry. I knew I was at the edge of an abyss, a black hole, black like the ground around me. I would fall if I moved; I might be falling now. Panic shot throughout my body for no reason that my frightened mind could tell. "Yes," I made myself say.

"Good." He winked at me and turned his beatific face up to the ceiling, and I saw that even with his neck stretched he had double chins. Somehow the sight of his creased, ample flesh reassured me. If he could look away, perhaps I wouldn't disappear. His chins smiled blindly at me. "Cars," he said to the air. "What do you think of when you think of cars?"

"I don't drive—any more," I heard myself say.

"Is that so?" he asked, looking at me with interest.

"Yes," I said. Again, that wasn't enough. I could tell. I looked down at the stump where my left arm used to be. I thought of jail. My heartbeat accelerated once more, and in a rush I said, "I learned to do everything else—except tie my ties. But I couldn't learn how to drive. I put a spinner on the wheel—you know, like the kids used to use in the fifties. You can palm the wheel with one hand with a spinner except I can't and I kept driving into the curb—my car, I used to have a TR7, you know, red and I dropped a new engine into it and I used to do my own tune-ups." What in the world was I doing? He didn't care about my old car. I didn't care, for that matter. And the rabbit inside my head raced faster and faster, chased by nothing but itself. I

[3]

thought of waking up in the middle of the night and finding a record still spinning on my turntable, black vinyl, amplified click-ka-click click-ka-click, spinning. I wanted to shout, and I clamped my jaw shut so tight it hurt.

"It's all right," he said, touching his fingertips lightly to my forehead.

"I can't—" I said, feeling my jaw begin to wobble.

"You will."

"I can't control it."

"Yes," he said, his fingers staying on my skin, "I know."

"You're a shrink, aren't you?" Behind his veil of calm concern was a mask, and behind that another.

"Not really," he said. "Why?"

"Nasty profession."

"Nasty problems?"

"What are you if you're not a shrink?"

He appeared to consider my question seriously, sorting among various answers for the right one. With a sigh, he chose. "I'm a neuropsychiatrist," he said. The fact seemed to amaze him, for his eyes widened and his whole face lit up. "I study brain function," he told himself. "Mind, really." He took in air and held it for a while, eventually letting it out in a long, accepting breath. "That's what I am. What are you?"

"Investigator," I said, "private investigator." It was my turn to be surprised. I knew that was right, but I couldn't find one scrap of evidence in my head to back it up.

I must have looked annoyed, because he asked, "Nasty profession?"

Laughing like some other man, I said, "Yes, it sure as hell is." I began to cry even while I was making the last barks of laughter. If there had been a way I would have run as far as possible from the defective sack of meat and juice in which I was trapped; one of us would have run, at least—the one that was terrified. The rest of me was busy laughing, crying, breathing in and breathing out.

Levine took his hand away. "You've had a blow to your

head," he said calmly, "and so your brain has been shocked —physically insulted. I'm trying to assess the extent of the...insult."

"And?" I wiped my face with my good hand and dried it on the sheet.

"What is the extent?" I nodded carefully. "Hard to say," he replied. Then he chuckled. "That's easy to say, isn't it? And not very informative. Let's see if I can do better. All of your wiring is in working order. I know because your reflexes are fine. Your basic mental functioning is returning to normal." It seemed to me he laid a slight stress on the word "basic" and I cringed as though he had struck me. "Yes," he said. "You are experiencing some confusion and some difficulty in ordering your responses appropriately. But I don't see any reason to worry, and I'm the expert. You have a lifetime of what?—forty years?—behind you, and you can't escape that so easily as you imagine." He paused and drew a finger under his eye, following a crease in his skin. "Too bad, perhaps, but you were Jantarro"—his eyes sparkled—"and John Kenneth Galbraith Jantarro you shall be."

"Call me Cagey," I said abruptly.

"See?" he said, flipping over his plump hands. "Your nausea is natural and will pass fairly quickly if you stay still, as will the pain you are experiencing. I can tell from the tightness around your eyes. By the way, unless the pain becomes severe, I'd rather not give you any medication for it. Alters your responses and may mask important symptoms. So the only concern is your memory loss, and that isn't anything to worry about. Some temporary amnesia is common after concussion. You will remember." Again there was a slight stress, this time making it a suggestion and perhaps a gentle command. Smiles broke out on his face again. "A week's rest in the hospital will see you on your feet again in full possession of all your past life, whether you like it or not."

I heard him clearly; I was even interested, but only with a

part of my mind. Something very simple was wrong. I was missing something fundamental, like the baby who plays with his toes and doesn't know they belong to him. "A week," I heard myself say, "that's too long. I can't take a week. There isn't enough time."

He had drawn a chair forward, and now he leaned over me with a shiny object in his hand. He peeled back one of my eyelids and peered into my brain with a searchlight, looking for an insult. "Don't worry," he murmured, "it will all come back." His breath was warm and smelled of cinnamon. I wondered how he could have missed the rabbit, still fleeing in a circle. He let the lid fall and went in through my other eye. Maybe the rabbit was invisible, like Harvey. Out of sight, out of mind. Invisible, insane.

For the next two days I kept falling asleep in the oddest places. Once they found me dreaming away on the cold tiles of the bathroom floor, and they lectured me on the need to stay in bed. When I went to sleep in the elevator on the way down from my floor, they threatened to strap me in bed unless I behaved. Eventually they took away all of my clothes including my pajamas, figuring, I guess, that the sight of a big, naked, one-armed man making a break for freedom would cause enough fuss that they'd hear about it right away. And the craziest thing of it all was that I never wondered for a moment about the importance of trying to get out, even though I hadn't the slightest idea of where I was headed or why. I was like a windup toy, relentlessly pushed by a spring and stopped only by walls, an old-fashioned toy from my childhood, before they made them able to navigate and plan.

Most of the pain went away—or maybe I just got used to the daily trek up the hill with the boulder. This was the old Jantarro, the one who squeezed the pain down from his torn shoulder, along the phantom forearm and out past ghost fingertips—out into the world where it could become a thing to be borne and put away at night. Levine was right.

[6]

The old Jantarro was insistent. I had reconstructed my life to the point where I helped Glenda pack for Florida, kidding her about representing a man who had sold swampland to people who couldn't swim. I made a fuss about carrying her bags down to the limo that would take her to the airport, kissed her goodbye, and went back to my place. I remembered making coffee and wondering whether to do the hard or the easy crossword puzzle, but I went blank after that.

My nausea had passed off, except for those times when I fell over and shook up the jello again. I didn't go on crying jags any more, and I didn't laugh much either. And so long as I avoided the big, black hole in the ground, my heart kept me going at its normally sedate lub dub. "On the mend," as Levine put it, grinning so hard I thought he'd rupture something essential. According to him, most of my gray matter had slid off the west wall of my skull and was happily settling into its old ruts. Past meets present. Soon.

But however soon it would be, it was too slow for my feet. When they couldn't carry me, wrapped in a sheet, down the hall and toward the stairwells, they itched to do it. I actually got cramps in my thighs from the stop-go pressure I was putting on myself. Escaping, I thought. The old Jantarro had done time before the mistake was cleared up, and it seemed sensible that he'd want to break out of a situation as confining as this one was. But that didn't fit anything except my reasoning mind. The rest of me seemed to be headed somewhere in particular; and since it also seemed to be located in the vicinity of the black hole, my reasoning mind didn't want to know.

It didn't want to know, but it got told. I stepped back, out of the way of the woman who was maneuvering the lunch cart through my door; and the concrete-block wall brushed my arm, sending the hairs on it straight up like quills on a threatened porcupine. My cheek went to the wall of its own accord, caressing it, nuzzling it, feeling the memorable roughness. And I dropped through the hole.

• • •

[7]

It was an underground garage, smelling of damp concrete, gasoline and sharper odors that were male and fear, mingled with dust and trapped in corners. A strange blue light suffused the heavy air, and I knew it was the parking lot beneath the city hall. Only nearby sounds were carried to my ears, and the nearest one was a tapping on the glass beside me. Sharp as an etching, the words "safety glass" stood out in the corner of the window of the car in which I was sitting; and just above them, knocking to get in, was the gaping, black muzzle of a .357 Magnum. The worn leather on the rear seat was sticky, making it difficult for me to slide out. Yellow. The car. Their hair. His, straw-blond, straight, and falling limply from a part as white as a scar. Hers, nearly silver and spilled in coils on to her bomber jacket.

She was someone I knew and couldn't place, in spite of the fact that she was tall, lean, and as lovely as a woman can be when she's holding the arm of a man aiming a cannon at me. Her fingernails were long and purple in this pale, blue light; and she ran one gently down the side of his face to show us both that she belonged to him. He shrugged her away and waggled the gun to tell me to move. Even though I looked hard, I couldn't see anything in his eyes that might help me—no uncertainty or unwillingness, no pleasure at what was about to happen that might be turned against him. In his black cords and black turtleneck sweater he was no one, come to kill me.

He stayed on the other side of the car from me, pointing with the Magnum across the trunk at a stairwell in the far corner underneath a small, red exit sign. When I didn't move he raised the gun to my face, and I began to walk past him to the way out he had chosen for me. Overhead there was a muffled rumbling from the cars bringing the people to town, to fancy restaurants, to the movies, to anywhere at all. A furious itch tormented the end of my stump where it met the prosthesis, and in a ghostly counterpoint the cool air played through fingers I had lost three years before. Behind us I heard the dead thump of the car door shutting. I must have hesitated, because he shoved the barrel hard into the small of my back. I stumbled forward. We were half-way to the stairwell.

The squeal of power steering cut into the silence: some-one was locking his wheels into a tight turn. Then it stopped as abruptly as it had started. Four shuffling paces later, the squeal came again, and I knew there was a car on the down ramp. The growl of a big engine in low gear, and another shriek from the steering. Louder this time. Maybe only one floor above. I increased my pace and he said, "Stop." When I kept on going, he rushed me from behind and drove us forward into the pair of concrete pillars at the base of the ramp. The gun was rammed up into the soft spot at the nape of my neck, and my cheek kissed the ce-ment so hard I could taste it on my twisted lips. He levered my good arm up to my shoulder blades and breathed into my ear, "Still."

The lights from the descending car raked the ceiling at a crazy angle, and once more the power steering complained. Hidden behind the pillars, I tried to place the car on the ramp. My body was more compressed than ever, slackening the pressure from the gun a bit. What the hell. I sprang out along the rough face of the column and leaped on to the car. The gun went off.

"Good stuff," said Levine. "What else?"

My lunch was cold, and I pushed at the slice of pale meat beneath the slimy gravy. "I couldn't see the car," I said. Pork, maybe, I thought. Or turkey. "I mean, it was there and I know it was yellow, but when I try to picture it, there's nothing. Only pieces of it—the lid of the trunk, where it cut across his legs, and the inside of the back seat. How can that be?"

"Weird, isn't it?" he said. This sort of thing genuinely pleased him; his face made that clear.

"Maybe I dreamed it."

"Nah," he said, shaking his head. "You don't usually dream with your lunch, do you?"

"So why couldn't I see the car?"

"Perhaps you didn't want to."

"Why didn't I—"

"—want to? You're asking *me!* About what *you* want?" Fat smiles tumbled over his face, and his eyebrows shot up like two startled blackbirds.

I laughed. "Crazy, I guess."

"You bet," he said firmly. I sank the plastic fork into the mound of mashed potatoes. It went in easily. Quietly he asked, "Scared?"

I removed the fork. "You bet," I said.

2

I WOKE from a dream just before dawn the next morning. There was no light in the windows yet, but the glow from the hall seeped around my door and threw an angular slash along the wall across from me. I studied it for a while, the edge of an imaginary door. It didn't matter, I told myself, whether I remembered what had led me to the garage. I could go on being a private investigator without that knowledge, and cases would keep coming in the way they always had. If I could do it without an arm, I could do it missing one day from my life. I just got hit by a car. It happens all the time. And that would be that.

I flipped the pillow over to its cool side, settled my head carefully and determined to go back to sleep. But it didn't work. I wasn't tense or anxious, I was simply wide awake.

And the dream didn't evaporate the way that dreams usually do, retreating back into the warm, dark spaces they breed in; so, with nothing better to do, I ran it over in my mind.

I had been trapped in a big house with a dying man. The house wasn't at all like the house I had grown up in, but I thought of my father's house anyway, of the way I felt small in it even after I had reached six feet three, of the way each fragment of it spoke of the past—not prompting specific memories but, rather, memory itself. My father hadn't died at home as the man in my dream was about to. He'd been taken from the old-folks home in an ambulance and had died on the way. The man in my dreams was wrinkled like an apple doll, and there had been an odor about him, something neither pleasant nor unpleasant, only pronounced. I had discovered him by accident while I was looking for a way out of the house, emerging in his bedroom suddenly and feeling acutely embarrassed, as if I had happened on a private act. Lying with him in the bed were an old woman and a baby, but somehow they didn't belong. I turned to leave them in peace and found the woman and the child blocking the door. Both of them were crying noiselessly. I reached into my pocket and took out my wallet, looking for some money to offer them. It was then that I had woken up.

I rolled on to my right side and worked at getting my stump under the covers. Good old Oedipus, I thought. Even a blind man could have seen what my dream had been about. My eyes closed once more. To lull me I let my mind pick a piano piece to remember and run through. Piano music is my pacifier, my route to no-thought, my delight. It selected Schumann—something light and simple. In less than half a minute I was stuck on identifying the piece, and then when I had figured it was from his *Carnaval*, I went hunting for the passages that had the letters from his name hidden in them. I was on my back by this time, eyes wide open.

Another name popped into my head. Another German name. Georg, Fritz Georg. What had he written, I wondered? Slowly at first, then with increasing rapidity, large chunks of memory landed on my consciousness like bricks from a collapsing building. The house was his house. I had been there. He was the old, dying man—my client. Recollection was coming fast now, a jumble of sharp-edged events that threatened to flay me and bury me. My stomach rolled with nausea and my head ached horribly. I tried to grab on to something fixed, to get a purchase in all this confusion, but each time I gripped an image it fell away and another one replaced it. There was nothing to do but give myself over to the tumbling memories, to spin with their force, to join the pitch and yaw of remembering.

A large garden and a lawn so green in the sun it hurt my eyes to look at it, the smell of almonds and with it the impression of tapestries hung like pictures in a gallery, the crack of a syringe as it hit the bottom of an empty waste basket, boredom and anxiety mixed, the feel of a phone cradled against my ear—and with all these came the staccato bursts of two-way radio conversation, indistinct and wrapped in roaring noise. Money. Paper money—a tall stack of it and a plastic grocery bag—sat on a dining room table like a meal for a poor man. And then I remembered walking down a driveway of gravel that crunched underfoot. And before that I had taken a taxi from my apartment. And before that there had been the phone call.

It was the day Glenda left. I had thrashed around my apartment with nothing to do, feeling that all of this freedom should have made me happier than it actually did. I had read the bridge column in the paper, fretting over a strange convention for showing possession of the aces in the minor suits which looked like a great way to go down in five clubs. The phone rang and a man introduced himself as Fritz Georg.

"They have taken my wife and my child, Mr. Jantarro."

"When?"

"Three days ago."

"The police?"

"They...have been involved since the beginning."

"Why me, then?"

"I need someone—you—to stand by me. Tomorrow the note said they will be released if I pay." His German accent became more pronounced.

"Do you know who 'they' are?"

"No. Please, Mr. Jantarro. I will pay you well."

"I am not a good bystander," I had told him. "A lawyer might be better." I didn't believe it myself. With the exception of Glenda and her partner—my attorney—no attorney appeals to me.

"Please." He had said it like a man unaccustomed to the word.

I arrived early the next morning, paying off the cabbie at the gates at the end of the long driveway and waiting while the cop on guard radioed down to the house. It was a big, stone mansion; and although it seemed to have been built fairly recently it sat on the manicured grounds like an old Victorian dowager, squat, fat, and imposing. The cops ignored me, which was just fine by me until I discovered that my client had collapsed under the strain and been put to bed. His nurse or housekeeper was guarding his door, planting her stout, middle-aged frame in front of it and hanging on to the sides of her white dress as if for extra support.

"He is not well," she insisted.

"I'm sorry to hear that," I told her, and I explained again about his call and my reason for wanting to see him. The hall outside his bedroom was longer than the one on the ground floor, with dusty carpet underfoot instead of polished slate, and oil and vinegar portraits of severe people in place of the tapestries that hung like dead flags in the entranceway. The whole place smelled of almond extract. She looked off to the right as she made up her mind, conflicting urges twisting her plain face so hard it must have hurt. Without saying anything, she suddenly turned on her squeaky, crepe heel and opened the door, holding it for me to follow her in.

Fritz Georg was old. He was death minus a day old. A man in a tight black suit was just disposing of a syringe as I came in, wrapping it fastidiously in paper and letting it fall into the wastebasket. Georg's eyes swam through the chemical fog and found mine. "I'm Jantarro," I told him.

He lifted a hand a few inches off the covers and dropped it back. "Zhanarro," he said, and I nodded. He opened his mouth to speak again, but only a rattling snore came out. I watched as he sank deeper and deeper under the sea of tranquility. The doctor looked up at me. "Merweiss," he said, with a small formal bow, "Anton Merweiss." He picked up his patient's wrist and felt for a pulse. The woman put her hand on Georg's other hand, patting it gently. He seemed to be stretched between them, his skinny arms a length of old rope, frayed and ready to part. His head was a knot in the rope, all ridges of skull and shadowy declivities that led to the grave. He had no real flesh on his body, no lines on his face from laughing or worry, no color in his skin from the sun or strong drink. All the paraphernalia of living had been discarded in readiness. My client was only breath and bone.

I remembered going into the living room in search of someone who could tell me what was happening. They had a communication console set up in the middle of the room, manned by an earnest-looking boy wearing earphones and a tiny microphone that he kept adjusting in front of his lips. He spoke in a steady stream of low, almost inaudible tones, as if this were a golf game and he didn't want to disturb the players. It seemed to me he needn't have worried. Five cops in suits sat together in the motionless silence of a prayer group. And out on the lawn, a half dozen or so of the Emergency Task Force did push-ups beside their tented assault rifles. Nobody wanted to know about me.

In the kitchen I found a guy named Antonini drinking a

coffee and eating a tuna sandwich. He was in charge and he was full of himself. He was also young, so it was a forgivable sin; and I forgave him as soon as he started to spill a little on me. The housekeeper had got the note, opening it along with Georg's mail. No one had seen anybody delivering it. She had sat on the news for an hour while she made desperate efforts to find Georg, who had gone into town on business. Finally she had called the cops. The note was typed and simple: two-hundred-fifty thousand was the price, and a cab would come today to get the money. The bills were to be put in a Miracle Mart shopping bag. That was all it said. None of the usual stuff about no cops and no fooling around. No threats, no warnings. Just the plain demand. Antonini had done all the things a cop should do in this kind of situation. He had marked every bill in the two ten-inch stacks of fifties; he had unmarked cars scattered around the city and two helicopters chuffing over at the airport; and there was an array of bugs and tracers ready to remark on the location of the cab or any other vehicle that might be involved in the payoff. He was planning to catch the bad guys.

That bothered me. My client's best bet was to play it straight, to treat it like an unsavory business deal. Antonini's way, too much could go wrong, and wrong always means dead kidnap victims. I raised this possibility but he brushed it aside. He had a plan, he said. Men were standing by to impersonate the cab driver—fat ones, thin ones, black and brown ones. He'd have a man on the inside. That would make all the difference. He wiped fishy mayonnaise off his mouth and grinned. It was nine-thirty, and I spent the next hour trying to dissuade him to no avail.

And that was all I remembered. The kid from the console had come in to tell us that the cab had made it through the front gates, thirty minutes ahead of schedule. Antonini had grinned again, nervously this time, and we had got up to meet it. And then nothing. I lay there watching the light in the window go from gray to pink and from pink to white daylight, forcing myself to walk in my imagination out of Georg's kitchen and up the gloomy hall to the front door. But it was no good. Each time I opened it, there was no one there. I was making up fanciful cab drivers by the time I quit.

I was excited, though. The beginning was there and so was the end; all that was lacking were a few hours in between. I would leave the hospital today, I decided, and find those hours. What was the good of being an investigator if you couldn't do a little work for yourself every now and then? Excuse me, Ma'am. I wonder if I could ask you a few questions about myself.

I hummed a brighter Schumann tune and fished around in the closet for my fancy plastic arm—the one with all the neat little motors and myoelectric switches. My head hurt hardly at all, I told Levine when he did his rounds. He smiled as widely as if he'd just won the lottery and said we'd see in two more days.

"Feeling pretty cocky, huh?"

"Just closer to normal." I explained about the things I had remembered.

"Could you handle a visitor?" he asked, holding his head in his cupped hands. He looked like a boiled egg with a face drawn on it. "Seeing as how you're so frisky and all."

"Hell, yes. If whoever it is waits an hour or two, we can go out to lunch together. I want to have a shower and a shave."

"He's been waiting four days as it is," said Levine, "and I don't think lunch is on his agenda."

"I don't understand. Why the wait?"

"I told him he had to. You needed the time, the rest."

"Who is it?"

Levine traced a curved line from his mouth up to his ear, and he scratched at a bushy sideburn. "He's a police officer. Calls himself an acquaintance of yours. Bench. You know him?"

I knew him, all right. "Yes," I said, "I know Bench." We

[17]

went back to my beginnings in this business, Bench and I. We played games. He would try and get on any case I had that looked halfway interesting, and we'd race to the finish line. I'd won more than my share. Like the time the city hired me to figure out where most of their budget for roads and their public works commissioner had disappeared to. The cops had been at it for months. In two weeks, I found them both in the same place. That bothered him. Or the time the prostitutes hired me because the Curtis kid was gunning them down like clay pigeons and all the cops could do was tell them to stay off the streets at night. I was only a day or so ahead of him that time, but I got there first. That bothered him a lot. But still we got along as well as two people can when one of them is a public servant. Until he sent me to jail.

I lost my arm in the slam. And after that, something seemed to go out of the game. The board of inquiry cleared me and made him apologize. I didn't mind so much—about him. It wasn't really his fault, and I dealt with the people who were in fact to blame. But he took a real dislike to me and changed the rules. Now he makes life uncomfortable for me whenever he can. He was going to do it again today; I could tell.

"I can hold him off a bit longer if you want," said Levine.

"No," I told him, "I can handle it."

Levine shrugged. He paused at the door as if he wanted to add something but he just shrugged again and left. I lay back on the pillow, surprised that my head had begun to throb, and I wondered why I felt uneasy. Bench came in slowly, making a show of closing the door behind him, taking his time, being the fussy official. "I think," he said while he had his back to me, "you're in big trouble."

3

"WHY am I in big trouble, Bench?"

He turned from the door and considered me for a moment, no expression on his face. It always reminds me of a boxer's face—the boxer dog—with its squashed nose and blunt, pushed-out muzzle. Bench is a compact man, barely tall enough to be a cop; and if it weren't for his over-short hair and his funny little moustache, you might think he was an accountant because of the precise way he dresses and moves. The moustache is there to cover up a repaired harelip, and the cropped hair is his idea of the kind of military grooming that the police regs ought to require. His suits are all the same gray wool, his shirt is always white, and his tie is a plain, blue knit thing with a squared-off bottom that never hangs higher or lower than an inch above his belt.

Bench took a chair and placed it exactly parallel with the side of my bed, sitting down with deliberate slowness. He pinched the end of his pug nose. "Because, Jantarro," he said in that flat, nasal voice of his, "you'll be going inside again."

A ripple of anxiety made the hairs on my arm stand up. "That's nothing to joke about," I said. "You of all people should know that."

He shook his head, no, in two small measured moves. "I'm not joking," he said, and then he pressed his lips together so tight I could see the tiny scar between the hairs of his moustache. His gaze went down to his fingertips, and he held the pose for a second or two. "You know, Jantarro," he said abruptly, turning his hands around so he could look under his nails, "I never did want to bust you for that insurance thing. Not that I didn't think the evidence was good, because it was." There was no dirt under his nails—ever— but he picked at them anyway. "I was being sentimental, I guess. A guy like you, I figured, wouldn't do it." He looked up at me. "That sort of thing."

"It's okay," I said. "You already apologized."

Two lines of pink appeared on his cheeks, and the skin on his face went tight. He closed his eyes. "But I do want to bust you on this. Oh, Lord, I do. And do you know why?" He opened his eyes to see if I did. "Because you're a jerk-off, Jantarro, that's why. It's not even because you fucked up the Georg thing. I mean, that alone would do it, I reckon." He was speaking quietly. He leaned forward until his hands were gripping the edge of my bed and he thrust his face at me like a weapon. "It's because you're a jerk-off," he hissed.

I felt as if my feet were in shallow water. There was a sensation of cold clamminess that shouldn't have been there. It wouldn't go away when I moved. "How did I—? What went wrong with the Georg case?"

He wasn't going to answer me. He had a full agenda from his four days of waiting, and he wasn't taking questions from the floor. "You're a jerk-off because you think that cops are stupid. You piss on cops. You piss on me." He pumped the air in front of him, both hands spread out, palms down, suppressing something that lay between us. "She worked here—at St. Albans. Now, we know that. Only a jerk-off would think that we didn't. But Jantarro figures to play sick so he can slip inside and get on the fast track to Helene Georg and the cops will wind up with their mouths open in surprise when he pulls the monkey out of the hat. The cops will never guess." He looked at me with a genuinely pained expression. "You are an asshole." The water was up to my knees now, and my nuts had begun to retract. I didn't feel good at all.

"I was out for a day, maybe two, Bench. I still don't remember everything." There was something in my voice that made his lips curl. A whine, maybe.

"Yeah," he said, waving it away with an economical gesture of his fingers. "Doc Smiley told us." Doctors were jerk-offs too, apparently. The pain had crawled across my head and was trying to suck my right eyeball into my brain. I tried to struggle into a sitting position, but my arm wobbled and I almost tipped over. "Okay," he said, "that's one. Two is the way you sat like a smug little shit while Antonini did his job. Jantarro has a secret and it's something the dumb cops will never guess. They can run around and do their thing, but Jantarro is cool because he's going to bust the thing wide open all by his wonderful self. Like I said, a jerk-off. Too bad it blew up in your face. Too bad for the Georgs. Maybe it'll never be bad enough for you. But I'm going to try."

My right eye was tearing faster than I could clear it by blinking. I felt light and queasy, unreal. I was going to push back on him, let him know that he'd got it wrong about me; but as I searched for the words, he swam further and further away, until I lost him.

. . .

Antonini opened the Georg's front door, and over his shoulder I saw the cab crawl level with the porch and stop moving. The driver got out slowly. Antonini groaned. And it pleased me. It looked as if his little plan was in ruins; and now there was a chance that he would agree to play it straight—learn something from the driver, maybe use the marked money and wait till it surfaced—but basically let the swap go ahead. I wandered back into the big living room to pick a seat that would let me listen in on the grilling the driver would get.

Antonini played it wrong. He was mister tough, bullying and threatening. The only thing you get with that approach from most people is hostility, and with hostility you get distortions and half-truths meant to mislead. Screw-you-too-Jack is the attitude. I coughed, caught his eye and jerked my head toward the quiet corner by the big picture window. He was reluctant but he came.

"Stay out of it," he said as soon as he joined me. We were facing out onto the garden, a perfect Eden maintained by hired gardeners and untroubled by the presence of an Adam and Eve. Even though it was late October, most of the trees still had their leaves and there were blotches of color here and there like lumps on an artist's palette.

"Sure," I said to him. "No sweat. It's just that I thought if you wanted to tag-team it, I could be the soft guy." I was careful not to look at him. "Give me five minutes, maybe. You know, run around like you were in a killing mood and I was the only thing between you and dismemberment." A line of huge blue spruces bent their tips together in the breeze, catching the sun and shining like the spume off the sea.

He sighed deeply. "Why not," he said. "But only five. And I'm staying right here in the room."

"I want you to," I assured him.

"Five minutes," he repeated.

"My name is Jantarro," I told the driver with a smile,

[22]

"and I'm not a cop, so you don't have to answer my questions."

She looked at me with big eyes and ran the zipper of her bomber jacket up and down nervously. It was a wonder she didn't catch her long, platinum hair in it, because it hung loose past her shoulders. "So what are you, then?" She was trying to be tough herself.

"Do you know what's going on here?" I asked her. She shook her head and gave Antonini a mean look. "Well, it's like this. The man who owns this place"—I waved the plastic, left hand in front of me—"has lost his wife and kid. Somebody kidnapped them and wants money in exchange. The note we got said that a cab would come to take the money to the payoff. It was supposed to be at eleven. You're a little early, but I think that's you." I smiled at her again. It was easy to do.

Her shoulders dropped and she got a disgusted look on her face. "Why the fuck didn't anybody tell me?" she asked. "That's different. I thought it was...like a drug thing. You know?"

"Tell me about it," I said, and I sat down on the couch next to her, my big knee next to her shapely knee. Her jeans couldn't have been any tighter.

It was plain sailing after that. She screwed up her eyes in concentration and played back everything she knew like a tape recorder. She did the night shift. When she quit, she always went to a greasy spoon called Charlie's for a coffee and a little chit-chat. This morning—about six, six-thirty —she got a call there and was told to look behind the phone, where she found a note offering her fifty bucks if she did what the note said. There was another fifty in the envelope just for reading the note. No, she wouldn't recognize the voice again—just a man's voice, quiet, level. Educated, maybe. Yes, anybody could have known she was at Charlie's. There weren't any other cabbies who looked like her; all anyone would have to do was ask around; all the drivers in town knew her. The note? No, she had thrown it away. But she remembered exactly what it said. For a hundred bucks you do that, get it right. It was easy. Be here at eleven. Pick up a parcel. Take it to the TD Centre, to the base of the elevators that go up to the top floors—from forty-five to sixty—and wait. When somebody calls for a package for Gilchrist—spelled like Jesus, you know?—give it to him. That's it. An easy hundred. Worth staying awake for. Figured it was drugs, what with the note and all. And could she have the fifty, please?

While Antonini went over the ground again, I slipped outside for a look at the yellow cab. A couple of ETF guys were fitting a beeper under the rear bumper and another one inside the interior light. I grinned at them and they let their eyes slip down me as if I were as interesting as a block of ice. I peered into the front seat. A pair of mirrored sunglasses stared blankly at me from the dashboard, and next to them was a pack of Rothmans and a green Bic lighter. The usual clipboard was on the front seat, a pencil dangling over the edge from a string tied to the metal clip. She had a plastic St. Christopher glued to the top of her meter, and below it a couple of driving gloves prayed silently.

The ETF men backed off a bit and I opened the rear door. No one jumped on me so I stuck my head inside. She was Ellie Peters, according to the cab license that hung from the back of the driver's seat in its neat little plastic envelope, and in the picture she was wearing a frilly blouse that made her look like a country and western singer. I flicked the edges of the plastic laminate with my good thumb and they seemed okay—tight, but not brand new—but these things are easy to fake. My hand went down behind the seat and found nothing but grit; there was nothing under the floor mats; and in the front I found two gum wrappers and a full ashtray. I wasn't looking for anything special, since this was the car that was supposed to pick up the package, not deliver anything. But if you don't look, you don't find; so I checked out everything I could.

Antonini had called the dispatcher, I learned when I went

back inside the house, and he had assured us that this was indeed Ellie Peters. It was time. I watched while a nervous young cop in a new suit carefully loaded the money into the shopping bag and held it out for her to take. She pushed hair out of her face and grinned at us all. "Hey," she said, "how about this." The cop's arm was drooping.

"A receipt," I said, making it light. "I think she should sign a receipt." The cop with the bag let his arm fall. She looked surprised and a little apprehensive. I got a pen and a piece of notepaper from my pocket, giving them to her as I said, "Just write, 'received from Mr. Georg two-hundred-fifty thousand dollars for delivery,' and put the date on it and sign it. The lawyers will want it in court," I told Antonini confidently. He didn't say anything, so she did as I had told her. I read the thing, smiled, folded it and put it in my pocket. "Make the messenger at the TD Centre give you one too," I advised her.

We all stood in silence for a minute, the young cop with his heavy load, Ellie Peters looking at it and looking away again, Antonini with a nervous smile stuck on his face, and I, thinking.

"I'm scared," she announced.

"Yeah," I said. I went and got a vase of asters from the sideboard and handed her the whole thing. "Here, take one for luck." She chose a purple flower and stuffed it down inside her jacket. I put the vase on the sideboard again.

"Let's go," Antonini said. She took the bag, swung it experimentally and walked out to the cab.

I rode with the young cop, and Antonini went with a couple of his older men. The idea was to arrive at the big tower about fifteen minutes ahead of her, so we could get positioned along with the rest of the cops who would be crawling all through the complex by now. She drove alone. It was the best way to handle it; a man inside with her would have been too much of a risk. Besides, she was tracked by cars in front of her, behind her and on all the parallel streets. She wasn't going to get lost.

[25]

The TD Centre is a giant, black erection of glass as soulless as it is possible for a building to be, and this unnatural tower of offices rises up from a barren concrete-slab plaza. It was lunchtime when we got there; and men and women dressed for the denatured stillness of offices plunged out of the revolving doors to scurry across the windswept desert in the daily noon frenzy. It was a good time for a payoff. Antonini and his men forced their way through the crowd and disappeared into the building. I lingered outside, along with three other men I recognized as cops and one I wasn't sure about. Then we waited. The wind tore at my pant legs and threw dirt in my face; people barged into me and didn't apologize; I stayed still and tried to make up my mind how to handle it.

When it happened, it went so fast that I almost got sucked into the surge of officials who ran for the tower. Ellie Peters drew up with a squeal of brakes and left the cab at the curb, blocking one lane of traffic. She got out on the passenger side and bounced into the tower looking jaunty and not the least bit scared. Right on her tail, the three lingering cops disappeared through the revolving doors one after another like stooges in a magic act. Brown Plymouths began to pile up at the side of the road behind the cab, disgorging men in suits who made for the building on the run. Things were beginning to get a bit crowded at the entrance and the outflow had slowed to a trickle, making me wonder if Antonini had tried to hold everyone inside. It would take till Christmas to get everyone's name, let alone anything useful.

I had dirt between my teeth now, and I knew what I was going to do. The man I wasn't sure about was a cop, and he stopped me when I got close to Ellie Peters's cab. "I'm sorry, sir," he said, "it's taken."

"It's all right," I told him. "They want you inside." I kept my plastic hand tucked into my jacket pocket, because there aren't too many one-armed cops. He looked skeptical. "Antonini says to move it," I shouted above the wind and the cacophony of horns protesting the loss of driving room. "They've got them bottled up in there and the crowd's going nuts." I pointed to the base of the tower where a mob was gathering at the barred entrance. He danced a bit, uncertain, and then hoofed it to where the action was. I opened the back door and slid into the cab.

I watched her slip out of the tower door and cut her way through the crowd, neat and unhurried. Because she was only the delivery girl, she was the one person Antonini would let past him. And anyway, he knew where to find her if he needed to. She didn't see me until she was in the driver's seat and I said, "Taxi?"

The color drained out of her face and her mouth fell open. "Oh," she managed, finally. "You."

"Me," I agreed. Another thirty seconds went by. "I think you'd better go," I told her. "I'll explain as you drive." As if in a trance, she twisted the key, put the cab in gear and moved out into traffic. "It's under the front seat, isn't it? Matching Miracle Mart bags." She didn't say anything. We almost sideswiped a couple of parked cars as she wandered across lanes trying to get a grip on things. "It's okay," I said. "You were pretty good. It was really your handwriting that did it. It didn't match what was on the trip sheet. Hard to think of everything." She had speeded up, taking corners too fast and fishtailing a little, jumping reds—going nowhere. "I just want to see that Georg gets his family back. I don't care about the quarter of a million. He doesn't care about it. I'm along for the ride just to see that he gets what he's paid for. That's fair, isn't it?" I thought about the clerk on the fiftieth floor who was right now opening up a Miracle Mart bag full of plain paper strips and wondering what the hell all the cops were doing there.

She had made up her mind. She drove purposefully now, no slewing or jerky stops. In a minute we were sailing down the ramp into the parking lot under city hall, spiralling down to where it was quiet and private. "Okay," she said at last, "let's talk." She killed the engine and turned around to smile at me. I got to explain it all one more time before the Magnum tapped on the window.

"Jesus," I said.

Bench asked levelly, "Want me to get a nurse?" It was a request for information, devoid of concern, and in his place I would have been as cool. I had screwed up royally. There were no two ways about it. The fact that Antonini had missed a dozen bets didn't make me feel any better. Sure, he should have found the bag of blank paper under the front seat, he should have checked her out more thoroughly than he did, he should have kept her under his wing even after she had given the bag to the messenger in the TD Centre. None of that made me look less sloppy. Lying in bed under Bench's icy gaze, I couldn't imagine how I had been so stupid as to let her lead me right into a trap. I even wondered whether I should have tried to play it alone. That's how guilty I felt.

"Well?" asked Bench. "You want that nurse?"

"No," I told him, "I can handle it."

"Me, I wouldn't figure you to be able to take a decent shit by yourself."

"Do you want to know what happened, or do you want to dump on me some more?" As I heard myself ask, I realized I didn't much care which option he chose. But he wanted to know, so I told him everything.

"The receipt?" he asked. "You still have it?"

"I don't know. If I do, it's in my jacket." He got up and looked in the closet, shaking his head as he came back. He had a thoroughly disgusted look on his face.

"That's the lot, then?"

"Yes." I tried to think. "You in charge now?" I asked him.

"What do you think I'm doing here?"

"That was going to be my next question. Are you going to arrest me?" I watched the emotions war on his face. I knew what he was debating. If he did charge me, it might only result in a lot of bad publicity for the department: "Private cop shows up force, gets charged for pains." That sort of thing.

"I want to," he said.

"I know you do."

"I don't give a fuck what you know, Jantarro. Not from now on. I'm running this thing now, and if you get in my way I'll..." He got up abruptly and left before he finished his thought. I had a rough idea of what he meant.

4

I SIGNED MYSELF OUT the next morning and took a long time getting down to the street. Then I stood on the sidewalk and let the honking and squealing of the angry traffic push at my aching head, while I considered my options. There weren't any, of course; but it required a good ten minutes for me to see that. And for me to see that just because I had a bruised conscience I didn't have the right to go around feeling sorry for myself. I was alive and I wasn't in jail. Those are the two main things in my business. In fact, I was pretty lucky because I might still have a client, and in order to find out if that was so I was going to have to move. I wasted another couple of minutes thinking up how I could apologize—or explain—and then I sighed up a lungful of car exhaust and shuffled around the corner to the cab stand at Victoria and Oakland.

I made the first driver in line put down his newspaper and take me to work. If he talked to me on the way, I didn't hear. In fact, the only things I did notice were that I had a greenish smear of dirt on the pocket of my jacket and that at a certain point the sidewalks vanished and the houses retreated further from the road. I sank back into the seat and contemplated the inside of my eyelids after that.

"This it?" the cabbie asked. I told him it was and wondered for a moment whether I should ask him to wait, but I decided it was just my cowardice and sent him back downtown with ten bucks of my money. All by myself I climbed the steps to see my client.

The bell chimed solemnly—it tolled, I thought—and I noticed how rough the stones of the house looked in this gray light. I saw that the house was as oppressive as a prison, dense and forbidding, and I was afraid that I once knew that but had forgotten it. I pushed the button again, and the door opened before the sound inside died away. "My name is Jantarro," I said a little too loudly. "I would like to talk to Mr. Georg."

The maid, whom I hadn't met last time, said nothing but stepped back to let me in. The beefy woman in white was trundling up the hall towards us, disapproval radiating from her like heat from a fire. "It's all right, Eva," she said to the maid. "I'll deal with Mr. Jantarro." The maid gave me a quick look and scuttled off. Mr. Georg's nursekeeper tilted her head back to meet my eyes directly. "We thought you had gone," she said.

"Yes," I replied. "Mr. Georg?"

She paused, uncertain, pursing her lips and tugging sharply at her clothing.

"You will upset him," she declared.

"It would upset him more if he didn't hear what I have to say."

[31]

Her eyes turned suddenly keen and she drew her dress tight around her in a protective gesture. "You have news of the woman? His wife and son?"

"I have a report to make to my client," I said and began to move toward her, feeling a little like a character dropped into a Wagnerian failure. The long hall of wood paneling seemed phonier than it had the last time and the tapestries had clearly been loomed on some machine in post-war Belgium. The scent was more like cyanide than almonds, and it made my head throb.

It might have come to a tussle if a voice from behind her hadn't called out, *"Was machst du da den, Renate?"* It was a peevish sound, nearly querulous and nearly weepy. She let out a burst of German and used my name. Georg came into the light, frowned at her and said something severe. His tone had deepened and now had the edge of command to it. "Please, Mr. Jantarro, do come in," he said to me. I couldn't tell from the end of the hall if he welcomed my visit or if he was just being polite.

He turned and, propped on a walking stick, went back into the living room. I followed his shrunken figure across the fine Oriental carpets toward the big window at the other end of the room. Under the leaden sky the garden lost its color, and seen through the window it might have been a set in a boring black and white documentary. I imagined that when the director shouted, "Action!" not a single thing would change.

Georg backed up against an armchair on which cushions were piled high, and slowly he bent his knees until the place where his buttocks should be met the padding for his bones. "I must apologize," he said as soon as he was perched, "for not being able to greet you the last time we met." His eyes were watery and pale blue, the color of washed-out denim, but they held steady as they fixed on mine.

"You managed," I told him. I sat on the edge of a chair facing his. "You had other things on your mind."

[32]

"Yes," he said with a little hiss at the end. Silence seeped through the glass from the garden and surrounded us, I, stiff as a West Point cadet, and he, an ancient child in a high-chair holding his breath. We would die here, immobile and wan, and people would come to give us a desultory dusting from time to time. And nothing would ever happen. Suddenly he said, "*Es ist niemand im Haus, Herbst in Zimmern.*" It was as if a parrot had burst forth in speech.

"I beg your pardon," I said.

"You do not speak German, Mr. Jantarro?"

I thought of high school and the silly books with dry, rust-red covers. I recalled what was supposed to pass for conversation in them: Stops the bus here? How comes one to the marketplace? "No," I said, "I'm afraid I don't."

"That was Trakl, a melancholy poet of my youth. Death and bats and ravens, he liked to write about. It seemed less...less romantic then. The lines I quoted could be translated this way: 'No one is at home; autumn in the rooms.' It describes how I feel."

"I understand," I said.

He peered at me through the rheum on his eyes. "I believe that you do," he said.

I took a breath and he turned his head away. "Do you know what happened?" I asked him.

"The police have told me what it is that they know, but of you they have not spoken at all. When I asked, they said that they could not be responsible for your movements." His head was coming round to me again, and I saw a faint smile escaping from his mouth.

So I told him what had happened—everything I remembered. I had agreed with myself that they were basically one and the same thing. When I finished, he seemed to have shrunk even more, and for a minute or two he said nothing but only moved around inside his clothing a bit. I thought of dried leaves in a burlap bag. I said, "I'm sorry," and despised myself for the weakness of it.

His hand gave a little flutter, and his shoulders twitched

in what might have been a shrug. "You needn't be," he said. Once more his gaze drifted out of the window, and I was afraid he would leave me here to suffocate in the thick air. After a long time, he said, "You will need a photograph, if you are to find them."

I let out an old, stale breath. "I've got one. The police had lots of copies." I brought it out of my inside pocket and put it on the table between us. He turned to look down.

Georg said, "I am almost eighty." Helene Georg gazed up at us, eyes set wide in a triangular face, round and dark above high cheekbones. "We are from the Alsace. All of us." Her brow was unlined, and the way her face was lit for the photograph made her skin seem translucent. In the shadows her eyes were caves in a high ridge of quartz. "Helene is fifty-six," said Georg. Incredible. She looked twenty years younger than that. Light and dark, open and hidden, beautiful and enthralling. "In English, people always say 'Alsatian' but that makes them think of guard dogs and camps. I say 'from the Alsace.' Helene was fifteen when I married her. Nineteen-forty-six. My memory is still very good." He stopped as if to test himself on some difficult piece of history. "My son was born just after that," he said.

Hugo Georg was another proposition altogether. They had put a suit on him for the picture. A white shirt and a tie. His black hair was combed into straight rows and looked as if it had been wetted to hold it down. It was a recent picture so he would be in his late thirties, I calculated. That was an age when you had children, worried about paying off the mortgage and getting bald. Too much squash playing hurts the knees, the job is beginning to pall, and your wife is developing new failings.

Retarded is the wrong word for it, I decided. There was a quality of otherness in Hugo's face that declared quite clearly he was not just running late on the same line. He was moon-faced, distant from us by a quarter of a million miles, and shining for no earthly reason. No mundane con-

cerns had etched lines of character into his skin, no awareness of what it meant to pose for the camera had made him
assume an expression. Hugo simply was.

"Mr. Georg," I said. "Was there any warning? Had anyone threatened you?"

He turned to face me. "Are they still alive? Tell me, Mr.
Jantarro. I must know. Are they still alive?"

I waited without speaking. They had been taken three
days before the payoff was made, and it had been another
four since then. They might be alive. Stranger things had
happened. "I have a lot of ground to catch up on," I told
him, "if I'm to do anything useful. I need information. You
have to answer my questions."

"*Jawohl,*" he said without any irony. He made an effort
to hold himself straighter.

"Was there any warning? Did anyone give you any reason to suspect that something like this would happen?" He
just shook his head. "Did anyone notice strangers hanging
around the house—the property—before the kidnapping?
Someone who looked suspicious or who shouldn't have
been there?"

"The police—" he began.

"I know," I said. "The police have been all over this before." His eyes had glazed over. I was losing him. It was
like trying to talk to an overtired child. "Look," I said,
placing my hand on his knee. It was frightening how in-
substantial he felt. "Look, it may not be worth it. The
police are doing their job, and they have a small army of
men. Maybe one more man won't make any difference."
For some reason I didn't believe a word I said.

"No!" he said. He looked alarmed. "You must do it. You
must try to find them. The police will try, of course,
but..." The peevish sound was back in his voice. "I cannot
simply leave the fate of my family to public officials. I
must do what I can. That is why I hired you, and so you
must try. You are...you are me in this matter, my legs, my
brain, my...force. Simply to sit and wait would be intolera-

ble." He sent his tongue out to moisten his lips and perhaps to taste what he was about to say. "You must keep me informed. You must tell me as soon as you learn anything. Before you tell anyone else."

This was nothing new. Most clients want to use me as an extension of themselves and to buy the copyright on what I find. And I told him what I always tell them. "You are my client. I work for you. I get results because I know how to do things my clients don't know how to do. That means you've got to let me do it my way. My job is to get your wife and your son back, is that correct?"

"Of course, but—"

"If I need to do something to accomplish that job, should I do it?"

"Well, yes, within . . . of course."

"Good."

"I need to be kept informed."

"You shall be." I knew what was bothering him, because it was bothering me too. "I will always prefer to report to you rather than to the police."

"It's not only that."

"Is there any reason that I should know about why the police are to be avoided?" There almost always is. When there is an investigation in one part of a client's life, there is also a fear that it will spread to every aspect of that life; and none of us is without things to hide. The difficulty is getting the client to tell me what the skeleton is all about. I had an idea in his case.

"No. Of course not. There is no reason."

"Was your wife having an affair?" There was no easy way to deal with it.

"No," he said emphatically.

"You are old. Your wife is very attractive."

"No."

"You're telling me she isn't interested in sex anymore?"

"She would not do what you suggest." His voice was a plaintive whine. You couldn't believe a voice like that.

"She wouldn't run away and leave you?"

"Then how do you explain the taxi driver and the man who almost shot you? How do you explain them, Mr. Jantarro? My wife has left me for two lovers? Two lovers who are willing to be violent, to plan, to extort money?"

I saw a side of him that was new to me. Cunning crouched in his eyes, ready to spring and destroy the slow, the weak. It was the man who had made all that money, the man who had built a mansion in a new land. I had been taking him for a gentle old man, castrated by age, Hugo's father. "Yes," I said slowly. "I hadn't forgotten. It is likely that it's a professional job. But it wouldn't be the first time that someone has hired professionals to deal with a spouse."

"The only professionals my wife knows are doctors. She is a nurse, Mr. Jantarro, not a criminal."

"But you are worried that the police might be thinking along these lines. They might just figure it was a wife's little parting shot and let it go at that. Am I right?"

"The police are officials. They will think whatever is convenient for them to think."

I leaned back in the chair and sighed. "It's all right, Mr. Georg," I said. "I don't think she set it up and I don't think the cops will either." I ticked off my points on plastic fingers. "One, as you say, these were professionals. Two, most lovers don't feel the need for the company of a middle-aged retarded man. Three, it seems a strange way to get a dowry. If she wanted money, there were probably easier ways to get it from you."

Georg seemed mollified, even a little triumphant, his eyes darting at me and away again as if forgiving me in small doses for being so stupid. "*Sehen Sie?*" he said, not appearing to realize he had spoken in German. "*Na, na, na,*" small bursts of annoyed satisfaction.

"I still need names," I told him. "Someone who was a lover might have used his relationship to set her up, found out about her, her schedule. Give me a name."

"My wife was loyal." Smug.

"I don't believe you."

"*Unmöglich.*" Tired. "It is no longer easy to cry. I am dried up. I cannot even—" He waved in the general direction of his crotch. "*Trink* more tea, Renate tells me. '*Glä-sel Mineralwasser, Fritzchen.*'" He mimicked the nursekeeper's jerky nervous speech. "*Mehr Wasser, Meer-wasser,* hee, hee, hee." His high-pitched laughter sounded hysterical, and I wondered if I had lost him for good.

"Mr. Georg." I tried to get his attention, but he was somewhere else, and I had the crazy urge to peel back an eyelid, as Levine had done with me, and to go searching in his shriveled brain for the information I needed. What did I care, I asked myself? It wouldn't be the first time that a client had given me a job and then prevented me from doing it. But I wanted to get the information. I wanted to take it from him if he wouldn't give it to me. I pictured the old wiring in his head, tangled and fraying like the cloth-covered lines that sag between ceramic insulators in the attics of old houses. Dusty old steamer trunks full of yellowed clothing, moth-eaten, stale. Sepia photographs of rigid people reduced to types by the action of time on memory. Stains of mold on everything. I pulled myself back to reality with a snap of my head that set my skull buzzing with a dull pain. It wasn't like me to get so far off the rails.

"Helene," I said to him. "Hugo." I tried to say the words caressingly, to slide them in through his ears. "Helene, Hugo, need your help. Help."

He looked up brightly, a bird that has heard a noise. "After the war," he said, listening to his own words, "after the war, they shaved the heads of many women." He checked what he had said against some picture in his attic and nodded when he was satisfied that he was correct. "The French told us we were freed. Nazi elements had to be *déraciné,* uprooted, exposed to the light. The weak men in the village said, '*Oui, oui, d'accord.*' And the colonels affected not to hear the German accents. And so they started with the women. Girls who had slept with Nazis, mothers who had fostered them. And they laughed as they cut. And they took what they wanted, for after all these were Nazi whores, *putains*. Helene was outraged. My little Helene. A girl. She was a Jeanne d'Arc against the French. Pregnant—?" He searched around with sightless eyes, trembling a little, hunting for the truth. "Yes," he said with a smile like a rictus. "Pregnant, then. She organized the women, the other ones who had not been humiliated, and she made them all shave their heads too. What shame, what shame. Women from the moon, and the men were frightened."

It was like listening to an old Edison recording, crackly and uneven. The voice was distant and stripped of resonance, almost overwhelmed by the noise of life around it. Abruptly he jabbed his cane to the floor between his legs and levered himself upright, swaying briefly before he found his balance. "Renate!" he called. "Renate!" He began to walk away from me. From the front of the house came the sound of someone hurrying. I stood up.

He stopped and wrenched himself around to face me. "I quoted Trakl," he said in a voice with some life in it. "I remember this: 'Cold metal treads upon my brow. Spiders search my heart. A light dies in my mouth.'" He stayed twisted towards me; a door banged near us and then there were footsteps in the hall. "That is how it feels, Mr. Jantarro. That is how it feels."

Renate took him away without deigning to look at me. I let myself out and went to find a cab. I still had a job, but it was raining.

IT RAINED for two days, a cold miserable rain that got into
every corner of my being. One by one I watched my leads
shrink away. The real Ellie Peters had been found trussed
up like a parcel in a dark corner of another parking garage,
alive but unable to say anything useful about what had
happened to her. She had simply been sapped from behind.
Her hair was long and white-blond, and her nail polish was
the same strange shade of purple I recalled from the garage.
The cops hadn't wanted me to talk to her, even though they
knew she had nothing to offer. I had to phone around and
find out which hospital she was in, and then I had to dress
up as something Hippocratic and slip into her room when
no one was looking. She was glad to talk, but she had
nothing to say. I was running around behind the cops,

wasting my time on stupid things like the procuring of hospital whites. That and getting people to open up to me.

It took me an entire afternoon at St. Albans to persuade a friend of Helene Georg's that she should talk to me despite the orders that the cops had given her. And when she let loose, I got a paean of praise for Helene that would have done nicely as a eulogy, but which was no earthly good to me. It also couldn't have been true. No attractive woman married to a man twenty-five years her senior goes straight home after work every day for five years in a row. It just doesn't happen. I told that to the friend and she said, "That's what the police said. Why do you men always go around looking for dirt?"

"Because things grow in dirt," I told her. She made a disgusted noise. She probably didn't understand, so I explained that mushrooms grew in the dark in horseshit, and detective work was like hunting for mushrooms. She looked as if I'd put her off fungi for good.

From Antonini I learned that the bug on the back of the taxi had worked all right, but that no one had thought to use it once the fun started inside the TD Centre. They had used it to find the cab after the blank paper strips had been discovered, but by then a squad car was already there because I'd been bounced off the front of a new Buick and the owner was sore about what I'd done to his car and what I might do to his bank balance if I sued. It seems my fake arm came loose in all the excitement, and the guy thought he'd performed the amputation. His wife had called the cops while he was alternately puking up his guts and moaning over his new car. Antonini said the guy was planning to sue me first. Nobody saw either of the kidnappers, although they dug a slug out of the concrete wall, and by the weight they figured it was a .357 Magnum.

I had some fun goading Antonini into revealing all of this, but it was the kind of fun you get peeling potatoes. It was too easy and there was nothing very worthwhile when I'd finished. Besides, Bench caught me at it, and that plugged the only source of information I had inside the department right now. He actually began to slice Antonini to pieces right in front of my eyes, and I left before he could fry the bits. On the way out of the station, I borrowed the desk phone to call my lawyer to say that if a guy got in touch about a Buick, our position was that I was recuperating nicely but not out of the woods yet, and until we knew how extensive my injury was we didn't know how much we'd be demanding. She took it all down and only asked two questions. That's why I like her. That and the fact she's Glenda's partner.

Glenda. I phoned her twice. Once she was in a meeting, and the other time she was just plain unavailable. She phoned me but got my answering machine. The only message she left was the sound of a phony kiss—the kind that ends with a loud pop. At least, I think it was Glenda. Feeling really bad about it, I called Louise, and the message on her machine used words like 'sharing' and 'concern' a lot; there didn't seem to be much left to say, so I gave her a phony kiss, but the pop didn't come out right. And it kept on raining.

The day after I saw Georg I remembered the flower vase with the cabbie's prints on it. It just came into my head as blithely as a kid who's two hours late for dinner and hopes no one will notice. That shook me. How much had I forgotten forever? It was one thing to miss a whole day; you notice that kind of a gap. But the little stuff, the momentary awareness, the fact seen only for a second, things like that could disappear by the thousands and I'd never know they were gone.

I got the vase and covered it in a plastic bag. Anything but a Miracle Mart bag, I told the maid. The lab I had chosen to do the work was the best around, and they handled it as reverentially as if it had been Ming. The prints were so-so, they said, insinuating that I'd screwed up somehow. A good left thumb and a pretty left index, but the rest was smudged. I allowed as how there were some who would not disparage a good left thumb and a pretty left index, and I made sure to accept the manila envelope containing the report with my own version of the digits in question. The man at the desk didn't seem impressed.

The prints were in my pocket and they could stay there until I decided how best to use them. Who knows, I told myself, a day may come when I needed something to make me welcome at the cop-shop. Until then, I'd squish around in the rain hunting for mushrooms on my own without help from the public service.

"Nope. Never seen her before." The bartender at the Ward Nine was sure. "Seen them all. Wouldn't forget one like her."

"Can't help you, friend." The guy behind the bar at Mallory's gave the picture a quick look and then went back to fiddling with the color on the TV. I had to buy a drink before he'd pay any attention to me and my problem. "She married to the guy?" he asked, putting his finger on Hugo's face. I explained. "Too bad," he said. "My sister has a Mongoloid, you know?"

The hostess at Twinkles screwed up her puffy face and peered at the picture. "Could be," she said. She looked at me anxiously to see if this was the right answer. I pushed her gently and she drifted the other way. "The hair was different, cut on an angle. Real smart. It did look like her though."

"You too? What'd she do, kill somebody?" The Collegiate was a long shot. Not near St. Albans and not the right crowd. But I was tired and the streetcar wouldn't come, so I went in to get out of the rain. The bartender was a man of sixty with a brush cut like something out of the Knute Rockne days. He was wearing a black and gold crew neck sweater that had BMOC stitched on in felt letters.

I asked him, "You've seen her?" I was curiously annoyed; he'd broken my string of negatives.

"Yeah. Sure." He stood at the end of my booth and kept

glancing toward the back of the restaurant-bar. I invited him to join me. "I got to run this place, fella. I can't do it sitting down." He jerked a thumb at the back. "Tell you what. You come on back with me and I'll give you the story between plays. How about that?" I left my wet raincoat in the booth and followed him.

"You said, 'You too,'" I reminded him. "Who else has been asking?"

He held up his hand. "Wait till the huddle, fella. The coach says patience pays off. You remember that and you'll score more often."

I sat at the dingy bar while he went back and forth between the three tables of customers and the kitchen. Old photographs of boys in striped jerseys and leather helmets lined the wall behind the bar, and next to the glass case holding pieces of pie there was a smaller glass case featuring a tired looking football with writing all over it. Hand-lettered signs said: Quitters Never Win & Winners Never Quit, and Nothing Ventured Nothing Gained, and Winning Isn't Everything. Under the last one someone had written in ballpoint: *It's the spread that counts.*

"What's the score?" I asked him when he finally sat down next to me.

"The police," he said. And then he looked at me hard. "You're not a cop, are you?" I shook my head. "No, I guess not. Yeah, well, two cops were in here with the same picture. And I told them. I mean, why not? It's my duty, right? It's a free country, so I can say what I want, just like I'm talking to you."

"What did you tell them?" Even though winning wasn't everything, I wasn't going to quit.

"That she was in here." He had swiveled on his stool and was surveying the place with a worried look.

"Regularly?"

"Just the one time."

"You sure, sure it was her I mean?"

He turned to face me with exaggerated slowness and

placed two gnarled hands on the bartop, splaying his fingers. He said, "December one, nineteen-forty-two, extended season because of the war, Packers and Pittsburgh, fourteen to seven Packers. September four, nineteen-oh-eight, Princeton and Rutgers, three to nothing Princeton. Go ahead," he challenged, "ask me anything. I got a memory like you wouldn't believe."

"I believe you," I told him. "It's just that sometimes things that happened a month ago are harder to remember than things that happened twenty years ago.

"Who said anything about a month?" He grinned at me.

I did a rapid calculation. "All right," I said, "ten days ago."

"Uh-uh." He shook his head slowly, savoring his pleasure.

"Okay. When then? When did she come in?"

"Two days ago." He leaned back and rested his elbows on the bar behind him. When he saw my shoulders slump his grin got a cynical twist. "The cops handled the pass just fine. They took it and ran. I guess you don't have what it takes any more. Is that it?"

"Two days ago," I said. Now I was pissed off that my luck was still bad.

"Yup. Count 'em, one . . . two."

"Well, thanks anyway," I said, squaring my shoulders as I stood up.

"Hey! You don't believe me!" He was standing too, hurt and bellicose. He tried to suck in his gut but it only made his face go redder.

"It's not that," I said. "I believe you believe you saw her. It just couldn't be, that's all."

"Oh yeah? Oh yeah? Well, let me tell you something, mister. I saw her all right. She came in about two-fifteen, two-twenty. In a hurry. No smiles or nothing. She wanted a Kisko. 'What flavor?' I said. 'Anything,' she said. So I gave her grape. A lot of people like grape. She paid me with a ten."

[45]

"What's a Kisko?" I asked him.

"You don't know what a Kisko is?" He took me by the arm and pulled me to the front of the place where he opened a freezer and took out a handful of frozen tubes in bright plastic colors. "People eat them," he said.

My coat was gone and it was still raining.

No more bars, I told myself under the hot shower. No more coffee shops, restaurants or hotels. I rubbed the loofah hard across the end of my stump to punish the infernal itch, and I almost felt good for the first time in two days. No more noes, maybes and yeses from people who wouldn't know Helene Georg from a ... well, from a Kisko. Wherever her mushrooms grew, it wasn't in the ten-block square area around St. Albans.

You can't wash your right elbow with your right hand. A fact. So I scratched it back and forth across the loofah which I had jammed under my stump, wishing all the while that Glenda would come back and do the job properly. I decided to give Louise another call, and if she didn't answer I'd find out if Nancy Potok was still in town. I liked Nancy well enough, and there are some things a loofah just can't do.

I buried myself in a terry cloth bathrobe and padded into the kitchen to make a hot toddy, but I stopped by the phone and maybe because I felt guilty I tried once more to reach Glenda. I let it ring ten times and then somebody answered. I gave her the name and room number and together we let it ring ten more. She said she was sorry and I said not to worry.

In half an hour the drink had got to me and I was seeing things clearly. For the past couple of days I had been reduced to breathing air already used by dozens of cops, and that was no good. I needed to get a line into the department, to know what they knew without the hit and miss business of schlepping along behind and picking up discards. Since Bench would have stopped up Antonini but

good, that left only one possibility—short of offering someone a bribe. JoJo was that possibility. I also needed a lead of
my own, one that hadn't been chewed up by the cops and
spat out as useless. But first things first.

First JoJo. I felt guilty. JoJo Polifemi is by way of being a
friend of mine. One of the things that friends do is help you
out, but there is a blurred line between asking for help and
using someone, and I pondered the line and my position in
relation to it throughout my second drink. Satisfied that I
was only asking for help, I dialed. He sounded pleased to
hear from me and why didn't I drop by the studio tonight.
Sure. Nancy could wait. Or Louise.

As it turned out, I didn't get to JoJo's until nearly midnight.
I had changed into slacks and a sweater and was poking at a
steak that was destined to be dinner when Bench called. In
flat, bored tones he told me that there was something he
wanted me to see and he'd be round in five minutes to pick
me up. He promised me that it wasn't the inside of a jail
cell. He promised me that the sight he had in mind was
much worse than that. Not possible, I thought.

I changed out of my wool sweater and into a windbreaker,
because it's hard to draw a gun from under a sweater without calling time-out. With my left arm strapped on and my
shoulder holster strapped beneath that, I have enough
leather on my body to satisfy any bondage freak. It's one of
the reasons I only carry a little Chief's Special. The really
big guns need really big holsters and make me feel too
much like an android in bivouac. There are other reasons.
It's harder to kill anyone with a .38, and this toy of mine is
only accurate at kissing distance. It makes a nice bang,
though, and that's usually enough. Tonight I was pretty
sure I wouldn't even need the bang; I just wanted a friend
along for the ride.

All the way down Yonge and into the rail yards off the
Lakeshore, Bench was grim and preoccupied. The rain
would fling itself against us in gusts like buckets of nails

from the night sky, rattling on the windscreen and the roof. I tried to think about the fact that my windbreaker didn't cover my ass and I was going to get wet. I knew where we were headed—not the place but the occasion—and the prospect of a wet butt wasn't enough to keep my mind off Bench's promise and the chance that it might be fulfilled.

It was a one-ring circus. The cops had set up a circle of klieg lights that made the patch of ground they hit seem to leap up above the scrub land around it. The police cars huddled together in a tight arc outside the bright disk of light, and two of them sent their red beams sweeping through the dark, painting the rain the color of fresh blood. The loud cackle of static from half a dozen walkie-talkies sounded urgent and meaningless at the same time. Men in raincoats and men in uniform capes shifted uneasily from foot to foot and murmured quietly.

Bench moved slowly into the electric day, drawing me with him.

A railroad cop had found it. He stood beside his company's track at the edge of the circle, legs wide apart and head high, protective and brave. He had been crying, but the rain had obliterated his tears and only the raw puffiness under his eyes gave him away. That and the way his arms hung limp against his legs. Behind him in the dark an orange flare sputtered, and beyond it, further down the line, another one glowed weakly.

It lay in the middle, between the rails. A black, shiny mass slicked by the rain to the sheen of new tar. One foot protruded from the mess and an arm as well. It was a man's foot, but the arm was a woman's arm, slim-wristed, effete, and very white.

Not for me, I thought. They haven't left it here for me! I turned my head away and felt the vomit rise within me. I forced myself to look again. Hard. Clear.

A faint and irregular seam ran down the middle of the mass, just a suggestion of what once had been a boundary between the two of them. Their difference, their separateness was gone. I told myself that they had been embracing at the end, a voluntary clasp. I noticed that some oily ash was running from them and gathering in a puddle of rain. The railroad cop was staring at me with disgust. He must have thought that I was crying too.

"I wanted you to see," said Bench quietly.

"Are you certain?"

He nodded. "Yes," he said. "The tests will tell for sure, but we found her ring, and the shoes are the ones he was wearing when he was snatched." He paused to see if there was anything I had to say, then he continued in the same reasonable tone. "They were moved here. Dumped. No burn marks on the ground." He moved a hand in the general direction of the mess. "The ME says it was done maybe two days ago. But like I say, the tests will tell for sure." His calm voice was like the rumble of distant freight.

"Georg?" I asked. "Has anyone told him?"

He nodded slowly. "We informed the nurse. He's sleeping now and when the doctor gets there in the morning they'll tell him. One of my men will be there. Maybe I will." For the first time since he had picked me up he looked at me full in the face. His eyes caught the flash of red lights as they hurried past. "I thought that as his representative you probably should be there too." He looked back at the ground. "I wanted you to see."

"WHAT HAVE YOU DONE NOW?" JoJo stood at his half-opened studio door swathed in a bright pink kimono and hands on his silk hips. "Look at you! You're all wet and...icky!"

A voice came from behind him, reedy and muffled, a child's voice from beneath bedclothes. "Jo! What's the matter? Come back, I'm cold."

Our eyes met and he shrugged slightly. "I didn't think you were coming," he said quietly. Then he saw something in my eyes he didn't like and he pulled me inside by my lapels. "I'll get rid of him," he said quickly. He turned around and around, looking for a place to put me. The only soft places in the studio were his bed and the pile of cushions next to it. Finally he propped me on a crate of welding supplies, and I slumped like a putty doll, drooping with the pull of gravity. I could feel the blood rush through every vessel in my head and it made a kind of impersonal roar. I was detached, everywhere and nowhere.

Squeals and thumps came from around the corner, and an angry exchange of voices, high and low. JoJo came back carrying a tall gangly young man in his arms, handling him as easily as if he were straw. The man had his face buried in JoJo's neck and was making mewing noises that might have been weeping, and as he was carried past where I was sitting he lifted his head, wiped his long hair out of his face and said, "Bitch." His eyes were unfocused, stoned. They disappeared into the hall and more scuffling sounds drifted into the studio.

JoJo was standing in front of me, measuring me for a lift. He is short and dark and built like a construction worker. His broad, flat face always has a haze of stubble on it, no matter how many times a day he shaves. Muscles and curly hair crawl up from his chest and run down his arms like roots from a tree. The beefiness is real, not the stuff of weightlifting. He works in iron, welding beams and plates into unlovely sculpture that sells to no one and so lies all around his warehouse studio like ruins from another world. They are self-portraits, I suppose. João-Jose Maria Polifemi y Silverio, Portuguese immigrant's son, gay sculptor. It's complicated.

He had decided how he would do it and he moved toward me. I waved him back. "I can walk," I said testily.

"Okay," he said lightly. "I'll make some tea. What kind would you like? Rose hip? Mo's 24? Peppermint?"

"Scotch," I said. He smiled slightly and padded off to the cubicle he uses as a kitchen. Wearily, I got to my feet and followed. He filled the electric kettle and plugged it in, then he got down two mugs and put a tea bag in each.

I sat down on a stool and laid my head on the strip of plywood he uses for a counter. The water was rattling in the kettle and JoJo got out jars from his cupboard and spoons from the drawer. "Take your jacket off," he said. "And your pants too. They're wet. Don't worry," he added without turning round, "I won't make a play for you."

It was like an overdone roast, I thought. Burnt meat. They used to offer up burnt animals to appease God, and I wondered whether anything could possibly be appeased by the sight I had seen. If so, I hoped I never met it.

"Go on. Do what I tell you. Get out of those wet clothes." JoJo rapped a spoon sharply on the table beside my head. "There's a robe on a hook by the bed. You can put it on if you want." There was the right mix of sympathy and authority in his manner, so I slid off the stool and went to change.

I couldn't help looking at the bed and the tangle of sheets on it. I thought of Glenda and wanted nothing more than to crawl inside her and never come out. I shook my head and it hurt. An I-beam projected into the lighted area of the bedroom rising out of some piece of art hidden in the dark recesses of the warehouse, and I hung my jacket on the end of it, hesitating only a moment before I draped my pants on it too. The robe was burgundy terry cloth and looked fairly clean so I put it on. I had to take it off again to remove my gun and holster.

JoJo put a mug of something hot in front of me. "Honey in this one and brown sugar in this," he said prodding two jars with stubby fingers. He sat down beside me. "Now," he said, "tell mother about it."

I told him. JoJo is a good listener. He doesn't fidget or interrupt. He doesn't chime in with experiences of his own. He pays attention to what you tell him and to the way you tell him as well. When I finished he was frowning, his forehead buckled like a crumpled fender.

"It's not like you, Cagey," he said. "You've seen this kind of thing before. All right, all right"—he patted the air into a vague shape—"killing is never pretty. But you're not hung up on the beauty of life. So what's the matter?"

"You're full of shit," I told him. I took a swig of the pink stuff in the mug and burned my tongue.

"Sure I am." He was bending the spoon into a coil, working on the bowl with his strong hands. "But it never got to you before. I'm full of shit. You're full of shit. We're all sacks of shit." He had got the bowl flattened out and was trying to make it stand on the tail of the strip of metal. It looked like a stainless steel cobra. "Big deal," he said.

"I'm all right." I heard myself say it, and I wondered how big a lie it was. I wanted to be home and in bed.

"Remember the business with Sammy Ott?" he asked, still twisting metal. I remembered. Sammy Ott had been mailed in pieces to five very rich business men. The man who had got the head hired me to see to it that he didn't get any more wet mail. I came to know parts of Sam really well. "Or that girl," he went on, "what was her name? Alice something or other. Killed with the silver-tipped bullet."

"Mercury. Mercury-tipped."

"Whatever."

"I'm okay."

"Sure." He didn't like the cobra, and he squashed it flat with one thump of his fist. He got up and put his mug in the sink with his other dirty dishes. He put the honey and the brown sugar back in the cupboard. For a moment he stood with his back to me, arms down by his side. Then he turned. "I'm glad you came to me, Cagey. I'm glad I'm your friend." He picked up the squashed spoon and flipped it back and forth from one hand to the other, as if weighing something. "I'd like it better if you talked about your feelings. It's what friends do. Sharing." He looked at me.

What did he want? I tried to think of something to share, but I felt like nothing inside. A kind of desperation filled me, a last-chance feeling, a now-or-never need to say the right thing; and all I could do was to face him blankly.

"I'm tired, Cage," he said sadly. "I'm going to bed. Ask

[53]

me now and let's get it over with." His face began to stiffen into a peasant mask.

"Ask you what?" I said stupidly. I was having trouble following him.

Anger settled into his jaw, curling his lips and swelling the muscles in his neck. "Ask me if I could penetrate the cops for you." His voice was oddly light and sing-song. "Ask me if I wouldn't mind—just this once more—sticking my cock up the backside of some queer in brass buttons to see if I can push something out of his mouth that might be helpful to dear, sweet Cagey."

The words lay between us, ugly and painful. Never before had it been so explicit. Usually each of us led up to it carefully, pretending that I'm not using him, papering over the awkward moments with jokes and innuendo. "That's not why I came," I said. "They're dead. It's all over. Lost."

"I don't believe you. You called before you knew that. And you came anyway." He was sneering now. "You've never let a case go yet. Are you telling me that this one is different? That you're quitting because it's getting rough? Is that what you want me to believe?"

What did I want him to believe? My sense of loss was so great that I hadn't given a thought to whether I would continue with the Georg case. There might not even be a case to carry on. Who was he to know better than I what I would do, what I wanted? Angrily I shouted at him, "You can believe whatever you fucking well want." There was more I wanted to say, and my mouth hung open as my tired brain searched for the words. But nothing came, so I stomped into the bedroom, dumped the bathrobe on the bed, and pushed myself into the damp clothing that hung like dirty laundry on his piece of rusty steel. Wasn't it ironic, I thought, that the killer fruit had developed scruples just when he didn't need them.

I climbed into my own bed with the Scotch bottle and made believe that I was really okay. When I woke up at three in the morning, I called Glenda. She answered on the second ring. She's always been a light sleeper. "It's me, Cagey."

"Cage. What's wrong? Are you all right?"

"I'm just fine," I told her. "I miss you."

"That's nice." She let the sleep back into her voice.

"When are you coming back?"

"What?"

"Home. When are you coming home?"

"Oh, Cage, I don't know. I mean, you know how these things are. The Florida courts are..." She yawned and then I had only distant beeping on the line.

"Glenda?"

"What?"

"Good night."

"Night, Cage."

7

MERWEISS WAS CIVIL but correct. With measured bows and handshakes that were just firm enough and just brief enough, he saw to it that we were seated and offered coffee. Bench was muted and laconic. He laid his arms along the arms of his chair, straightened his back and let his eyes close halfway. The man he had brought with him was positively brilliant in the way he managed to convey the proper degree of solicitude without slipping into genuine concern. He arranged his creases and handled his coffee cup like a scion of old Eastern money. The police college gets better and better.

Punctilio is not my strong point. But this morning I had no difficulty in behaving myself. I was too tired and chastened by the events of yesterday to do anything other than follow directions. It's a good thing no one asked me any-thing, because I'm not sure I could have responded even monosyllabically.

We sat in silence while the good doctor went to check on his patient. This time we had been put in the library, which was on the second floor and only two rooms away from the bedroom. If things went wrong, Georg could be hurried back to die in bed. I attempted to read the titles on the spines of the books, but the Germans run their titles from the bottom to the top, and it made me dizzy to read upside down. The older volumes were stamped with that Gothic script which is almost illegible anyway, so after identifying Schiller and Lessing I gave up. Goethe would be in there, and if my high school teacher hadn't lied, so would Kleist. There might also be that collection of kitsch I had once been shown, known as a Bibel and containing frag-ments of sentimental writing torn from the works of Ger-many's romantic greats. I wandered lonely as a cloud. That sort of stuff.

Merweiss came back to give us a last-minute briefing. He folded his white hands in front of him and considered us down the length of his nose. He splayed his hands protec-tively across his chest. He had judged that it was better to have but one interview, one occasion on which the sad af-fair would be discussed, and for that reason it would be up to us to convey the news along with any other matter we wished to raise with Herr Georg. Bench sighed and began to stir. The scion cleared his throat politely. I glared at Merweiss, willing him to get on with it.

His patient would be sedated, the doctor told us, steep-ling his fingers and canting his head to the side. How much of what he heard would make sense to him, no one could predict. As well, we should not be alarmed by inappropri-ate responses. An old mind, a mind under the influence of medication, might not react the way our minds would under similar circumstances. Was there an appropriate re-sponse to this kind of news, I wondered? "Doctor," said

Bench heavily, driving the word through his flattened nose, "I think we understand." Eastern money smiled a clubby smile of approval. The doctor cleared his throat and nodded. Then he left.

"Lord," said Bench when the doctor had gone. He scrubbed his forefinger back and forth across his moustache like a man pretending to brush his teeth. I made another stab at waking up but the coffee was finished. We waited.

The nurse opened the door, and the doctor brought Georg in. He was propped in the corner of a wheelchair, his head lolling against the high leather back. His eyes were open and fluid ran out of them onto his cheeks. Not tears, just a pale discharge. He would have been drooling, I thought, and they would have wiped his chin before they entered the room. I couldn't see his making any response, let alone an appropriate one.

Bench buttoned his suit coat and sat forward in his chair. "Mr. Georg," he said, and he waited to see if the old man's eyes could find the source of the noise. Georg's head continued to move to some private need or maybe just to the demands of gravity on life. "Mr. Georg?" Bench tried again, louder this time. "Can you hear me?"

From behind us Merweiss spoke in German, softly at first and then he, too, tried raising the volume. Georg showed no signs of hearing that either. Bench looked at his partner and then at me. His partner's smile had a fixed quality about it now, and he shrugged delicately at his boss. Merweiss came to stand beside the old man, his hands on the grips of the wheelchair. "It is impossible," he said.

Georg opened his mouth and mumbled something. We all bent closer to listen. *"Ma vie,"* he said clearly. And then, *"Pauvre Hélène."* My life. Poor Helene.

"French!" said the scion, as if he had invented it.

We looked at Merweiss. "It has happened before. The mind..." he said. "Languages are funny things. He has three—they speak French and German in the Alsace, you know—and sometimes he gets lost in one or the other." He shook his head.

With a warning scowl in my direction, Bench screwed up his face and said, *"Monsieur Georg, pouvez vous nous écouter?"* I hadn't realized he spoke French.

The partner translated for me in a fast whisper: "Mr. Georg, can you hear us?"

"Don't bother," I told him.

Georg heard Bench. He smiled and looked around to find him. I hoped he wasn't going to try to move his body, because his bones didn't look as if they could take the strain.

"Votre femme et votre fils sont morts." Bench gave it to him straight. Your wife and son are dead. The scion couldn't help himself and he whispered it like a ghost.

It seemed that the message had made it through the drugs. "Ahh." Georg spoke slowly, taking care with each word: *"Jeanne d'Arc...morte pour...morte pour la patrie ...Bon, bon, bon."* He smiled and it was pointed in my direction. I couldn't imagine what he was thinking about that would have pleased him.

"Nous essayons de trouver les meurtriers." We are trying to catch the murderers.

"Bon, bon, bon." He patted his own knee.

Merweiss coughed and we all stood up. I looked at Bench and he shrugged. There was nothing more that we could do. As they wheeled him out, Georg looked directly at me and said, "Find them."

Her name was Renate Ebers. She had been born in Austria, trained as a nurse there, and worked in this country for the last thirty years. Helene Georg had hired her a little over a year ago to take care of her husband, and she had grown very fond of the man. She did not like his wife.

All of this came out in a rush, with much blushing and tugging of clothing. I had been leaving Georg's house, hanging back to let the cops get out of the way, when I had felt a pull at my coat. Nurse Ebers was signaling me with furious, covert gestures to stay behind. I made her make me coffee and bring me a handful of aspirin before I would listen to her.

"And the boy," she said. "I didn't like him either." She had managed to get a hand so deeply wound into the fabric of her uniform that I wasn't sure she'd ever get it out again. "God forgive me, he never did anything wrong, but I just could not like him. Not that it mattered very much. His mother took care of him. It was not part of my job, but when you live in the same house with someone it is important to be..." Her gaze dropped to the kitchen table. "When I heard the news—last night—I was glad. God forgive me." She stopped and before she could think of anything else to confess to, I gave her my cup for a refill.

"Mrs. Georg," I said. "Why didn't you like her?" I saw her back stiffen. She took time to put in the cream and sugar, stirring the coffee while she thought.

"She was not good for him," she said turning around. Our hands met as she passed me the cup, and she blushed. Was it simple jealousy, I wondered? Was this unattractive woman envious of the beautiful and wealthy Helene Georg? They were of an age, both nurses, and both in Fritz Georg's household.

"How?" I asked.

She flapped a hand and looked around for something else to fuss with. When she found nothing, she got a chair and sat down opposite me. "She would excite him, and that was not good. You have seen him. He is old and needs a peaceful life."

I frowned. "Excite him? You don't mean...sexually, do you?"

She turned brick red and sweat broke out along her hairline. Very carefully, as if the words might slip, she said, "They would talk. I heard them. Not what they were saying, of course. But the tone. The sound. He would say something and then she would reply. Louder and louder, faster and faster, until they were almost shouting. Afterwards he would be weak as a baby. She would come to tell me that I must put him to bed. He would be fretful, troubled. I could tell, even though he tried to hide it."

"What did they fight about?"

"It was not fighting," she declared firmly. And then more quietly she said, "He never fights."

"Argue, then. What did they argue about?"

She was going to tell me that he never argued either, but she closed her mouth. When she opened it again, she said, "I don't know. I did not listen. I told you."

I pushed my chair back. There wasn't any point to this. "It doesn't matter," I said, getting up. She looked alarmed.

"You are leaving?"

"I'm sure you want to help," I told her, "but Mrs. Georg is dead, and I don't see how all of this can be important now."

"Wait."

I stood looking down at the top of her head, which was bent over her clasped hands as if she were praying. Maybe she was. I noticed that she was beginning to lose her hair around the crown.

She looked up. "I honestly don't know why they were fighting—arguing—because I didn't listen." She held out her hands in an appeal. "But something was wrong. Something very bad. Of that I am sure."

"But the worst has happened," I said. "She and the boy are dead. Are you saying that whatever was wrong was somehow responsible for her kidnapping and death?"

She looked terribly worried. "That cannot be. Of course you are right. But I am still afraid for him. I know it is not sensible. But I am afraid."

"Do you think that he arranged to have her kidnapped and killed? To make it look like a professional job?" This was the thought in the back of everyone's mind, and it might as well come to the front for a walk in the air. I don't like to think of a client as guilty of the thing I'm hired to uncover, but it wouldn't be the first time it had happened.

I expected her to react with horror, but instead she gave the matter careful thought. Maybe the murder of a wife who excited one was not a particularly bad crime in her book. "No," she said slowly, shaking her head. She craned her neck to look up at me. "I do not think so."

I sat down again. "I don't think there's any possibility that they'll try again. That they'll kidnap him. They've got their money. It'd be too big a risk. So where's the danger? What are you afraid of?"

"I don't know. Mr. Jantarro, I am not a foolish woman. I do not cry and cling to men. I do not cringe from the world and pretend that it is feminine to be frightened. I am not hysterical. But I feel that something is wrong." She held her head defiantly, challenging me to disagree with her.

"Tell me more about Mrs. Georg," I said. "Did she have affairs? Did she drink too much? Did she bet on the horses?"

"Bet on the horses?" She snorted and gave a mirthless laugh. "Bet on the horses and risk her precious money? No, Mr. Jantarro, she didn't bet on the horses or on anything else. She didn't drink or use drugs, either." She stopped and looked directly at me.

"Do you have a name you can give me?" I asked.

"She was always too discreet."

"A place, then. Anything that would give me an idea? A new activity she took up, perhaps. You know, a sudden interest in skating or poker." She shook her head. "Maybe you've got her wrong, then," I suggested.

"Oh, no," she said with certainty.

"How can you be sure?"

"A woman knows these things," she said with a little smugness. It was almost ridiculous, this dowdy fireplug of a woman allied with an elegant beauty in a tangle of knowing and disapproval. I smiled a thank you and got to my feet. It wasn't so much that I was tired, although God knows I could have used a week in bed, it was more a case of listlessness. I moved—and felt compelled to move—but I had no real direction.

In the hall, she said, "There was a man before my time. I remember his name from one of their...discussions. But that was probably too long ago."

"What was his name?" I asked. She was likely right. It was a recent lover I was looking for, not a burned-out affair from the past.

She screwed up her face with the effort of memory. "Demeny," she said. "A man called Demeny. It must have been a terrible thing because they argued about it all night. I think he built this house."

"Demeny?"

"Yes. Fritzchen—I mean Mr. Georg—he kept shouting that it was he and not Demeny who had built it all. 'Every brick,' he kept saying. 'Every brick.'" She smiled shyly. "I think he meant every stone," she said.

"Yes," I said.

Clutching the wings of her dress once again, she stayed between me and the door. "I will tell you one thing, Mr. Jantarro." I raised my eyebrows. "She was a very good nurse."

"I'm sure she was."

"And Mr. Jantarro?"

"Yes?"

"You won't stop, will you? You'll keep trying to find out who did it. You won't stop."

"I can't stop," I said.

The aspirin wore off at Jarvis and Charles. Maybe it was earlier, but I noticed it there as I walked into police headquarters. My head felt like a pot of porridge on the boil, thick and full of small explosions of steam, and for a second I considered turning around and heading to Levine's office to find out if this was how I was supposed to feel. But I figured he wouldn't know how I was supposed to feel since he'd never jumped into the windshield of a moving car. Besides, I didn't want him to get me free-associating to porridge.

"Come to turn yourself in?" It was the desk sergeant, a benign old Irishman who'd been a week away from his pension for as long as I could remember.

I waved at him. "Bench in?" I asked in passing.

"Ho, laddie," he hollered. "I'd better telephone up. You just cool your heels while I tell him you're here." He had actually come out from behind the counter, and although he wasn't touching me, he was ready to do that and more if I kept on going. His smile was still in place.

"Good idea, Sarge," I said, and I went back to the desk with him. He sent the message and got the reply that I was to wait.

"You have any aspirins, Sarge?"

"No aspirins," said Bench, coming up behind me. "This isn't a goddamn flophouse." The desk sergeant faded away to work on a pile of forms. Bench looked at me, panting slightly. "What is it, Jantarro? I have work to do. There are one or two murder investigations on my mind, in case you hadn't realized that." As if to emphasize his busyness, he scrubbed the short hairs on the top of his head.

I took the lab's fingerprint report out of my jacket and handed it to him wordlessly. He started reading and then peered at me over the report with an annoyed, puzzled expression. He read some more, and when the light dawned, he went very still. Abruptly he turned on his heel and marched back into the gloom of the building, smacking the envelope once against his thigh.

"Boyo," called the desk sergeant when I was near the front door. I turned around. "Here," he said. He had put three white tablets on the counter with a paper cup of water. "It should be whisky," he said as I drank it down.

I HAVE MONEY. A lot of money, by most people's standards. But I also have a thing about that lot of money, because it represents my left arm. It had been mangled and crushed beyond repair by a pair of sadistic guards, and it was taken from me in the prison hospital by a bored doctor who had never had the chance to do an amputation before. I sued the hell out of everyone and anyone connected with the place. And I won. Some of the losers couldn't pay very much, so I took what they had and made sure that whenever they get a little now I take that too. I keep one man employed almost full-time to see to it that I don't miss anything they might have come by. The government in its various manifestations could pay, and it did.

Every month—or more frequently if I want—my accountants send me a detailed report on my money: where it is, what it's in, how much there is. It's like having a kid at college and getting a report from the dean. I pay their fees and initial my approval. Then I forget about it until the next report. I never spend it.

For a while I tried to explain to people that the money was my left arm and that nobody chops off fingers to pay for groceries. They pointed out that I was earning interest and that I could spend that without disturbing the "corpus," as the accountants call it. Nobody understands, so I quit trying to explain. Like anyone else, I live on my income and I have to work for it. Part of working for a living entails getting paid, and old man Georg hadn't given me a cent since I'd turned up at his bedside nearly two weeks ago. So the problem was to investigate Georg to figure out who had the power to sign checks and to get him or her to sign one for me.

I phoned Renate Ebers and presumed on our new-found intimacy. With a little reluctance she revealed that her own checks were signed by a man named Postitch, and she thought he was with a law firm called something like Boofers, Gregley. It was close. The firm was Bofors, Gergeley and they did have a Norman Postitch—one of the partners, in fact.

"I am so very pleased to meet you." Norman looked like a clown: frizzy yellow hair that glistened like acrylic, a large sad mouth, and a gabardine suit that was nearly turquoise. His bow tie was pink and drooped like his mouth. "So very pleased to meet you," he said again, waving me into a seat opposite his desk.

"That—"

"That?" He let his eyes go wide, but he still looked distinctly unhappy.

"So pleased that..." I said.

He thought for a moment. "Oh," he said, "yes, very f-f-f-unny." He was annoyed with himself for stuttering.

"Habit of speech," he said rapidly. He settled himself into his own chair and wriggled a bit to make sure he was home, looking about as he did so to check that the drawers and the pencils and the pictures of his family were where they had been when he had got up. "I'm so sorry that you had to wait," he said, and he winced when he heard himself.

"It only took an hour to get to you," I told him. "And at my rates that's not going to cost more than you can afford."

"Yes," he said and smiled, bringing his mouth up to a level position, before he let it fall back into its normal droop. "Money, then?"

"No one's paid me, and no one's made any arrangements to pay me."

"Oh, my g-g-g-goodness." Irritation. "Sorry. My fault. Mr. Georg t-t-told me he w-w-was going to hire you. He was t-t-to tell you...speak to me. Power of attorney." He fanned a hand above his desk to show me how easy everything was when you had the power of an attorney.

I put my bill on his desk and told him how much I wanted. He nodded and pushed a button on his phone. When the secretary came in he waved at the bill. She took it and left without a word.

"Look," I said when she had gone, "I need instructions. Apart from two words out of the mouth of a drugged-up old man I've had nothing telling me what to do or whether I should be doing anything at all." I swallowed. I didn't want to lose the case, not at this stage. "Those two words were, 'Find them.' I'd like you to confirm that I'm supposed to find the people who kidnapped his wife and child and killed them."

"Confirmed," he said and slapped the desk.

"Now I need some information. Background stuff, really. The kind of thing that has to get cleared out of the way before I can see what's important. I take it that it's Georg who has the money and not his wife. I mean, he's the rich one, right?"

Postitch fingered the ends of his bow tie and his Adam's apple bobbed a couple of times. "That's c-c-correct," he said, looking uncomfortable.

I smiled and shrugged at him. "It's just a case of figuring out if anyone benefits by the death of his family. A quarter of a million sounds like a lot, but the kidnapping could have been a cover for a murder by someone who stood to inherit even more than that, someone who would otherwise have been an obvious suspect."

"Like Mr. Georg?" He didn't look shocked at the idea.

"Well," I said, "he'd be the most obvious, wouldn't he?" In the little silence that followed Postitch held himself perfectly still. "But there would be other possibilities."

"Y-y-yes?"

"It's likely that Mr. Georg is going to have to change his will, isn't it? Now that his wife and son are dead. Are there any prominent candidates for the position of heir?"

It seemed to pain him to breathe, as if he might at any moment unwittingly give away his client's secrets. "I don't think..." He let it trail off into a slight shrug of apology.

"Power of attorney," I reminded him. "You *are* Georg for things like this. Think of the main thing—catching the killers. You just confirmed that I'm hired to do that, and you're about to pay me to do it. Don't get in my way by being overdiscreet. That wouldn't make sense and it surely wouldn't be serving your client's best interests."

He put a finger to his lips while he thought. Finally he sighed and said, "I s-s-suppose it's okay. Mr. Georg's w-will leaves almost everything t-t-t-to charity. He s-set up a t-trust for his wife and s-s-son. I-i-income g-goes to them." He smiled and got his mouth to make it past the horizontal this time. "I don't think the C-Cancer Fund would k-k-kill for it."

I frowned. "You're saying he cut his wife and kid out of his money? Why would he do that?"

Postitch made his eyes go wide. "I didn't ask." His tone suggested that if he, Georg's lawyer, hadn't asked, then I certainly shouldn't. "Besides," he added, seeing my puzzlement, "the i-income is quite adequate—or w-w-would have b-been."

"When did he do this?"

Postitch hesitated. "Six years ago," he said.

Six years ago. I could root around forever trying to unravel ancient history or I could go for the killers in the best way I knew how. If Georg ever came around I would ask him. It would be the simplest way. "One more thing," I said. "I want access to the autopsy results on the bodies. The only real hope I've got is if you draw up something that makes me Georg's representative."

"Power of attorney," he said and we both laughed.

"Exactly," I said.

He reached for a pad and began scribbling furiously.

"You're not an attorney, are you?" asked the stringbean in the Luftwaffe field-gray uniform. He slid a hand along his shiny Sam Browne, feeling for the bright plastic buttons on his shoulder.

"No," I agreed. "That's the beauty of it. To be an attorney you have to go to classes for three years and pass all those exams. But it only takes a few minutes to get the power of attorney." I showed him the document Postitch had given me with its big red seal like a bloody supernova at the bottom. "It's a wonder everybody doesn't do it."

He took it and frowned. "I don't know," he said.

"That's because you're not an attorney," I told him and I smiled to show him that under our uniforms we were brothers. He sniffed, stamped a heel, and then pulled out a pair of half-glasses from his top pocket. Glaring at me over the lenses, he shook the document fully open and waited until I broke eye contact.

What I liked about the Institute of Forensic Science was the way in which the decorator had found so many shades of lead. A lesser man might have tried to prettify the place, to take your mind off the fact that a few feet away bodies were stacked in the morgue coolers, prisoners of death in an overcrowded penitentiary. Above me were the bits and pieces that the pathologists and the technicians worked on, poking and probing, burning and staining, until they made the dead tell tales. I wondered what Helene and Hugo Georg were saying.

The guard was moving his lips as he read. It's the old Norman French more than the Latin, I find. "The same old habeas corpus stuff," I told him confidentially, and I held out my plastic hand to take back the paper, looking as meek as I could.

"Hmph," he said, and he tapped the document with his spectacles as if he were about to criticize its wording. Then he said, "Who do you want to see?"

"Dr. Henry Wilms."

"You have an appointment?"

"It's about a case he's working on. I can't say any more." I shot a glance over my shoulder and then lowered my voice. "Bench won't let me." Without waiting for a response, I took the paper out of his hand and walked briskly to the bank of gray elevators.

Wilms was on the fourth floor, I remembered. I'd worked with him a bit when I was piecing together the Sammy Ott case and we'd got along just fine. He was their head man and it was a good bet he'd been given the Georg case. If he hadn't he would know who I should see.

I stopped outside his office. He was talking, and I caught the odd word that leaked out. "...distended...clearly cirrhotic with extensive scarring...collection of plasma in quantities associated with ascites..." I knocked.

"Come in," he called.

"Sounds to me like he should quit drinking," I said as I went in.

"Jantarro!" Wilms grinned and his tanned chipmunk-cheeks bunched up under his sharp eyes. We shook hands and then he cocked a thumb over his shoulder. "He has quit drinking," he said. A file lay open on his desk and beside it was a pile of slides and the dictaphone he had been talking to.

"Yeah," I said, "I guess that's one way to look at it. Cured by his own disease."

He shook his head. "Nope. The one for the road was a twenty-five caliber slug that turned left at his ribs." He waved a hand at the file. "This is just thoroughness."

"Thoroughness," I said sitting down, "I approve of that." He raised his bushy eyebrows in a question. "I'm working on the Georg case," I told him.

"I see," he said carefully, and I knew then that he was too.

"For Mr. Georg," I said, wanting to set up a confiding mood. He nodded. "I just wanted to be sure that the bodies I saw were really those of Helene and Hugo. Thoroughness," I added.

"I approve," he said. He blinked a little while he thought. "Is there any doubt?"

"From what I saw they could have been barbecued lamb. There's always doubt. Doubt is what we're paid for, you and me."

"Yes," he said. And then, "I can't tell you anything, Jantarro. You are specifically off limits. The word came down."

"From someone who never doubts," I said.

This time when he said, "Yes," he said it slower and more thoughtfully.

"You once explained something called correspondence matching to me."

"Correspondence rating. Yes. Records to tissue. Twenty-five scales, one to ten, themselves ranked in terms of likelihood. It's all probabilistic."

"Teeth and birthmarks and that sort of thing."

"That's right. First you assess the fullness of the records and give them a score. Then you go back and forth between the records and the tissues looking for correspondence. In the ideal case you've got HLA blood typing on the record and you can sew it up pretty quick. Mostly, you have to settle for the old ABO and some dental work. Although, it's surprising how many people have been worked up at some point in their lives for a surgical procedure. That helps a lot."

"Yes," I said, "and then you get a number at the end. Out of a hundred, right?"

"Right."

"Right. But I bet where there has been mutilation of the corpse—water damage, that sort of thing—"

"—or bad burning—"

"—yes, I bet that it can get pretty difficult to come up with a high score."

"You'd be surprised," he said.

"Really?"

"Uh huh. I've seen scores of eighty-two and seventy-five, even with bad burning."

"That's pretty high."

"At ninety you're wasting the pathologist's time."

"How low can it get before it's a case of mistaken identity?"

"Oh, around thirty you're fairly certain it could be somebody else."

Now came the tricky part. "I guess it would help if you knew what kind of experience the person had gone through before death. I mean, if they'd been shot first and you knew that. Of if they'd come in contact with a certain substance and you found traces of it on the body."

"Sorry, Jantarro. That doesn't come into it at all, and you know it. You're fishing for the results of other tests. I can't do it."

I got to my feet. "I won't push," I told him.

"It wouldn't do any good."

"That's why I won't do it," I said with a smile. He stood up and went to open the door.

"Come on," he said, "I'll walk you part way."

We went down the corridor in silence and he stopped outside a laboratory that had the door open. Inside I could see bottles on the main table, all filled with pale fluid in which pieces of unidentifiable matter floated. They were straw-colored, and umber and burnt sienna. I thought of the color of memories, fragments of the past gone sepia with age. After a while, death is dun like everything else.

"Thanks," I said.

"Gasoline," he said without looking at me. "Ordinary gasoline. That's all. On the inside too." And then he shrugged and said, "Good luck."

I went home to get some aspirins, some Scotch, and a chance to think. In that order. My head was killing me. Blasts of pain went off in time with my heartbeat, and each one rocked me slightly. I gobbled a bunch of the white pills and washed them down with my first Scotch and water. Then I waited for something to happen. When after five minutes nothing did, I administered myself my second drink and took my third to the big easy chair in the living room. Okay, I instructed myself carefully, we're sure it was Helene and Hugo. The high scores and the fact they found his shoe and her ring add up to certainty. Well, reasonable certainty, anyway. I smiled. This was thinking. Now all I had to do was go from here and figure out what to do. I leaned back and waited for the ideas to come, but all that happened was that my head seemed to bounce slightly with the pain.

I got up and put on a tape of Gould's new version of the *Goldberg Variations*. I like piano music, and Glenda had bought it for me as a going away present before she left for Florida. It was a sort of joke, because the piece had been commissioned to put the insomniac Count Keyserlingk to sleep at night, and Glenda had figured some soporifics are better than others. The real joke was that I hadn't had time to listen to it yet. Besides, Gould couldn't make a narco-leptic nod off; he attacks the piano like a typesetter past a deadline. He perks me up.

You're a kidnapper, I said to myself, sipping and listening. Why do you burn your victims' bodies?

I was caught by Gould. He was playing this variation much, much slower than he had done in the fifties' recording. I would have been willing to bet it was twice as slow. I let myself enter his portrait of Bach and my pain receded. Maybe it was the effect of age, the difference between Gould at twenty and Gould at fifty.

Ashes to ashes? Was that it? Had they been burned as part of some bent religious rite? No, you burn your bodies to prevent their identification. That's why you do it. In which case, you're not a very bright kidnapper if you don't do the job thoroughly—and that means stripping the bodies of clothing and jewelry. Gould picked up the pace and for a moment I marveled at the tattoo of diamonds rattling my head.

But—but I'd got away with the money in a neat little move that your ordinary snatch-and-run dummies wouldn't have thought of, so here I was, smart again. Maybe I started smart and then got frightened, lost my cool. I took a long pull on my drink. I had been cool enough to pour gasoline down my victims' throats before I torched them. The cold drink felt good in my stomach and I closed my eyes. The torrent of sharp percussive notes entered my head, eroding my will to pay attention, and I disappeared down stream in a dizzy whirl.

I awoke just before the tape ended. My Scotch and water was now a pool beside my chair, and I watched for a minute as the nylon carpet tried to soak it up. My right arm was still asleep and my left one buzzed faintly as it protested against the odd angle at which I'd abandoned it. A message, I thought. The bodies were burned to give someone a message. What would it be? Stop? Too late? Be afraid? Maybe that's what Renate Ebers was trying to tell me.

I fought my way out of the chair and stood uncertainly for a moment, groggy and slightly irritated. Instead of the canon on the tenth interval which the last variation ought to be, Bach threw in a graceful joke for the wakeful Count. He combined the original aria with two pop songs from the Baroque hit parade, ones that translated loosely as "Come a Little Closer, Honey, Been a Long Time Since," and "I Left Because I Couldn't Take the Mess." It was a limpid and beautiful piece of music, and it always made me sad.

In the silence after Bach, I realized I was hungry. I thought about running the tape again, but instead I put on the television so the noise would keep me company while I went to the kitchen to make a late lunch. Someone was doing terribly exciting things with a wok, to judge by the laughter and applause, and I stolidly beat tuna fish into a blob with mayonnaise. "Remember the crunch," I heard the chef say. I smeared the concoction on white toast and made a mental note to buy celery. A glass of milk went above the plate and to the right—about two o'clock, I would say—and next to the napkins sat two Oreos, possibly stale. I stepped back and applauded myself, but with me it's the sound of one hand clapping. Well, one and a half. Glenda always says it sounds like someone spanking a doll.

There were four things I could do, I decided halfway through the repast. I could follow up on this Demeny, just because his was the only name I had. I could go back to the Ebers woman and see if she knew more than she was telling me. Or I could go back to St. Albans and work at breaking through Helene's reputation. All of these assumed that the kidnapping was somehow tied into her past, and that was a long shot. Only, it might find me the inside man—or woman—if there was one. The fourth thing I could do was to get in touch with Groper or Benny the Fat to see if the mob would be willing to feed me a tidbit. Always presuming that they weren't involved in the first place. If they were, Georg could get himself another boy. I didn't think they were involved for the simple reason that I've never known them to use a woman in a key role. But it was possible that they'd become equal opportunity employers.

[75]

Getting up to look for a third stale Oreo, I thought about the mob. The syndicate. The Mafia. The Cosa Nostra. And three or four other Italian groups. And the Chinese Triad. The Maltese had their own. So did the Greeks. And the Vietnamese had brought with them some people who were prepared to supply their community's needs for a fee. And on and on. It was foolish of me to think of in the singular—*the* mob. But I guess I wanted it to be an *it*, a single thing that I could place over there, on the other side of town, unrelated to me and mine.

There was another reason I wanted it to be unitary. If there is one *mob* and if you deal carefully with the right people—observe all the necessary protocol—you stand a chance of doing whatever it is you want to do without tripping over a loose end. That's what I wanted to believe. Because if you do get in their way, it's ball game over. They seem to have an endless supply of crazies who will do whatever they're told for money. And crazies can't be defended against. That's why I have this fantasy about the mob. It's the same one most people have about their government, come to think of it.

Have another Oreo, Count Keyserlingk?

"HE SAYS to go on up." The young man delivered the message and then he propped a work boot up on the pile of wood where I was sitting and tilted his white hard hat back off his forehead. His eyes held some amusement and he pushed his hands into the down vest he was wearing as if to help him contain it. I couldn't stop myself. I let my gaze travel slowly up the side of the unfinished skyscraper all the way to the top where Demeny was supposed to be. When I unbent my neck I saw that the kid was grinning openly. A dare is a dare.

"Sure," I told him. "Coming with me?"

"Wouldn't miss it," he said with a laugh. We ducked under a huge vat of concrete dangling from the end of a cable that fell from a crane on the roof, and he led me through all the puddles and the muddy spots on the site. The rain had quit and the air was fresh and warm, unnaturally so for late October. It was the kind of day to go for a ramble in the country. Or to fly a kite.

At the door to the wire cage, he stopped and gave me a hard look. "You sure you want to do this?" he asked. I shrugged at him as nonchalantly as I can with all my leather on. "Last guy who did threw up all over the cage, slipped around like a guy on skates, and screamed a lot."

"That must have been fun," I said, and I walked into the flimsy elevator. He got in, fixed the door shut with a twist of wire, and punched a button on the junction box hanging near his head. Nothing happened. He grunted and pushed it again. We stayed where we were, the cold damp of the giant structure chilling my back while the lovely day beckoned from the front.

"Shit," he said, giving me a sheepish grin. "Loose connection." He undid the cage and stepped out to fiddle with a bundle of wires that were held to the wall of the building with string. Just for something to do I followed him out of the cage. He teased a yellow wire as thick as a pencil out of the bundle and ran his thumbnail up the exposed portion until he found a worn stretch of insulation. Then he wiggled the wire between his hands. The cage started up without us, but he didn't seem concerned. He gave the wire another jiggle and the cage stopped and began to descend. Carefully he smoothed the cable out against the others and smiled at me. "It's okay now," he said.

"Sure," I agreed.

I followed him back inside, and he tied up the door once more and pushed the button again. With a jerk we started to climb up the side of the building. The cage ran between strips of old board that had been nailed together into a long two-sided chute that stopped us from swinging in the breeze. But we bounced against the boards and each collision bumped us out a little toward the empty sky and the hard-looking road across the way. Along about the fifteenth

[78]

floor, when it was clear I wasn't going to throw up, he relaxed a little and began to talk.

"You in construction?" he shouted over the wind. I shook my head. "Money?" he yelled. I shook my head again. He looked at me carefully and then nodded slowly. "Demeny's a good man, you know?" It was getting harder to make out his words the higher we got, because the wind had a clear shot at us above the surrounding buildings.

"Yeah?" I said, and I lost count of the number of bumps.

"Yeah. A good boss."

Who did he think I was? "That's good."

"Works hard."

We were bellowing at each other now like belligerents, and rocking back and forth in the enclosed space, I felt like a boxer trapped into ten rounds with a stranger. The cage hit the top and the jolt nearly knocked me off my feet. We were in a little hut built out from the roof and suspended over nothing. The kid jammed his hat down tight and undid the wire catch, motioning for me to go first onto the plank that led around the cage. The wood creaked under my weight with every step I took, so I thought about the way the deck used to creak on my father's boat, the one that he built himself in the backyard where the neighbors would gather and crack jokes about Noah.

It was like landing on Mars. I was glad to get there but I was immediately ready to go home. The roof was an immense, barren expanse of black, a parking lot in the sky broken only by a shantylike construction half a block away to my right. Directly ahead of me, a hundred yards off, three figures stood close together with their backs towards us. And from where I was they looked to be at the very edge of the world, perhaps debating whether to fly away or to sail down. As I left the shelter of the elevator hut the wind hit me and ripped my jacket open, flapping it like the cape of some mad movie baron and showing my gun to the kid. I could see the look of alarm in his eyes, and he moved sideways to put some distance between us, as if that would have helped. I left him behind and plowed through the air toward Demeny.

At the midpoint I tried hailing him. Waving my arms I shouted his name two or three times, but I might as well have been in another county for all the effect it had. Tacking to the right, I thought, could put me in his peripheral vision, and he would be aware of me sooner than if I stayed on a straight course. I'd hate to startle a man at the edge of the world. After another thirty yards somebody's head moved, so I stopped and shouted again. All three men turned. Then they began to walk toward me. I buttoned my jacket but the wind trapped inside ballooned it out until I felt light enough to float away, and I realized that there was nothing on the tar-flats to hang on to, nothing to connect us to the world below.

Demeny had to be the one in the middle. The other two flanked him and moved out to position themselves slightly in front of him, the way that bodyguards will. The short one—the one I had spotted as Demeny—was wearing a track suit of dark blue and he kept bouncing up and down as he walked, like a fighter, nervously dancing on the balls of his feet. I was unsure whether I was imagining things, the way the meeting was working up to a confrontation, a showdown in which I was outnumbered three to one. Four to one, if you counted the kid I had left somewhere behind me. I turned to find him, but he was nowhere in sight. He was probably just staying out of the wind. Maybe he was loosening a board in the elevator hut, so I'd drop like a turd from a tall cow when I tried to get down. It was the constant wind, I told myself, that was unnerving me. Was it to be a shootout up here in the great corral in the sky? Or was it to be the old loose-board trick? You can't have it both ways, Jantarro.

"What do you want?" Demeny's words flew past the two men and barely kissed my ears on their way to the wild blue yonder. The trio stopped a good ten paces short of me.

"I just want to talk to you," I called to them. They had a

quick, huddled conference and they all shook their heads. No talk? Who doesn't talk?

The big one on the right filled his lungs. "Can't hear you," he hollered.

"Talk," I screamed. What the hell was going on? I began to close the gap between us. The musclemen moved closer to Demeny, ready to block my way. When I was about six feet off, I stopped and held up a finger to get their attention. With careful mime I displayed my empty hands, and then keeping both of them out where they could be seen, I slowly moved my right hand to the outside of my jacket pocket. I turned slightly so that my right side was toward them and the jacket was flattened against my body by the wind. With exaggerated gestures I made them see the pocket was empty and that I was going to put my hand into it. I checked their faces to see if my message was getting across; they were rapt and suspicious at the same time. Slowly I slid my hand down the side of my jacket and into the pocket, bringing out a card with my name and occupation printed on it. It snapped and twitched in my outstretched hand, as the wind threatened to snatch me and my job away.

It had taken me a couple of bad experiences to learn to carry some ID in places well-removed from my gun. The first time, I had reached without thinking and got clubbed by an oversuspicious type who never even apologized. Maybe that's too hard on him. When I came round he was gone, and since we never met again, he never had the chance. The other time, I wound up having to shoot a man. It was that incident that taught me the lesson, although you'd think it would have been the other way around.

The big one stepped forward and reached for the card. I didn't let go until he pulled it hard. He retreated with his prize, like some stone-age primitive with an anthropologist's note paper, curious and fundamentally skeptical all at once. He held it for Demeny to read, moving his lips as his boss took in the words. Demeny tapped the card with a finger and it flew out of the big man's hand and tumbled along the roof until it disappeared, then he bounced out from behind his men and came over to me. "Jantarro?" he shouted into my ear.

"Yes," I shouted back.

He put his head close to mine, and as he reached up to loop an arm round my shoulder he said, "Come on." Nodding toward the cage, he pulled me with him across the roof. At the hut he went first and didn't disappear through the floor. The kid was in the cage waiting, and he looked relieved when he saw Demeny and me so chummy. Eagerly he rushed to tie up the door and punch the button that would drop us slowly to the ground.

After the fifth or sixth bump I shouted at Demeny, "What was that all about up there?" The kid put his eyes on Demeny's face, the worried look back in them. Demeny made a wig-wag motion with his hand and just bounced up and down silently. I shrugged and watched the cars and people get steadily bigger.

When we got out Demeny said, "This is my boy, Jimmy."

"Hi, Jimmy," I said, and took his hard handshake.

"Now bugger off," Demeny told the kid. Jimmy smiled bashfully and did as he was told. "He's going to be an architect," Demeny said, as we picked our way carefully through the site. It was funny how leaden and clumsy I felt, as if the gravity down here were stronger than it had been in the sky. Demeny fished in the pouch pocket of his track suit, brought out a bunch of keys, and fitted one into the lock of the trailer door that had 'Office' written on it in paint. Inside there was a beat-up old desk with a chair behind it, and on the other side of the room two folding chairs leaned against the wall. The shelves were full of papers in messy piles along with samples of brick and odd-shaped bits of metal. The walls were covered with plastic paneling in a fake wood-grain.

"Sit," said Demeny, and he went behind the desk to take

a beer out of the small fridge under one of the shelves. I unfolded a bridge chair and sat. Demeny uncapped the bottle, took a pull, and then remembered his manners. "Beer?" he asked me, hoisting the bottle in front of him. I shook my head. He drank again and set the bottle down on a bunch of papers that were spread out on the desk. He sighed deeply and scrubbed at his face with both hands. It was a square face, blocky, and once it might have suggested strength; but now the flesh hung loosely, muscles gone to fat and skin gone slack. Wisps of mouse-colored hair stuck to the top of his head, adding to the aura of decay and defeat that surrounded him. I thought that this is how an old gladiator might look. He poked a finger into his ear and jiggled it. "So?" he said.

"Helene Georg," I said.

"So?"

"You knew her."

"Built the house for her old man."

"Tell me about it?"

He pushed out his lips and rubbed them back and forth against each other. "What's your...interest?" he said.

"I'm investigating her kidnapping. And her death."

His eyes widened at that. "Dead? That wasn't in the papers," he said.

"Not yet," I agreed. He sucked thoughtfully on the beer bottle, keeping his gaze on my face. I got the impression that he was recollecting more than stalling for time.

"That's too bad," he said. "Her old man hired you, hey?" I shrugged. "Yeah, well. What do you want to know? There isn't a whole lot I can tell you. I knew her maybe ten years ago."

"Must have been something. They still talk about you."

"That so?" His eyes narrowed and he didn't seem pleased. I waited for him to speak again, and now I knew he was putting the pieces together in a story for my benefit. "You never met her?" he asked. I shook my head. "Well..." he said, and leaned back in his chair, tilting it onto the back two legs as he swung his feet on to the desk. "She was only the sexiest woman I ever met. That's what you've got to understand. Give you a hard-on when you walk into the same room with her. That kind of sexy." He plucked at the chest of his track suit with a distracted air. "It's not like she *did* anything, you know? I mean, no bump and grind. No wet lips. None of that whore stuff. She didn't need anything like that." He looked up and for a second I thought he was staring at me, but he was seeing right through me into the past. "I used to think it was the way she smelled," he said to himself. "Like those phono ...phemo...whatever, those smell molecules that animals put out so they can find each other and get it off. But I don't know. Didn't matter a damn, really. There's some guys, the world can be ending and they're busy trying to figure out why."

"But not you," I said.

"What?"

"You and the sexiest woman you ever met. You don't stand around using your head, right?"

He let his head fall back and he laughed a loud, raucous laugh. "Frank Demeny gets it off," he laughed. "Frank Demeny gets a hard-on, he uses it." He raised a clenched fist and shook it in a mock salute to himself, to manhood. "Is that what you think?" I shrugged. "Sure," he said. "Sure, most times that's just what I do. I read somewhere every man's got sixteen thousand shots in him, and I'm doing my best to go out with an empty gun. Why not?" Suddenly he dropped his feet and leaned forward, his forearms flat along the desk and his head low between them like some big cat. "But you got to understand something else, too, mister private detective. That"—he stabbed a finger at my crotch— "doesn't lead me around. I'm no dog on a short leash. I do what I decide to do." He sat upright again and tapped his skull. "I can think." He gave a short barking laugh. "Besides, she didn't want it." I lifted my eyebrows. "I know what you're thinking," he said, "but you're wrong. She wasn't a prick-teaser. She didn't get you all hot and bothered just for the fun of telling you no. It's like I said. She didn't *do* anything. Maybe she knew what was going on, but it was just the way she was. If you got steamed up, well, that was your own problem. The guys on the job used to say she was a dyke. Could be, I guess, but I don't think so. I think she just didn't want it."

"So what was all the fuss about?" I asked.

"Didn't her old man tell you?"

"You tell me."

"My side of it, right? Why not? I guess it's a good thing that you think maybe there's another side to the story. Sure you don't want a beer?" His hand was already snaking back behind him for another bottle. He got one and jerked the cap off using the edge of the desk, taking a long pull before he spoke. "It's simple really. Her old man reckoned that the two of us were making it. Don't blame him. I was coming on pretty strong, snorting and pawing the ground— all that stuff. Anyway, he takes me aside one day: 'A valk in de garten,' he says. So we do a tour, all cool and how-is-the-work-coming. Then, wham! He says he's going to bust me. Now, you got to understand that ten years ago I'm— what?—forty-five, I'm still a comer. Nearly twenty years I been coming on, from brick layer to my own building business. Had it all and lost it once already, by then. And here I am on the comeback trail, and I'm so close I can taste it. And this old fart says he's going to bust me. He spells it out—on his fingers, you know? One, I'm going to have you charged with theft, he says to me. And he can, too. I've been taking stuff off his job to use on another job. Cash-flow problem. Everybody does it. But the way we got it set up, the stuff on his site belongs to him. So he's got me. Two, he says, I'm going to make sure you can never borrow money again from any bank. Damned if he doesn't know where all my lines are and for how much. And three, I'm going to let it be known—that's the way he said it—let it be known—that you cooperated with the Chinese when you were a prisoner of war."

He squared his shoulders and gazed at a space between us for a minute. "Korea," he explained to me. "The Chinese were in Korea—"

"I know," I said.

"Yeah."

"Did he?" I asked him.

"I was just a kid, you know?"

"Soldiers are."

"Yeah." He made a sound halfway between a laugh and a cry. "He did, all right. Everything except that last thing." He looked at me hard. "It was a lie. That last thing. I never did."

"But the rest—"

"He turned off my money like bending a garden hose. The cops were down on me quick as a flash, but all formal like. You understand this, you understand that. And always Mister Demeny. The deal was I got to finish the house first before the charges went in. Georg doled out the money every day, and the men went up to the old house to get their pay. Can you feature that? Like hired help, for raking the leaves." The bottle was empty and he set it down carefully on the desk, considering it as if a genie might emerge from its brown mouth. "Built the fucker, though," he told the bottle. "And Georg hands me a check at the end—just before the cops took me down and booked me."

"Have you seen her since?"

He seemed surprised to find me there. "Who? Helene? Are you kidding? She's bad news for me."

I looked around the trailer. "But you made it back," I said, half question and half accusation.

"Yeah. Banks aren't the only places got money, you know. And I'm a good builder." He turned his head to the wall behind which the unfinished skyscraper rose. "This is the big one. Then Jimmy does the work." He looked back at me with something of pleasure and pride mingled in his expression. "What's a kid for if he can't support you in your old age?"

"Anything else you can tell me, Mr. Demeny? Anything that might be helpful on her kidnapping?"

"Did I hate him enough to do it, you mean? Sure I did. Still do. Did I do it?" He shook his head solemnly. "Nope."

I got to my feet and opened the door. It was dusk, all orange and purple. "What was that business on the roof?" I asked him with one hand on the doorknob.

He grinned. "Let's just say I thought you were the man come to read the meter, and I thought you should see it from the right perspective."

"Troubles with the gas company?"

"Something like that."

"Hope you straigthen them out."

"Have to," he said. "Can't cook without gas."

10

THE EVENING was warm. The moist air dissolved the day's accumulation of city smells and drifted them past my nose like a replay of everyone's life all at once. Not unpleasant. I loosened my tie and walked, warily at first, afraid my head would pound each time my heel hit concrete; but when the brain just ticked over quietly instead of complaining, I lengthened my stride and breathed in large quantities of civilization soup. I felt languorously excited, the way I feel when I have cracked a case and don't know it yet, like someone enjoying a birthday present without unwrapping it.

But I always peek. So I lifted a corner of my mood and tried to see what I had got that made me think I'd cracked anything except my head. There was nothing there. What did I have? Demeny? He was a possibility, of course. Right now everyone was a possibility. But when I thought consciously about him, I wasn't impressed with his chances, and therefore not with mine either. On the surface he looked pretty good. The revenge motive was right out there where it couldn't be missed, and the money motive could be made to stand up without much difficulty. When the money dried up, he might have found private backers; and he might have made it from oblivion to that obelisk of his legitimately with luck and with sweat. But chances were it didn't happen that way. Chances were he found backers so private that you couldn't find them even if you looked real hard. And once you get involved with the mob's money, everything has to go just right or they call in the loan and you with it. Suppose, I explained to myself, he ran into some problem. What would be more natural than that he'd take the funds he needed from the man who was responsible for dropping him in the shit in the first place?

But.

But what? I asked myself. Well, for one thing, he'd have been better off robbing a bank. And if he had to kidnap, then he should have picked someone other than the obvious. The mob wouldn't have let him go ahead and pull a stunt like this, where the fallout could only land on them. And they would have known about it if it was their money he was working with. Another good reason for calling Groper, I thought, and I shivered and told myself it was getting colder.

Even without the mob's money as a factor, it was just too pat for Demeny to be the one. His arrest record made it certain that the cops would be on him sooner or later, and he wasn't so stupid he couldn't see that. He hadn't mentioned any visits from the cops, and I wondered if for once I was out in front. That was another puzzle, because all the cops had to do was to run Georg's name through the computer to get a cross-reference to Demeny. If he wasn't on theirs, the feds would have him for sure.

I stopped to buy some chestnuts from a street vendor. "What do you think?" I asked him. He handed me the little brown paper bag full of hot nuts and appeared to consider my question.

"The weather," he said.

"Nice."

"Sure it's nice. Too nice. Something is wrong. Should be getting colder not warmer. I think maybe the Russians fooling around with the weather. Make the seasons go backwards. Soon we have summer again," he said gloomily, shaking his head.

A plastic hand is good for holding hot nuts while you peel them. I can also take things out of the oven with it, although they get upset with me at the body shop if I melt the finger tips. I've discovered that a three-fifty oven is okay if I move quickly.

The vendor was right. Something was wrong. It was too nice. That was a lousy reason for excluding Demeny, but it was the reason I liked because it was the only one I could come up with, and I had a feeling he wasn't the one. A feeling. No matter how much I disparaged my feeling, my mood of suppressed euphoria wouldn't go away, so I smiled a secret smile and drifted on home.

JoJo was there, feet up on the couch with rock music boiling out of the speakers and steaming all over him. I was glad to see him. Pleased and a little nervous because of the way I'd left him the last time. My jacket was off and a drink in my hand before he opened his eyes. "You brute," he said, forcing his flat face into a moue; and then he grinned.

I turned the music down. "You say that to all the guys."

His grin faded slowly and he put his head back on the cushion and closed his eyes. "Where's Glenda?" he asked dreamily. It was a good bet he was stoned.

"In Florida," I said, "doing her lawyerly thing."

"Good."

"Hey, JoJo. I thought we had all that worked out. You're not going to..."

"Slip it to you?" His voice was low, smooth and edged with an anger I'd never heard before. "Touch your important body with my grubby tool? Hide the salami in your cupboard?"

"Cut it out, JoJo—"

"—Forget it, Cage. I'm bringing good news, not a social disease."

"Listen, JoJo—"

"—I said forget it, man. I don't want to talk. I don't want to talk anymore in my whole life about how I'm different. About how it's not really a disease. About gay rights. Or wrongs. Or anything. Talking is not what I'm into, you know, Cage?" Thin strains of some kid singing through his nose bled out of the stereo, punctuated every now and then by a rattle of drums like distant gunfire. My drink was gone so I got another. He liked to dramatize, I reminded myself. The first time I met him he was doing an impersonation of a victim of police brutality at fifty-one division, gasping and running around clutching his genitals while he moaned that he'd say anything they wanted if only they wouldn't hit him anymore. I thought I was saving him; the cops thought they were getting rid of a pain in the ass; and he thought he'd found a partner for the night. We were both a bit surprised when we discovered friendship.

"What's the good news?" I asked him.

He reached into his pants pocket and pulled out a cassette. "I got it on tape. Pillow talk. I'm a spy, man!" He said it with a snarl that twisted his lips. He held the tape out for a second and then flipped it in my direction with a contemptuous snap of his thick wrist. It clattered against the coffee table.

For the second time that day I listened to things I didn't really want to hear, only this time the sounds weren't so clinical and the bodies weren't welded together by any permanent heat. JoJo lay there with a grim smile on his face, opening his eyes every now and then to see how I was taking it.

It was Arnie, a young married cop with two kids and cheeks still pink from the country air. He had joined the force a few years ago, and I had met him a couple of times when Bench and I were on speaking terms. Every mother's dream in blue, Arnie was training in police intelligence and could get his hands on anything he wanted; gay in a town where cops pounded on gays for amusement, Arnie was also training in disaster. And I had helped to provide a lesson in the second course. I took a breath and told myself that if it wasn't JoJo, it'd be somebody else.

There were whimpering noises in the speakers—short, regularly-spaced mewings. I thought how funny it was that I couldn't tell whether it was Arnie or JoJo, or whether the sounds were the cries of pain or ecstasy. In a moment I knew it was Arnie. JoJo stirred on my couch. "Good part coming, Cage," he said tonelessly.

Arnie screamed. "No!...Jesus, God...don't..." Then there were smacks and thuds. Arnie's raw breath was in the room with me. He screamed again, this time without words. Shaking I turned the machine off.

I heard myself say, "What did you...do that for?" But I knew. It was JoJo's way of making me live through what he thought I'd wanted him to do, his revenge for my presumption. A great anger had taken me by the shoulders and was shaking me. I was getting closer to JoJo. "You faggot!" I shouted at him.

He was up off the couch now, stretching luxuriously, letting his muscles pull his shirt tight. "What's the matter?" he said as if to a baby. "Does the big strong detective feel bad? Is the big strong detective going to beat up on the queer? So manly!"

For a moment it was what we both wanted. My breathing was deep and fast, and I felt dizzy with all the oxygen and no place for it to go but my head. What was I going to do? Was I going to start hitting JoJo because he'd hurt Arnie because I'd hurt him? And all for the reason that I needed to steal from the cops something that I should have been able to get for myself. My head hurt so badly I thought I might pass out. It was as if a crab had fastened itself to the back of my brain and was clawing at it. I made it to a seat and held my head in my hand for a moment, willing the pain to recede. "I think you'd better go," I managed to tell JoJo.

He looked at me menacingly for another minute, then at his hands. Abruptly he smacked a fist into his palm, and the sound was loud enough to make me wince. "Fuck you," he said through clenched teeth, and then he left.

Some time later I played the rest of the tape for myself. I caught myself at the tape deck pushing all the right buttons, driven by curiosity and telling myself that there would be time, later, to straighten things out with JoJo. I didn't hear Arnie's voice anymore, only the information I needed.

The fake cab driver was a woman named Harriet Gorton. Bench had found her prints on record from when she'd been busted for prostitution four or five years ago. So far, they hadn't found out where she lived. And Georg. My client. He had been a Nazi. Bench figured maybe he had his wife killed because she was going to reveal his past and that might involve him in the recent efforts by some prosecutors to have old war criminals deported.

Jantarro, working for a Nazi. Once again I was sorry I listened to the tape.

THERE'S A THEORY that every person or object in your dream is a part of you, a projection of an aspect of your psyche. If so, I was in pretty bad shape. According to my dream, I was a cave, hard, cold and empty. I was also a whole football team trapped in that cave by a one-eyed monster. The secret fire we'd built at the back of the cave was me too, as was the log we sharpened and roasted in that fire. The parts of me in numbered jerseys huddled, and number five gave the play: straight up the middle, power play, the backfield to carry the spear, which was me. Hut-hut-hut-hike! I was feet pounding, I was blood pounding, I was the ecstasy of a soaring attack. But could I have been the towering Cyclops whose sad puzzled face caught the pointed log? Or the huge eye that hissed and sizzed on the stick we had thrown? I must have been the charred hole and the urge to touch it. We woke up before we could see if we had escaped.

It was not the kind of morning the scriptwriter of my dream would have liked. Dawn did nothing with her rosy fingers but hide them in a fist of gray cloud, squeezing rain on to me and all the parts of me I could see from my window. I took a hot bath, shaved, and made some toast. The bridge column had a complicated coup to explain and it failed, leaving me still stuck in dummy without transportation. I did the dishes. And then I called Groper.

Rather him than Benny the Fat, I decided. Benny was always trying to play the angles and I didn't trust him. He wasn't deliberately treacherous, he just saw it as his God-given right to play all ends against the middle, and angles or ends I wanted nothing to go wrong with this approach to the mob. Groper had been a cell mate of mine for about three days before they moved him on to some minimum security place to do his eighteen months for trying to pass a bad check. He's done close to ten years all told, and because I listened to him recount the highlights of every single one of them in our three days together he considers me a friend. Because he believed me when I explained how I was framed, he's right.

"How's the boy?" he asked brightly. Groper never sleeps, so far as I can tell, and he is always alert and ready to chat.

"Chugging along, Gropes, chugging along," I told him.

"The little engine that could, hey Cagey? Choo-choo." He imitated the sound of a train whistle. Groper is not very grown-up.

"You got it, fella. Say, listen Gropes, I need a favor."

"Sure thing, Cagey. What's up?"

"I'm working on the Georg killing. You hear about that? The wife and kid?" It had been in the morning paper. Groper didn't read much but he had friends who did.

"The rich guy whose wife and boy were kidnapped?"

"That's the one."

"Whew! Way to go, Cagey. That's a nice job to get. I mean, a rich guy and all."

"Yeah, well," I said, "you got to earn a buck." You also can't rush Groper.

"Too true, too true." There was a thoughtful silence while we both considered the lash of the economic whip. Then Groper spoke again, his voice a little hushed. "But that was terrible what they did. Burning them like that. Who would do a thing like that?"

"That's what I'm trying to figure out, Gropes. And I need your help. See, I don't want to step on any toes unless I have to. It looked like the snatch was done by pros, and I wondered if you could put the word out with the big boys to see if they got a line on people working in that game. Now if it was one of their things that went wrong, then okay, maybe I should know that too so I don't back into anything. But if it wasn't something they were in on, then I could use a little information."

"Sure thing, Cagey. But it couldn't have been any of the big boys. They don't burn people that way."

"I hope not. And Gropes? Try this name on them. Harriet Gorton. She was in on the grab. She used to be a hooker. Maybe she still is. Gumball would know, right?"

"Gumball knows everything about women," said Groper with the kind of awe you might reserve for a nuclear physicist. "That it?"

"One more name," I said, feeling my throat tighten up against the words. "He could be a client of the big boys. Name of Demeny. Frank Demeny. Normally I wouldn't mess in their business, but it's possible he did it. Float that out and see what happens, will you?"

"Sure thing, Cagey. That it?"

"That's it." I almost forgot. "So how's by you?"

Groper launched into a long story about an aunt of his that had come to live with him because her husband had kicked her out, and that was good and bad because while he got home-cooked meals he also got questioned about his life and he didn't know what to answer. I told him I never knew what to answer either.

It's hard to find a hooker in the morning. I did a phone survey and found that most of the ones I knew took their phones off the hook. The rest just let it ring. I was being lazy, I told myself. What was wrong with the old-fashioned business of walking the streets and soliciting the information that way? A quick check out the window told me it was still raining, and I knew what was wrong with the old-fashioned way. But I was a detective, not a call-girl, and I couldn't get rich and stay dry at the same time.

I particularly wanted to find Lois West. She had worked with me on the Curtis case, and she was by way of being a president of the hookers' union—those that didn't work with pimps, at least. She had stayed cool when every hooker and would-be whore in town dressed like a nun and would only open the door to God because of the Curtis kid and his .22 target pistol. Together we set him up, and alone she drew him in. Back then she lived on College Street, among the university people who never asked her about her work. I figured her old address was as good a place to start as any.

I took a streetcar instead of a taxi. It was that kind of day, a stop and go, easy-does-it day. And as luck would have it I got an old one, paint peeling and windows that opened by turning a wooden-handled crank. Going back in time, I thought, not to the good old days—there never were any, even when I could fumble the ball with either hand—but to what was known already, what was given. Given. Gifts are given, I thought. But the past doesn't come free the way that gifts are supposed to. Beware of Greeks bearing the past. I dozed and dreamily resurrected the Cyclops from my dawn fantasy, letting that monster show me his face in the safe daylight where I was surrounded by old women dressed in black, teenagers skipping school, housewives on their way to a bargain. The thing about having one eye, I heard my mind say, is that you haven't any depth perception. At the same time I realized that Lois hadn't seen me since I'd lost my arm, and in all the mental pictures I'd formed of us together I had two hands to touch her with, two wrists to turn, two sets of biceps to flex whenever the occasion demanded.

I missed my stop. When I walked back, I found that the dark brown brick building was still there. That was something at least. She used to be in apartment four-oh-four, top floor, southeast corner. I got my shoes wet on the grass going round to check the windows, though I didn't have any idea what I was looking for. Shades were down. She'd had shades then, I thought I remembered. No name on the mailbox for four-oh-four. I pressed her buzzer and waited, then I pressed it again—a long buzz this time, the way I might if she had been late for a date and I was angry. At random I picked another buzzer, then another, finally getting a response from the speaker. "It's Jantarro," I said before I thought. The door clicked open anyway. I wondered what he thought I'd said.

My pounding brought someone to the door. "Who is it?" asked a female voice that might have been hers. This time I was ready.

"It's Jantarro," I said. There was a moment's silence, so I added, "Kenneth." I think I blushed. No one ever calls me that because no one is permitted to call me that—except her—and that was only because she chose to and persisted in it in spite of anything I did.

"Kenneth? Is that you?"

"Open up, I'm getting bored out here." She opened up and backed hesitantly away from the door to let me in.

"Look at you," she said, still surprised. "You look great. Even at this ungodly hour." She glanced down at her flannel nightgown and her beaten-up old carpet slippers, and her hand went to her face protectively. "Oh," she said, "don't look at *me*, though. I'm rumpled." I was surprised at how rumpled she did look, and not just her clothing either. Her face had new lines that connected with the old ones and there was a tired look around her eyes that no amount of sleep would erase. The hand she held up was bonier than I remembered, with a raw splotch below her index finger. Her hair was still red but it was shorter now and cut severely instead of bouncing in the coils that made it glint.

Our eyes met and she giggled a little sound of chagrin and pleasure mixed. It was awkward, but we went through the normal routines of people who didn't used to be strangers. She was reserved, holding her arms across her chest like a protective virgin and lowering her voice to the creamy public tones of a well-trained hostess. I apologized a dozen times—for just barging in, for not keeping in touch, for staying in after I'd barged. She made me coffee and retreated to let me drink it in mild confusion while she got dressed in mild annoyance.

Her place was nicer than it used to be. She had some new, black lacquer Chinese pieces that sat comfortably on a pinkish Chinese rug that hadn't been there when I used to know her. There was art on her walls now instead of the posters of Paris and some antique furniture exhibition. The big piece across from the couch where I was sitting was a drawing on yellowed paper of a naked, pregnant woman at the left, the silhouette of a man standing in a boat in the middle, and at the right, the man and the woman together. Under it all the artist had written TRANS FORM. I wasn't sure I liked it. But I did approve of the room. It was more formal, more serious, elegant without looking as if a decorator had done it.

"Like it?" I must have given her a funny look, because she said, "No, silly. I meant the room." She spread her hands to encompass it.

"I like it. I like it a lot."

"Good. I think it came together nicely. It was time to get out of wicker and Laura Ashley."

The change in her was stunning. She had put on a beautifully cut Italian tweed suit over a white shirt with little pleats on the front. An ivory necklace reminded me that she had breasts underneath the business clothing by the way it didn't fall straight down. She wore no other jewelry. Her skin glowed soft and pale, all the wrinkles effaced as if by magic. Mature was the word that came into my mind. Ripe in a way that could make me avid.

She smiled at me and shook her head. "It's all prosthetics, Kenneth. Like your arm."

I looked down at the forgotten limb and then up again quickly. "You knew."

"Of course. It made the papers, and I followed your career for a while. You were my hero, you know. Big, strong, ugly enough to be irresistible. And kind. Very, very kind." She smiled again, less wanly this time. "Not that there's anything wrong with prosthetics. Tools to do a job, like hammers or crotchless panties, for that matter."

"You're still—"

"—hooking? What did you think? That I'd outgrow it or finally turn away from the path of sin?" There was an edge to the last few words that had come from honing them on something other than me.

"Actually, no," I said levelly. "I hoped you'd still be in the life, because I want to ask you a favor."

"Oh, Kenneth, not a freebie. Please not a freebie. My accountant is all over my ass about the freebies I've been giving lately." She said it all with mock horror, but again there was the sharpness from some hidden knife that cut into her tone. I looked at her quizzically and she began to blink.

"Look," I said, getting up, "I've come at a bad time. I'm sorry, Lois. Give me a call sometime if you feel like it." By the time I got to the door I could hear her weeping, and I paused, torn between a desire to leave us each to our own problems and a feeling that I told myself was curiosity. Lois had never cried, when I knew her before. All bounce and

[100]

brass, that was Lois. And I wondered who this sad, elegant stranger was.

"Sorry," she said as I turned around. Then over a sob she said with difficulty, "Funny word, whore. It...it's related to the Latin word for dear. Did you know that, Kenneth? Oh, dear."

I went back to where it was still warm on the couch. "Do you think there's any more coffee?" I asked. She nodded a big yes and spluttered a laugh through her tears. Carefully, she took the porcelain cup and saucer into the kitchen. The fridge opened and closed, the water ran and in a moment the coffee maker made wet, puffing noises.

"I'm seeing a man," she told me abruptly from the kitchen. "Not a john." I said nothing. "He knows," she said. "And God help me I think I'm in love with him." China rattled a bit. "He says he wants to marry me. Can you believe that?" Her voice rose an octave. "I mean half the johns in the world will say they want to marry you. You're the first good fuck they've ever had, and they want to own you. It's crazy, isn't it? Though I suppose I can't go on hooking forever. I mean who would pay for it when I'm fifty? Unless I get married I probably won't even be able to give it away then." Her words had been coming faster and faster. Then they stopped. "Did you say you take milk? I can't remember."

"Milk and sugar," I called to her.

She came in with the coffee and set it down on the table with a graceful bend of her knees. Settling on her chair she smoothed out her skirt and looked at me sedately. "If you're going to whore, you should expect this kind of problem," she pronounced like some vicar's wife kindly stating the obvious. "Now"—all helpful and businesslike—"what can I do?"

I hesitated.

Then warmer, more genuine. "I mean it, Kenneth. You just caught me at a bad time. Whatever you need, if I can help."

"I'm looking for a whore." She started and then giggled the way she had when I first came. "Her name is—or was —Harriet Gorton. I don't know what names she used on the street, or even if she was on the street. Tall, be about twenty-five, six now. Long hair, white blonde. Now. Goes in for designer jeans, leather bomber jackets. Good-looking in a country and western way."

She flicked her gaze off to the side, thinking. I gave her time. "Where did she work? Did she have a pimp, because if she did it's not likely I'd know her. Only the independents, remember." She shot me a quick smile.

"I don't know any more than what I've told you. Except that she's into heavier stuff now. She was busted four or five years ago so I know she was in the life then. Any lead on her at all, I'd really appreciate it."

She shook her head slightly. "I don't know her. Not right off the bat, I mean. The description you gave me covers half the girls I know in the business. But I'll rack my brains and I'll ask around." She looked serious. "Is it okay to ask around?"

"Discreetly," I said. "She's got enough things on her mind that you're not going to scare her away. Besides, the cops are looking for her too."

"A race?" she grinned.

"A race. But Lois, be discreet because I don't want anything coming back on you. She's playing rough now and she's got some mean friends."

"Hey! It's the original tough cookie you're talking to."

"Thanks," I said, touching her finger tips with mine. She ran a hand over my fake fingers, lightly.

"It was very good to see you again. Old hero."

"Dear," I said. We both smiled.

12

"THANKS, SON, but I gave up drinking."

"It was either that or chocolates," I told him.

"I don't eat sugar either. Diabetes."

"Flowers, then. I should have brought flowers."

He chuckled. "I can't say I don't see or smell, though to tell you the truth, I don't know when the last time was that I saw something or smelled something consciously." I took the bottle of Johnny Walker Black Label from his lap and put it on the table beside us. He backed his wheelchair off a little to get a better view of me. "I've become habituated to this place, I guess," he said. "Most of the time I have my nose in a book and my eyes on the printed page." He turned his head slowly, as if it hurt him, taking in the sunroom where we were sitting, trying to see it. "I read a lot," he said.

John Scott had become a friend of my dad's when they were both in Spain with the Mackenzie-Papineau Battalion. I don't suppose I'd seen him since my father died almost eleven years ago. Scotus, my father called him, or Duns, because of some medieval philosopher who had disputed Aquinas's view of Aristotle—something to do with practice versus theory that I never properly understood. When he especially wanted to tease him he'd call him Doctor Subtilis. He had come back to teach but he didn't like it, so he published books instead—mostly small radical books that nobody ever read. I often wondered if my father didn't supply some of the money to keep the press and his friend going. Whatever the reason, both folded soon after my father's death, and Scotus had been in Sunnybrook Veterans' Wing for the past seven or eight years, not as a veteran of course, because the Spanish Civil War wasn't recognized by the government as a real war, stamped with the Good Housekeeping seal of approval. He was just here as an old soldier with complications that were identical to those that had caught up with soldiers who had fought in approved wars.

"Doctor Subtilis," I said out loud without really being aware of it. Thinking of my dad as much as anything, I suppose.

He was still looking at the rain on the sunroom window. "You remember," he said.

"Yes."

"Here to talk about your dad?"

It had never occurred to me, and for a moment I wanted to say yes. "No. Not really. I was just remembering."

"You're too young for that. Talking, constructing, rubbing against life to see what is generated—that's what you should be doing. There'll be plenty of time for remembering when you get to my age." He rubbed the stubble on his face but that only seemed to generate dissatisfaction, because he tightened his lips into two thin lines. "Listen to me. I sound like every old fart that ever lived too long. What happened to your arm?" Abruptly.

"Long story," I said, the standard line I use to fend off questions.

"Can't be that long. It was there ten years ago. Long is the stories I've got to tell. Fifty, sixty years, that's long. What was it? Cancer? An accident? A fight?"

I sighed and met his eyes. "A fight, I guess you could call it." I could smell the fat one as plainly as if he were there in the room with me, greasy, rancid like an old stew. His quick excited breathing was in my ear.

"Did you learn anything from it? No, I can see you didn't." He wasn't disapproving, merely stating a fact. "Not with the insurance company any more, are you?" I shook my head, told him what I did and he laughed. "Wouldn't your father love that. Wouldn't he just. Well, well." He chewed on that thought for a minute, working his jaws in little snaps. "If you didn't come here to talk about your father, what did you come for then?"

"I need some help. I want to talk to some old Nazis."

He frowned. "Nazi as a term of general disparagement, or Nazi as a term of art?"

"The real thing. German party members. From the Alsace, if possible." I thought of my client's careful choice of words. "Alsatians."

"That's pretty far out of my territory. Fascists was what they called themselves in Spain."

"Yes, I know. But there were Germans mixed in, weren't there?"

"There were." He went quiet, not moving except to lift his arms slightly above the armrests of his wheelchair. We must have stayed motionless for a whole three or four minutes, and I wondered if he could go to sleep with his eyes open.

"Well," I said eventually, "thanks for thinking about it. I'll check around with other people. It was good to—"

"Be quiet. You never could keep still, could you? I'm trying to come up with a name. I don't give up that easily, especially when this is the first chance to be remotely useful to anyone in longer than I care to remember." So we sat and were quiet some more. It wasn't really raining any longer, but the air was so wet that when it brushed up against the windows, drops formed and ran down in clear streaks, long lenses that gave distorted glimpses of the world outside. I tried to imagine how it would be for him, on the inside forever, and I wondered if he was angry and dead all at once like some lifers I had met.

"Dumbrowski," he said. "Stanislaw Dumbrowski." He looked pleased with himself. "Not exactly an Alsatian, but a Nazi for sure. We had him for a while, but he got away when we were overrun at ... wherever it was. He's in town, I believe. At least, he was a few years ago."

"You've been in contact with him?"

"No. I have some standards. Some of my contacts saw him. He was here. Working for the *Sun*, I think. City desk." He caught sight of his gesticulating hands and studied them for a second. "Mind you, he would be old, now. Probably too old to be working." His eyes came to mine. "But if you are what you say you are, you shouldn't have too much difficulty finding him."

We looked at each other, business done, out of amenities, separated by dead friend and father. "Goodbye," he said.

"Thank you, Doctor." He didn't hear me; a book was already in his hand and covering his face.

"Dumbrowski? I thought he'd gone to that great communist witch-hunt in the sky." The man in shirt sleeves turned back to the green, glowing monitor he was working on and punched a few more keys. "Forster!" he called without looking up.

From across the noisy press room someone shouted, "Yo!"

"Dumbrowski!" the editor yelled.

"Who?" came the reply.

Shirt sleeves swiveled in his seat and shrugged at me. "See?" he said. He returned to his monitor.

At the elevator a man came up to me. "I heard you asking about Dumbrowski." He drooped from a curved spine like a willow with only a few branches left, and he averted his eyes when he spoke.

"Yes," I said, "you know where he is?"

"What do you want him for?" He had to look almost behind himself to get that one out.

"I just want to talk to him, ask him some questions."

"Gee, I don't know."

"If you were him," I asked, "would you rather have nothing or a few questions?"

He thought about it, hanging his head. "You can find him at Marko's. It's sort of a chess club. A coffeehouse, really."

The big man behind the cash register pointed him out to me with a stab of his goatee. Dumbrowski sat at a table by himself and poked at a pawn in a game he seemed to be playing with himself. He sat stiffly erect in his chair, and as I watched from behind him for a moment, he smoothed his long white hair repeatedly with a nicotine-stained hand. He wore a white shirt with French cuffs, a pair of cavalry twill trousers, and badly scuffed desert boots. A dirty black overcoat hung across the back of his chair. I ordered a coffee and took it over to his table.

"Mr. Dumbrowski?"

"Correct." His whole body inclined briefly toward me. Dull, brown eyes toured me as if I were a potential recruit, but when they came to my hand a light went on in them. "Do I know you?"

"No. My name is Jantarro." I showed him my cup of coffee. "May I sit down?"

He drew the chess board toward him to make room for my cup and I got a chair from another table. "What is your business?" he asked as soon as I was seated. He had lit a cigarette and he puffed on it in small draughts. His forehead had wrinkled with some strain.

"I would like you to talk to me about Nazis," I told him. I didn't feel up to sneaking around the topic, and I wasn't about to pretend the kind of sympathies that might have opened him up more smoothly.

"I am playing a game in my mind, Mr. Jantarro," he said as if I hadn't spoken. He brought the hand with the cigarette down to the board and pointed the smoking end at the pieces in the middle. "These colored pieces of wood, I pretend that they are kings and queens, bishops and knights. I have known some real bishops and one or two men who could pass for knights. The rest I make up from films I have seen or from books that I read as a child. All it takes is a good imagination and I have a good imagination." The smoke curled up into his eyes and made him squint at me. "I think that you are playing a game in your mind, too. But instead of using bits of wood, you impress your imagination on flesh and blood. Wood has no feelings and doesn't mind, but...." He shrugged and smiled. "In short," he said, "I think you are crazy."

"Remarkable powers of diagnosis," I said, watching him over the rim of my coffee cup as I drank. "Shows some considerable familiarity with crazies. You don't mind talking to crazy people?"

He laughed and the gleam came and went in his eyes once again. "It can be amusing."

"Join me in my fantasy, then. It may be the best way to deal with me. I imagine that I need to speak to old National Socialist Party members and I also imagine that you are one of these people and you know others. Is this so?— within the game of course."

"Look around you, Mr. Jantarro." He flung his thumbs up to point over his shoulders at the five or six other old men in the room. "Every one of them is a person you describe." Could it be true, I wondered? Would old Nazis gather in a Bund like this? Somehow I had thought it wouldn't be safe for them to do that. But then who cared any longer? What would they have to fear, if their own consciences were tame? "Anton—at the cash—he is a Hungarian, so he doesn't really count. He was a party member, but he is a Magyar. The rest of us? *Echt deutsch,* as the poet says."

"Dumbrowski?"

"Poland's boundaries have moved a great deal. Besides, as you have agreed, so much is a matter of imagination."

"The Alsace has moved a lot, too." The room was hot and I suddenly felt the desire to be out of it, to be doing something straightforward, simple—clean. My headache had returned, and it seemed to push my eyes out with each throb. "Are there any . . . club members from the Alsace?" I asked him.

His face assumed an expression of distaste, gathering his mouth and causing a thousand lines to crack his lips. "Do you know what Hitler thought about the Alsatians? Characterless, he called them, because of the constant shifting of their nationality. They would be a gain to neither side, he thought."

I was sweating now. The coffee tasted of chicory, almost making me gag. "No Nazis from the Alsace?"

"I didn't say that, Mr. Jantarro." His voice had taken on a pedantic tone. The hand that had smoothed his white hair now preened him all over, straightening his cravat and his cuffs, tugging at the wrinkles in his shirt front. "There were indeed members from that part of Germany, and some of them did in fact distinguish themselves." He drew himself even more erect. "It is one thing to play games with you, but it is another to reel off lists of names. I play with wooden pieces, remember? It is you who deals in people."

"I don't want a list, Dumbrowski. I just want one name, someone who could tell me about what went on there during the war, someone who was in a position to know."

"One name. Someone who might know." A smile

flickered behind his gaze. "I think I could...imagine a name for you. He might not be willing to talk, you understand. But he was in a position to know. A club member, as you put it."

He had stopped talking for thirty seconds before I realized it. Something made me look down at the table. Dumbrowski's thumb was rubbing the side of his index finger in the crude request for money you see in old movies. I gave him a twenty of my own.

"Fritz Georg," he said. "Goodbye, Mr. Jantarro."

I THOUGHT I should think. And I knew I should eat. My mind and my body clamored for attention as I stood outside Marko's, letting the evening wind dry my sweat. I couldn't think of a good reason not to do either; I just didn't feel like it. I was restless, too unsettled by having what the tape said about my client confirmed. Dumbrowski's coffee had left its bitter taste in my mouth, and his words echoed mockingly in my ears. Worst of all, my head hurt so badly that I was afraid I might start weeping if I didn't distract myself with movement. So I turned right and began walking. Aimlessly. Unwinding my tension on a long, twisting strip of the city's sidewalks.

Where was there to go? I already had my lines out for the Gorton woman and Demeny. If I went for her I'd only be wasting my time, and if I went for him I'd run the risk of wasting my life over a money dispute that I didn't give a damn about. There was always Renate Ebers. She could talk about my client, the Alsatian, late of the National Socialist Party. But of course she would say she was not there, she did not know. Not tonight, I decided. No gloomy gatherings at the mansion beyond the sidewalks. The old men's faces hung before my mind's eye as in a gallery; Dumbrowski, Georg, Duns Scotus—my father. No, not tonight.

I had coffee and a doughnut at the Donut World on Davenport. The caffeine seemed to help my head. And then I walked some more—up along Church, I guess, because I wound up having another coffee and doughnut at a place off Dundas that was full of pushers and users, skinny whitefaced kids of sixteen, so frail it was a wonder they could turn the tricks and snatch the purses they needed to feed the habit. Two glue sniffers in a booth opposite mine considered me with eyes of glass, unblinking, like cheap, stuffed dolls. I wanted to shoo them out and bang some sense into their heads. Then I laughed at myself: Jantarro the childless parent.

And Jantarro the parentless child. I couldn't dissociate my problem with my client from my father. From my problem with my father. Stiff and composed, he looked at me silently from the past. Principles, boy, his piercing gaze demanded. Principles down to your marrow. Principles worth fighting for.

He had volunteered to fight for the Loyalists in Spain. I've seen pictures of him in uniform; the same sharp eyes I came to know later were then tinged with surprise, perhaps at where his principles had taken him; and his curly hair was almost blond, fuller than I remembered it in real life. Looking at the picture, you would have said that there was a scholarly man, an academic—and on second glance, you would have noticed something dangerous in the eyes, his uneven features, the set of his head. A scholar—or a revolutionary, you might have concluded a little uncertainly.

The battle along the Ebro, Sierra de la Llena, Tarragona. I worked it all out for myself with books from the library and old family photo albums. Dates, postmarks on letters my mother had saved, scraps picked up from conversations I had overheard between John Scott and my father. The retreat to Barcelona across Catalonia, the fall of the city to Franco and the scramble of two hundred thousand up into France in the winter of thirty-eight, thirty-nine. My first project in detection was finding my father, and I remembered how he stood unmoving as I proudly related to him all my discoveries about his place in the war. When I had finished he turned on his heel and left the room without a word.

Principles, I asked myself? Was I going to work for a Nazi?

"Nazi," said one of the glue sniffers, and I realized I had spoken out loud.

"You're crazy," said Levine with his face all happy smiles. "Right up my alley." He had me flat on my back, half undressed, and was busy sticking pins into me.

"Who's the one performing voodoo?"

He laughed. "Feel that?"

"Of course I feel that." He moved further up my leg.

"I'm serious," he said. "You should be resting, not running around. You've had a serious injury to your head; and unlike arms, heads come one to a body. You've got to take it easy or some permanent injury could result. Or you could miscalculate and get hit by a bus or pass out driving." He was up to my armpit. I would grunt every time I felt the needle and he would move higher.

"I don't drive," I said. "I already told you that."

He shrugged and regarded me benignly. "Your life," he said.

"My headaches too. What can you give me for those?"

"Nothing. And I want you to stay off alcohol." It was my turn to shrug. The plastic surface of the examining table felt cold against my bare shoulders. "Being tough is important to you, isn't it?" he said, pulling up a stool and sitting down near my head. I grunted the noise I had been making when the needles went in. He smiled and nodded, bobbing his head like a buoy in the wake of a motorboat. "Let me tell you about the brain," he said and he rubbed his hands together. I closed my eyes and let the sound of his voice push at my ears, comforting like the sound of surf or wind. He talked about something he called the Glasgow index and about how the brain was like a salt-water pudding. Axons, dendrites, aneurisms, and the death of cells. It was a curious bedtime story.

"Okay, Mr. Jantarro," he said after a while. "You win."

"Call me Cagey," I mumbled from near sleep.

"I'll call you crazy, if you don't mind. Can I have your brain when you die?"

I opened my eyes and found him grinning. "You've got one already," I said.

"Hundreds. All in nice, specially made jars. I'll put one aside with a label on it for yours."

"That bad?"

"Soon. If you keep it up."

"Nothing you can do about the headaches?"

"Nothing I can do. It's all up to you. If you take it easy for a couple of weeks—rest, lie around, read books—the headaches will go away."

"I can't," I said.

"Why not?"

"I've got a case."

"Give it to someone else."

"I can't."

"Why not?"

"I don't know."

He beamed. "Good. Good. You're learning, you're learning."

I swung my legs off the table and reached for my shirt and

pants. Neither of us said anything for a couple of minutes. Then I asked him, "Did you know Helene Georg?"

Levine began to wash his hands in the little sink in the corner of the examining room. "Is that what you're working on?" he asked without turning round. I said nothing. "No," he said after a moment's scrupulous attention to his fingernails. "No, I didn't. I met her once at a staff meeting about a patient we were both involved with. But know her? No."

"Who would I talk to to find out about her?"

"No idea." He grabbed a couple of paper towels from the dispenser and dabbed at his hands thoughtfully. "Not true," he said. "Her supervisor would be where I'd start." He tossed the towels into the waste basket and gave me an appraising glance. "But then, you could have thought of that all by yourself. So you probably want me to talk to her to see if I can get her to talk to you. Am I right?"

I was slipping my still-knotted tie over my head and struggling to get the fake hand to grasp the short end tightly enough to let me pull it up around my neck. The silk kept slithering out of the plastic grip. "It's a thought," I told him. "I spoke to Nurse Whitman who worked with Mrs. Georg, but she wasn't very helpful."

"Do you a deal," Levine said, watching my struggle with interest.

"A deal?"

"I'll set it up if you take a day's rest first."

"After," I said.

His eyes twinkled with amusement. "Shake on it?"

"Can't right now," I muttered. "My hands are tied up."

"Thirty years. Any idea how many bedpans that works out to? A conservative estimate of five a day times a short work week of five days is twenty-five a week. Multiply that times fifty weeks a year is ... is ..."

"Twelve-hundred and fifty," I offered. I poured her some

more wine and splashed a medicinal dose into my own glass.

"Twelve-hundred and fifty times thirty is..." I smiled at her. Liz Brook was a dumpy, plain woman of fifty or so. Her hair was dull brown, going gray, and she had drawn it back from her forehead many hours ago to put it in a bun that now looked like a tangle of hemp beaten to death by a porcupine. Strands hung down across her face and she kept flicking them back behind her ears every couple of minutes. She had changed out of her nurse's uniform into a black polyester sweater and a pair of creaseless flannel slacks. I've know bag-ladies who looked better than she did. I liked her.

"...three fives are fifteen, carry the one..." She was working it out on the tabletop with a finger dipped in wine. At first when Levine had called she had said she was too busy. I heard Levine echo her complaint and I listened with admiration as the smooth-talking son of a bitch had her laughing in half a minute. He promised I would buy her dinner—anything she wanted—which was why we were anticipating the delights of a Frank Vetere's deep-dish pizza and whetting our appetites with a wine that had once passed through Italy. "Thirty-seven-thousand five-hundred," she said with a kind of wonder as she gazed at the wet squiggles on the table.

"Change jobs," I advised her. "Go into something clean. Something pleasant and amusing."

"What, and give up healing the sick?" she shouted. We laughed and I filled our glasses again. Her laugh sounded like a spaniel greeting its master, yips of real delight that would roll over into song at the top of a breath, and I felt better just listening to her. Her face went sober suddenly and she fixed me with her slightly cockeyed gaze. "Why should I talk to you?" she asked.

"Because if you don't, I'll tell them to put anchovies on the pizza."

She flapped a rough hand at me. "No, Jantarro. No bullshit. I've been kidded by guys that'd make you look like a sophomore in high school. Why should I give out with Helene's life story? She's dead. I know about death. It's final." She reached for the bottle and topped up her glass. "I figure her story should die with her." She sipped at the wine, rapid little nervous pulls that looked incongruous from a hearty, unkempt woman.

"You'll have to tie it together with her son's story, then, and burn them both."

"Yes," she said quietly. "Poor Hugo." She fumbled in her bag for a cigarette, stuck it in her mouth and fumbled again for a lighter. It was an old Zippo and it took three tries to get it to flame. "Everybody forgets about Hugo," she said with a lungful of smoke.

"Middle-aged retarded men don't exactly figure in people's lives in a big way."

"Too bad. He was a sweetie."

"You knew him?"

She took another sip of wine, knowing she was letting herself be drawn and wondering if she minded. "Yes," she said. "A little. When Helene first started at St. Albans she brought him down to show him where she was going to be spending her time. He was really gentle. I remember the first time, we turned our backs on him for a minute—to talk shop I guess—and he was down the hall and into the patients' rooms. Making cooing noises and trying to stroke them. Funny damn thing was nobody seemed to mind. You figure a big retarded guy is going to come at you and touch you, you're going to scream or try to get away. A monster, like on TV, you know? But no. He was attracted to people and they were attracted to him." She lifted her eyes from her wineglass and looked at me and through me at the same time. "The way people are supposed to be, I guess. No fear. No hang-ups. Just gentleness."

The pizza came and she pulled off a huge slice and curled

it so the runny cheese and sauce wouldn't fall off. She stuck the pointed end in her mouth and bit with a satisfied moan.

Using a knife and fork I maneuvered a piece onto my plate and sawed away at the rubbery concoction. "What did Hugo do? I mean what did she do with him during the day?"

"For a while he was at an institute—Howard? Hawforth?—Institute for Special Education. But she took him out about a year ago. Maybe he'd gone as far as he could go. I don't know. She didn't say much about it. Then this last year she had him with her as much as she could. He used to sit around the waiting rooms a lot, looking at pictures in the old magazines. Sometimes the nurses would take him for coffee or for a walk. Sometimes the kids in training over at psych would drop by just to talk with him. I guess she used baby sitters a lot too."

She slid a piece of crust into her mouth and munched while she thought. "Something was wrong, you know. I could tell from the way Helene had lost a lot of her drive. She was one of the best nurses I ever had," she said defiantly, and she reached for another piece of pizza.

I took my first bite. It wasn't as bad as I had feared. Or I was hungrier than I had realized. "What was wrong, do you think?"

She shrugged and pushed away a strand of hair with a greasy finger. "She didn't say. Maybe Hugo was getting to her. How would you like to be stuck with a retarded child, even if he was a sweet guy? Maybe she was going through the change of life. Maybe she was bored. Who knows?"

I watched her arrange another slice to fit her hungry mouth. "You were questioned by the police, right?" I asked her.

"Sure. Everybody who knew her was."

"What did they ask?"

"Just about her. Boyfriends. Enemies. That sort of thing."

She munched on the slice, taking in more than half in one bite. "What did you tell them?" I asked her.

She waited until her mouth was empty, and staring at the rest of the piece in her hand, she said, "The truth. That she didn't have any boyfriends and she didn't have any enemies. That she was a good nurse. That she should have been a supervisor, but she didn't want to take any more time away from Hugo." She held up her other hand. "A life."

"Is that what you're going to tell me?" I asked her as casually as I could.

She studied me for a bit, her homely face tightening and relaxing as thoughts passed through her mind. She let out a breath and said, "It is, if you ask me the same questions." She ate the rest of the slice.

"Another pizza?" I asked. She nodded, chewing.

I ordered a medium with everything except anchovies.

14

THE NEWS was all bad. Normally it takes two cups of coffee in the morning to get the newsprint into enough focus to discover that reassuringly constant fact of life, but this morning I had to bear down especially hard to pierce a buzzing miasma that seemed to hover around my head. I felt like I was living inside a palpable headache, the way one does after a night on the bottle, and for a moment I considered taking the day in bed as Levine had ordered. Then the thought slipped away and I went to shower and see if I could wash off my fog.

Under the hot water I arranged my day, breaking it into two parts because that was all the complexity I felt I could handle. The first half had to be Georg. There was no point in my pretending to myself that I didn't care about his Nazi background. Comparing him to other forms of criminals and disreputable human beings I had worked for in the past didn't make him any more attractive. I simply was unable to use the same set of scales for him and for the others. The funny thing was that I didn't feel morally refreshed by that decision or warmed by the glow that comes from following a principle. I actually felt troubled and a bit depressed, as if something had gone wrong in my reasoning process, something I couldn't see.

There probably wouldn't be a second half to the day. I would probably tell Georg what I had found out about him and give him his money back. The cops worked for all of us, and they could butt their heads against this case while I rested mine somewhere soft and warm. Florida sounded warm and I knew Glenda was soft. I could take a bunch of days that didn't have to be divided into any parts at all.

As I strapped on my arm I caught myself arranging the second half that probably wouldn't be. Liz Brook had eventually come up with the mushroom that grew in the dark part of Helene Georg's life. Her name was Rose Morrow. She was a nurse at St. Albans. She was Helene's lover. It was all very simple, really, as JoJo could have explained to me. I heard his dry almost whining tenor: some people like sex; some of those like men and some like women; it's a little like red wine and white wine. So Helene had liked white wine—or was it red? I paused and thought about whether I'd need my gun, deciding against it in the end. Fortunately I had a clean white shirt. There was nothing very helpful in my new-found knowledge of Helene's sexual taste unless her need to keep it underground had led her into other more dangerous practices. Rose Morrow might have the answer to that, and in the afternoon that probably wouldn't be, I would go and see her to find out.

By the time I had successfully looped the tie under my collar and drawn it up tight, I was feeling competent enough to add another small part to my plan for the day. I would call Lois for news about Harriet Gorton, but it would have to wait until noon unless I wanted to roust her out of sleep. For a mad moment as I checked my image in the mirror behind the bedroom door, I felt almost good enough to call Groper to see what he'd come up with. The moment passed and I left the day divided into three pieces. What was good enough for Caesar was good enough for me.

It wasn't raining and the paper predicted record-high temperatures for this day in November, so I spurned my topcoat and took my naked headache outside to look for a taxi.

Georg was almost sprightly. "Come," he said, getting up quickly and swaying like a toddler, "we will go for a walk. My cane." He waved at the stick beside his chair. Outside he swung onto the flagstone path and led me into the large garden, all the while keeping up a running commentary on the beauties of the plants, the weather, and anything else caught by his senses. I followed silently, not really listening but only waiting for the right moment to insert my message.

He stopped under a massive blue spruce to finger the needles, rubbing them under his thumb and smelling his hand with evident pleasure. "I am like Lazarus," he said to me. He lifted his head carefully and took his gaze to the top of the giant tree. "I was nearly dead. I was ready to die. And when...when—" he dropped his head suddenly and rolled it gently to ease the neck muscles "—Hugo and Helene were killed I wanted to die." He placed the tip of his cane on the ground in front of him and leaned forward on it, a tripod to support his eager eyes and ears. More than ever he looked like a quick, sleek water animal, his hair combed straight back from a widow's peak, his pointed features, the suggestion of something feral and slippery. I was curious in spite of myself. What had happened to put life back in to the bones and parchment that had hired me? Perhaps Dr. Merweiss was good with extract of monkey gland, or perhaps he had made a deal with the devil.

"Today," Georg went on, "I am alive. I do not want to die." He lifted one of his hands off the top of his cane and set it down again. "Oh, I know I will die—and very soon I am sure. But now that is irrelevant. It no longer is important to me one way or the other." He smiled at me and I shivered. "Now tell me," he said quietly.

"I'm quitting," I heard myself say.

He nodded a little to show that he had understood the words. "You are unwell? You were injured. That I remember." There was a film of ironic amusement across his eyes.

"That's not the reason."

"I did not think it would be," he said. "You are no respecter of the flesh."

"I'm quitting because you were a Nazi."

Georg made his mouth shape a little "o" of surprise, and the film had gone from his eyes, letting amusement show clearly. "Scruples, is that the word? Unclean, unclean," he called, waving an imaginary leper's bell in front of his body. I had the check out of my wallet and I gave it to him. "What is this?"

"The money your lawyer, Postitch, paid me."

He let it go and the paper wafted down to the ground. "I have seen it before," he said. "The blind spot, the lawyer who dies without a will, the race driver who will not take the station wagon to the supermarket."

"What are you talking about?"

"You. The credulous investigator. Let me ask you," he snapped, "how you know I was a Nazi."

"I don't think—"

"Someone told you. Yes?" I didn't say anything. "Yes. If you had been told in a murder investigation that so-and-so had done the killing, would you believe that and stop work? Of course not. You would look for evidence that was concrete, that did not depend on what someone said. Is that not correct?" He bounced his stick on the flagstone like an impatient schoolmaster with a blackboard pointer. I felt stupid, thick in the head. I wasn't following what he was saying.

"Were you a Nazi?" I tried.

"No, no, no, Mr. Jantarro. That won't do. You may refuse to work for me because I am not forthcoming enough about myself. That is your privilege. You can choose the color of your client's hair or the color of his skin. That is your privilege." He paused and swayed slightly. His breathing was rapid and pink spots had appeared on his cheeks. When he resumed, his voice was weaker. "But then, Mr. Jantarro, you would have to live with yourself. However, you may not in good conscience refuse to work for me because I am a Nazi, former or otherwise. That you cannot—you *do* not—know." He pushed his weight back on to his feet and moved past me along the path.

It was bullshit. Unless Dumbrowski had been lying—or Scotus before him, which was unthinkable. It was possible that Dumbrowski had an axe to grind. Maybe he wanted to repay Georg for some past wrong, like Demeny. I would believe a Nazi but I wouldn't work for one, a voice inside me asked? The fact was I did believe Dumbrowski. But why? Was I spinning myself some fantasy in order to make quitting more palatable?

I felt the heat of the sunlight on my back and I smelled the earth and the exhalations of the silent monster beside me. Suddenly I thought I saw a shape looming up behind me and I turned quickly only to find more garden and the painful glare of the sun. For a split second I was aware of feeling wretchedly unhappy.

I bent down and with my plastic hand I worked at picking up the check that had fallen to the dead lawn.

15

THE *schwarze* with the overbite. That's what Helene used to call her lover, according to Liz Brook. "But I think Rose is pretty," she had added. So I had been expecting a mannish, buck-toothed, black woman with maybe nice eyes. I was right about the eyes, although it took me a good five minutes to get to them.

She was a goddess. A tall, lithe, exquisitely fashioned goddess. And if it was an overbite that shaped her lips into that sensuous pout, then orthodontists everywhere should hang themselves with their own dental floss. Helene must have had a strange sense of humor.

Rose Morrow let me have my confusion for a bit, even appearing to relish it. Then her body stiffened and her face clouded over. "My shift is finished," she said. Her voice was softer than it had been on the phone and the trace of Jamaica was more pronounced. "I would like to go. You *are* Jantarro, aren't you?"

"Yes," was the best I could do.

"The big ugly man with the false arm."

"What?"

"How you described yourself on the phone. You're not exactly what I imagined."

"Descriptions are hard," I said and grinned foolishly.

She gazed around the lobby of St. Albans, as if thinking about something difficult. "I agreed to talk to you," she said absently, "but not to stand about while you gawk." Abruptly she swung around to face me. "Is it really false— your arm?" I couldn't detect any feeling behind the question, not even curiosity. It just appeared out of nowhere, the way she had seemed to do. I nodded and mumbled something incoherent, annoyed at myself for wanting to hide the offending hand behind my back, and aware at the same time that it was an ugly artifact, as unauthentic as the pastel and linoleum lobby we were standing in.

My feathers were ruffled. "I can't promise not to gawk," I growled, "but at least we can sit down while I do it. There's a good place for lunch not too far from here. Who knows, maybe once I get the scent of food in my nostrils, my more basic appetite will take over." She lifted a pair of majestic eyebrows and permitted the corners of her mouth to rise a little. That was all it took. Like one of Pavlov's dogs at the bell, I grinned. "You've never seen me gawk at a corned beef sandwich," I told her. "It's quite a sight."

She sighed. "Shall we go?"

We took a table on the terrace in the sun. No corned beef sandwiches. In her case, crepes with a seafood filling, and in mine a salade niçoise. We agreed on a carafe of something dry, white, and French. It was clear to both of us that without discouragement I would make a grade-A fool of myself. I felt light, excited—as if I were running in a race. She was like a carving—grave, hidden and compelling. She was kind, so she talked about Helene's death; and the memory of that charred mess was unpleasant enough to bring me to my senses. When she learned that I had seen them she made me describe the bodies in detail, listening with her lids half closed over brown and gold eyes, and it was almost a release to haul the memory out in careful words where the sun could get at it. My appetite was gone and so was the wine. She noticed the empty carafe first and barely had her hand in the air before the young waiter was at her side, bending close to find out how he might please her. Men are idiots.

"My turn," I said, when the waiter had run off.

She said, "Perhaps," and then, "It depends."

"Let's start with an easy one," I went on as if she hadn't spoken. "Any idea who?"

She snorted. "That's easy?"

"Sure. I reckon that if you did know anything, you'd have gone to the cops."

"What if I wanted certain things kept private?"

"The love that dare not speak its name? That love's quite bold nowadays; its name's a household word." The sun had crept across the terrace and now looked her in the face, raising dark blue highlights in her skin. She fished around in her bag and brought out a pair of sunglasses, putting them on slowly. "We can go inside if you'd like," I told her.

"That's all right." I watched the blurred image of the sun on her lenses for a while, then I transferred my gaze to her hands. They were smoothing out the painted metal tabletop before she drew them onto her lap. "I have no idea, Mr. Jantarro. You're quite right. It was an easy one. I'm bewildered. Lost and bewildered." She sat there simply breathing, impassive, and withdrawn.

"Help me," I said.

"Why?"

"Because I'm trying to get whoever killed her."

"For justice, Mr. Jantarro? For money? For your own satisfaction?"

[127]

"For my client."

"Her husband."

"Whoever it is," I said, "he seems to care more than you do."

"We spent many years seeming not to care. I don't give a damn how it seems to you."

"But you agreed to see me. You must have wanted to help me, to do something to catch her killers."

"I was curious. I still am I suppose." She had turned her head to look out into the street beside us. "I wanted to see what kind of man he had hired. I wanted to learn why he bothered to hire anyone."

"What's so puzzling about that?"

"I had her love, Mr. Jantarro. *I* did, not he. I had her passion, her vitality, her being. There couldn't have been anything left for him. I should have thought he'd be indifferent to her going." Lilting, rounded words. Fruit from a tree.

"I don't think that's how it works," I said softly.

She snapped her head back to me. "Oh, you don't, do you?" she shouted. "You don't think that's how it works!" The tears ran out from under her glasses, emerging suddenly like water from a rockface. I poured myself some more wine and drank a little of it while I waited for her to speak again. She dabbed at her cheeks with a napkin and began to soothe the tabletop once more with gentle circular strokes.

"No one to talk to," she said, spacing each word out to be sure her voice wouldn't fail. "And now you want facts. I haven't any facts. Only feelings and wishes and sounds... sad sounds... joyful sounds... all bottled up... here!" She thumped herself on the chest with the flat of her hand, and then she curled her other arm around her belly, hugging herself. "And here," she said.

A small pain came and went at the back of my head in time with my pulse, a winking light to warn all the ships at sea in my thoughts, and a great lassitude spread over me weighting down my limbs. She was no longer a goddess. She was an unhappy, wounded woman. And I was uncertain how to respond.

"Babies," said Rose Morrow. "She loved babies. We both did." Her voice hardened and she lifted her chin a little. "Isn't that ironic?"

"I don't know," I said tentatively. "I like paintings and I can't paint, I like music and I can't play. I mean, I could try if I wanted to, but I don't. I just enjoy what others create." It sounded stupid in my own ears, but I guess there must have been something in it because she nodded slowly.

"She had Hugo, of course," she said thoughtfully. "Maybe that's why. You know about Hugo?"

"Yes," I said, "I know about Hugo."

"He was always a baby. But it was the little ones, the new ones that she really liked. We worked together on pediatrics for a while, and then she transferred to neonatal— the brand new ones, the ones with problems. But every time a baby died she would get very upset. So she worked in the fertility clinic after that. She wanted me to come and join her there. I didn't want to. There aren't any babies to nurse. Just all those women who want to be mothers and can't be." She raised her face to mine again and I imagined that behind the sunglasses her eyes were meeting mine. "There was something..." she said, and she stopped.

I needed coffee, but I wasn't about to do anything that would interfere with what she was about to tell me. Her head turned away slowly, as if she had lost interest in me and in her reminiscences. She looked down at her hands, and then she folded them on the table. She spoke to the traffic, and I had a hard time hearing her. "Why should I trust you?"

I said, "You have to trust someone." It sounded fatuous.

"Coffee, I'd like some coffee." She was looking at me with steely brightness.

The coffee came and she busied herself with the paper bags of sugar and the plastic pots of cream. I tried changing tack. "Did her husband know about you?"

"I don't think so," she said. "Does it matter?"

"Probably not. But we're trying to figure out her movements, and if she lied to him about where she was going, it would mislead us." That wasn't quite the reason I had in mind, but it seemed to make sense to her, because she thought for a second and then shook her head.

"We never discussed him," she said. "Not after the beginning. She would come to my place after work a couple of times a week. Sometimes three. I never asked what she told him." She drank a little of her coffee and then put more sugar in it. "How did you find out?" she asked as she stirred. "About us, I mean. It could only be one or two people."

"Was Helene planning to leave her husband?"

"At least you can keep a secret, even if some people can't."

"Had she talked to him about leaving?"

"Why would she bother? He was going to die any day." She said it with some bitterness.

"Is that what she told you when you asked her to leave him?"

"Clever, mister man."

We drank our coffees in silence, she reluctant to speak and I reluctant to make more wrong moves than I already had. I wanted her to open up to me, and the only way I could think to bring that about was to do nothing.

She shivered. The sun had moved off us and it was getting cold where we were sitting. She retrieved her bag, took off her sunglasses, put them in it, and got out her purse. Reluctantly I called for the check. "Are you sure you won't tell me?" I asked.

"Tell you what?"

"Whatever it is that depends on my being trustworthy."

She smiled. "Let me sleep on it. It always takes me time—"

The bullet caught her by the throat, snapping her head back and then forward again quickly. Fountains of blood drowned her last words and for a second her lips moved soundlessly. Then she crumpled and slowly fell off the chair to the concrete below.

I was on my knees beside her, feeling vainly for a pulse, aware with startling clarity that the warmth of her blood on my hand was her life disappearing. Voices above me gathered and rose in pitch and volume. Someone started screaming and quickly others joined in. A man's voice tried shouting something over the cacophony. Hands pulled at me, and I struck out at them blindly.

She had dragged her bag down with her, spilling its contents under the table, and as if it would bring her back to life, I swept them toward me and thrust them hurriedly into the empty sack. A sticky wallet, a silk head scarf, a bottle of aspirins. I was like a greedy looter until the sirens in the distance made me wake up.

I staggered to my feet. People backed away from me, and I realized I was drenched with her blood. I felt like a wounded bear, rearing on its hind legs, lusting to kill its tormentor. Only there was no one in sight to maul.

Without wanting to, I saw her head swing back and forth again, the way it would if she had been dancing. I remembered how she had shivered. It was a rifle. But up the block a fair bit because I didn't hear the shot. Second floor, to hit her neck like that. And all of a sudden I was running.

IT WAS HOPELESS. There was no way I could have found him. But I had to try. Too much anger had exploded inside me to be contained, too much rage for me to sit and wait and tell my story over and over again to the cops. So I ran for him.

I didn't notice the traffic as I tore across the street, and I was only half aware of the people who fell away as I lunged after nothing I would ever find. I had fixed on an old building with some big open windows. All the other places were modern, sealed in glass. I pounded up the stairs to the second floor and began ripping open office doors and terrorizing the occupants. It was hopeless.

I calmed down after a couple of men tried to wrestle me to the floor. Somehow I explained. Perhaps the howl of cop cars below helped them believe me; that and the fact that I must have looked more distraught than dangerous. They offered me condolences and tried to make me sit down. One of them even showed me where I could wash the blood off.

In the bathroom I splashed cold water on my face until I stopped shaking, and then I leaned against the tiled wall and tried to think. The rage was still there, but now I needed to channel it, to make it work for Rose—and for me. In a while I became aware that water was running down my neck. I looked for towels but there weren't any, so I fumbled in my pockets for a handkerchief. There wasn't one of those either, but instead my hand found a bunch of stuff that wasn't mine. I guessed I had been holding some of the articles from Rose's bag when I'd taken off and had stuffed them in my pocket unthinkingly. Now I put them on the shelf above the sink: a small, pink compact, a ring of keys, and a half-finished pack of mints. "I, Rose Morrow, give, devise and bequeath to John Kenneth Galbraith Jantarro..." I slipped a finger through the ring of keys.

She would have trusted me, I told myself. She would have told me what she wanted to tell someone. Maybe she would tell me still.

She had four rooms on the second floor of a Victorian town house on McCaul. High ceilings for the tall woman she once had been. Dark brown woodwork that would have glowed next to her shining skin. And long, narrow windows, elegant light, careful light. I went to one of them and aimed an imaginary rifle at the neck of a man walking a terrier across the street. It was about right. I turned and surveyed the living room. Even when you know what you're looking for, it can take two good men an hour to do a room properly—leaving no prints, missing no spots, putting everything back. So what did I imagine I could do? I gave myself one hour for the whole place. It would take the cops no longer than that to get their act together, and in case they were swifter, I would go out the fire escape at the back.

There was no point in trying for hidden stuff, I told myself. In the living room alone there were fifty places she could have stashed something private. Hell, they even made fake light bulbs that looked exactly like the real thing, and it would take me a quarter of an hour just to check those out alone. The desk was an obvious place to start. It was small, cherry slant-top affair that unfolded to make a little writing surface and to reveal some pigeon holes. Using my plastic, printless hand as much as possible, I sorted quickly through her bank books, her check registers, her overdue bills, and an Air Jamaica schedule. There was nothing for me, nothing I could use. The drawers held her passport, letters to her father—very formal and very touching—and a bunch of photographs. Nothing takes fingerprints like the shiny surface of photos, and I prodded them apart laboriously with my left hand, searching for God knows what and finding beaches, palm trees, coral-stone cottages, handsome children with splendid smiles, and old women with dark scowls and forbidding eyes. Sadness gnawed at my chest as I reassembled the picture-book of Eden left behind forever. I closed up the desk and stood for a moment feeling alone, feeling temporary.

There never was a garden, I told myself. There never was anything to lose. And there is probably nothing to find. Here or anywhere. But there is anger, I realized, and a need to move, to act. Swiftly I lifted the cushions off the couch, revealing only dusty muslin beneath. I ran my eyes along the small bookshelves, stopping only once to remove an untitled book. It was one of those bound notebooks of blank paper, and whatever she had hoped to fill it with had died with her, for it was still blank.

The drawer in the end table was empty, and the sideboard was full of glasses and liquor. Half of my hour had gone.

The kitchen was strictly functional, all the pans ranked neatly along the backsplash in a specially-built holder, spices with their labels facing front and in alphabetical order, a pair of rubber gloves draped over the shiny steel sink, and not a crumb on the counter. She liked spicy foods and pork, and she bought milk but didn't drink it. That was all I learned from her kitchen.

I had expected a lot of drugs in the bathroom medicine cabinet, because she was a nurse, I suppose. But there was just the usual collection of patent medicines. She'd had sinus trouble, by the look of it. And she also took birth control pills. That rocked me a bit. A fast, angry dream of what might have been between us left me more roiled up than ever and vaguely disgusted with myself. Bisexual, homosexual, sexual. Tawdry categories for tawdry thoughts, reductionist, life caging. She was dead, I reminded myself. Not any sex. Dead.

Her smell was in the bedroom. I hadn't noticed it while we were together, but here I recalled it, and I wondered how I could have failed to sense it then. Perhaps I had—I must have—and it had worked inside me, past my consciousness the way a scent is supposed to. It was like nothing else, I decided. That's the glory and the trouble with smells. Unique to her, it would never exist again outside this room. I would think it was something like freesias, something like a dark tea, something like the first whiff of red cedar, and it wouldn't be any of those at all. Exhausted and dispirited, I had the urge to crawl into her bed and draw my legs up tight to my chest, to sleep in her musk for as long as it took to lose this agitation that commanded me to run and twitch. I had five minutes left in my self-imposed hour.

Her closet held uniforms and a profusion of cotton dresses, skirts and blouses, all in bright, printed colors meant to be lit by a bolder sun than ours. A tangle of panty hose and underwear lay in one corner of it, waiting to be put into the laundry hamper. Her suitcase was on the top shelf of the closet, empty except for a bikini and a beach bag from a local travel agent. On the wicker bedside table there was a sculpture of a small, naked girl, frozen in the struggle to remove a sock. That stubborn impediment to freedom stretched like a cord from her little foot to her fierce and determined hands which were straining high above her head. I picked it up and felt I wanted to help her, and I knew I never could. When I put it back, I saw a fold of paper that had been underneath it. My name stared up at me, written twice, with a question mark after it each time. Had she asked herself who I was? Whether she should meet me? Whether, perhaps...? I told myself not to be stupid. The paper went into my back pocket. The cops would find out sooner or later that I had been with her, but that was no reason to let them have it in writing. And in about two minutes. My time was up. Quickly I rummaged in the catchall beneath the bedside table, discovering her jewelry and a plastic bag of marijuana, two Harlequin novels, and a box of Kleenex.

That's it, I told myself. Nothing. No trace of Helene, no clue as to why Rose was killed, nothing at all. Thank her for the visit and get the hell out of here, I urged myself. I stood for a moment and filled my lungs with Rose Morrow one last time.

That moment of silence let me hear the noise, a faint metallic scratching in the kitchen next door. I froze and strained to identify the sound. Mice under the sink, perhaps. Something expanding or contracting in the refrigerator. A cat on the fire escape. Yes, on the fire escape. I crept to the bedroom window and crouched down, peering through the bottom corner of the glass, trying to get a line of sight to the little iron balcony outside the kitchen door. But I could only see the railing and the branches of a dead-looking sumac beyond. It could have been the branches scraping against the railing, I told myself, and I willed my heart to stop pounding.

Just as I moved away from the window, the noise came again, and this time it was clearly the sound of a key going into a lock. I remembered there was glass in the kitchen door. If I went out through the hall now, I would be seen. Almost reflexively I put my hand to my left side and came up empty, vowing never to leave my gun at home again. The sense of being trapped fluttered at me, inviting me to panic. Slowly I let my breath out and I thought.

It wasn't the cops. They would come in through the front door. They might send a man around the back, but he would wait for the main force to enter before he made his move. It could be a friend, except what friend would move so slowly and quietly? Besides, the first sound had been the wrong key or a badly made copy, and a friend wouldn't have that problem. That left a plain break-and-enter artist. Or her killer. Her killer come to get something after putting her out of the way. My heart was hammering again, and I heard the bolt give only by straining against the pounding in my ears.

I looked wildly around for a weapon. There wasn't even a pair of scissors in sight. The kitchen door eased open, its hinges complaining slightly. Whoever it was, he was in.

I hid behind the bedroom door. There was nothing else to do. Sooner or later he would make his way in here and I would have to hit him from behind. I balled my fist and wondered if it would be hard enough. Of course, if he was the suspicious type and checked behind doors before entering rooms, I was done for. I would be trapped like wood in a vise while he hammered at me with impunity.

He was an amateur, I decided quickly. A pro would have been in and out with the stereo inside of three minutes. Even a kid beginning the business would be faster. This guy was still in the kitchen, and unless he had a thing for cookware, he was the killer.

He pulled stuff out of the freezer, and as it hit the floor I remembered that I'd left my jacket in the living room. Two amateurs in one small apartment means there's a good chance someone will get hurt. It made me mad—my carelessness, his clumsy intrusion, and most of all my cowering

[137]

behind a door. In the kitchen he swore and threw something hard against the pans, and it sounded as if it fell into the sink. I could be at the front door before he noticed and outside before he could react. Even if he had a gun in his hand I could do it. Give myself a good start by pushing off against the door jamb, keep low, and he'd be bound to fire wide. The fact that he'd put a bullet through Rose's neck didn't mean anything. He'd had lots of time to line the shot up; all of that hardware that snipers use would have made it a sure thing. Damn, I hated running.

I was dithering when he came out of the kitchen into the hall and saw me. He launched himself off the wall and threw his weight into the door, catching me halfway in and halfway out. My shoulders tried to meet in the middle, driving my breath out of the way. I moved to face him, but my right arm wouldn't work. The mechanical one came up fine, but the one with meat on it hung limply at my side, paralyzed by the blow from the door. I felt like a broken windup toy, a pathetic monkey with a drumstick poised to strike the air where the tin drum should be. No anger now. No fear. No adrenaline kick at all. I was only tired, weary to the point of sleep.

He backed up, roared like a madman, and put his head down for a charge. I said his name quietly. "Demeny." The effect was comic. He snapped his head up as fast as if I had hit him. Sticks and stones, I thought, but give me words anytime. He stared at me wild-eyed, trying to place me, wanting to understand. He looked frightened, and inexplicably I felt sorry for him. It must be horrible to have planned and carried out the killing of another human being. "You're a good shot," I told him. "Korea?" He nodded dumbly.

"Sniper," he said and wiped his mouth. His nose was running and the gesture smeared the mucus across his face. I wanted to offer him a Kleenex.

"It's hard to do it closeup, isn't it?" We might have been standing in the hall at a cocktail party, plunged into superficial intimacy out of drunkenness and boredom. "Kill someone, I mean." He looked blank, an unconvincing portrait of a person. I said, "It's one thing at a hundred yards— wind velocity, range, all technical—"

A moan escaped him and he lunged at me.

I tried to kick him in the balls. A good kick means that your arms have to swing out to keep you balanced. Mine didn't and as I made contact I fell backwards, hitting my head on the floor. He joined me there, writhing around and whimpering. We crawled painfully toward each other. It was such fun I guess we wanted to do it again. I nearly gave up on the way over. Hysterical laughter bubbled around in my mouth.

We bellied up to each other, exhausted lovers too stupid to get comfortable. I could smell the dust on the floor and the sharp, unpleasant odor of his pain; and I worried about getting a splinter in my head from the old oak boards. Demeny started to slap at my face, openhanded and with a regular rhythm, each slap causing a spray of bright lights inside my head. Without hands that worked, all I could do was to hunch my way up his body and out of the reach of his rough palms. So I pumped my knees up and down until that also made my head light up with fireworks. When I stopped he grabbed my shirt front and pulled me back down to where he could get at me with his hands again. I couldn't decide if I was more scared that it would go on forever or that it would soon be over. I had begun to take little naps after every second or third slap, and I wasn't waking refreshed.

The feeling had come back into my real arm with a vengeance, a burning sensation that was excruciating wherever the flesh made contact with anything. But still I couldn't move it with any strength. I made my fingers crawl across a bed of coals until I found his crotch, letting the weight of the arm fall on it and rolling in tight against him to add some pressure. I must have got to him because his shrill scream woke me up. His hand left my face and scrabbled at my arm. He tried to roll away and free up his other arm, trapped beneath his body, but he was up against the wall with nowhere to go. I pumped my knees again and this time made it all the way up to his head. A knee connected with his chin and snapped his head back to the wall with a satisfying thunk. Like a monomaniac I worked at bouncing his head off the wall until I fell asleep again.

When I woke up he was still. I rolled onto my back and watched the ceiling go round and round for a while. Then I tried to stand up. Finally after flopping onto my belly and levering myself up with my knees, I shuffled into the living room to get my jacket and phone Bench. My vision was screwed up, and everything looked the way it does through a telescope—far away and too close at the same time. But after a minute of scanning, I found my jacket, clamped it in my fake arm and groped around for the telephone. I had the killer and Bench would never hear the end of it.

17

THE AUDIENCE all wore uniforms. It seemed to be Russia, because of the uniforms and because no one was smiling. Their white faces stared with an intensity that was disconcerting, and I wondered if they were all serious students ranked above me in a scientific stadium, coiled tiers of dispassionate observers. I was at the bottom of the gyre, under the microscope. I tried to shout at them, to warn them, to abuse them with my words; but I was muzzled by a web of leather strappings that pulled my chin down toward my left shoulder.

Rose Morrow was beside me, the two of us alone on the shiny field below the spectators. She was glistening in armor dark as ebony. In one hand she held aloft a sword and in the other she gripped a chain of silver. Smiling at me, she pulled on the chain and I found myself drawn slipping and stumbling across the field. She needn't have dragged me with the chain. I would have gone for the asking. I realized I was naked and I tried to cover my genitals but my hands wouldn't move. Rose laughed and appeared behind me, reaching between my legs and cupping my testicles in her hand, squeezing gently and laughing. I smelled the bear before I saw it. The thing teetered in our direction on its hind legs, yellowed teeth bared and tufts of loose hair protruding from its upraised arms. I felt sorry for it. As soon as it was close enough, I lunged to embrace it, but still my arms wouldn't work. The bear's arms went around me and it rocked me gently. It smelled of tobacco. "Rose," I said.

"By another name," said a man's voice. "Dreaming?"

It was Levine. I blinked a few times, waiting for it all to fall into place. "I don't want another test," I told him.

He grinned and flopped his hands out, palms up. "Would I bug a guy who's promised to let me have his brain when he dies? Not me. I'll wait until I've got you in a jar. A couple of days at this rate, I estimate."

"You smoking?" I asked him.

"Nope, and nor should you."

I shook my head impatiently. Levine's image multiplied and the faces swam in a slow circle. I swallowed hard and closed my eyes. "Smelled tobacco," I said.

"Oh," said Levine, somewhere on the other side of my eyelids, "that was the cop who was in here. Had it on his clothes."

"Cops?"

"Mmhmm," said Levine. "They say you belong to them. I say you belong to me first. Isn't that just typical of our age? Social agencies tripping over each other in their desire to help."

I groaned. "What about Demeny?"

"Never heard of him. Was he in your dream?"

Levine had only one face again, and as usual it was wrinkled with smiles. "No," I told him, "only bears, beautiful black women, and lots of guys like you."

"Sounds interesting. Want to tell me about it?"

"Why? So you can tell me I'm in deep shit?"

"My goodness no. I don't need to tell you that. You know that already—without having to consult your dreams. Now, if you were interested in the source of the shit—diet, digestion, that sort of thing—I could help you." He sat there beside the hospital bed, relaxed and benign, and for a moment I was tempted to unload some baggage on him. But then I realized he'd only hand it back to me, and I doubted it would weigh any less even when it was neatly packed.

"Thanks," I said.

"See you in the jar," he replied lightly.

Bench had a worried look in his eyes, and Antonini was smirking. That meant only one thing. "You lost him, didn't you?" I asked.

"And who might that be?" Antonini was planning to enjoy this.

"Frank Demeny, Domain Construction. Going from easy up to hard—so you can understand it—he is a lousy B and E artist, a poor hand at assault, but a first-rate assassin with a rifle. He's the one that shot Rose Morrow."

Antonini looked at Bench before he spoke. He shouldn't have checked with the boss at the first surprise—not if he was trying to redeem himself for the payoff mess. Bench returned the look with no interest. "Proof?" Antonini asked.

"You going to write this down or trust your memory?" He opened his mouth, held it ajar for a second, then licked his lips and closed it. He took out a small notebook and clicked his ballpoint. "Aren't you going to wet the point?" I asked him. He just looked down at the book, waiting. The guy was learning. "Okay," I said, "a couple of days ago I went to see Demeny in connection with the Georg kid-

[143]

napping. He was a possible." Antonini lifted his eyes to mine, but I just shook my head a fraction. "No need for that now. Maybe later, if he doesn't confess, you can ask me again." The connection would be on their computer. I was only teasing.

"Obstruction of justice," Antonini said to himself, as if identifying a particular species of wildlife.

"Doubtful," I said in the same matter-of-fact way. "Make a note. Check it with the legal people. Be a good thing to know. Now, where was I? Today I had lunch with Rose Morrow—she worked with Helene. I was looking for a lead. She got taken out. Had to be a rifle and my guess is second floor, a block up the street. Am I right?" Antonini kept his head down but Bench grunted. "Now the connection. I'd arranged to meet Ms. Morrow at her place later this afternoon so she'd given me her keys—"

"—Bullshit and it's Wednesday." Antonini smiled at me.

"Wednesday?"

"Wednesday. Witness incorrectly identified the day of the week." He pretended to write that down. I'd lost a day again. I didn't like that at all. "But that's okay," Antonini went on, "because you made notes on all this, right? I mean, you didn't trust your memory, right?"

I sighed with the best imitation of exasperation I could muster. "Look, Antonini, do you want this or not? Okay, so you scored. I'd say 'touché' if I thought you knew what it meant."

"It means touched," said Antonini, tapping the side of his head with a forefinger. "And you can go ahead and say it. Everybody else says it about you."

Bench made a noise. "Like children," he snarled. He was right.

"I let myself into Ms. Morrow's apartment using her key."

"To keep an appointment with a dead woman?" Antonini was matter-of-fact too.

"To find out who killed her. I had a jump on you and it

seemed like a good idea. It turned out better than that. I had him. But now he's probably in Argentina while you ask me dumb questions." I took a couple of breaths. "Demeny came in the back door. Picked the lock by the sound of it. He and I went a round or two, but I won by the first knock-out. I left him on the floor and tried to phone."

"Did he say he did it?"

Did he? I tried to remember. "He was a sniper in Korea."

"So were lots of people."

"But he was the only one in Rose Morrow's apartment half an hour after she was shot. Come on, Antonini, for Christ's sake! Do you need it handed to you with bows on it?"

Antonini snapped his book shut and tapped it thoughtfully on his fist. He put it in his jacket and turned to Bench, who nodded at him and buttoned up his gray suit coat, automatically smoothing his tie inside the jacket. Antonini faded to the back wall, letting his boss come forward for round two of the tag-team interrogation. I thought I could handle it. Bench settled himself on the chair, ran a finger lightly under the edge of his moustache, and sucked thoughtfully on his teeth for a moment. "See, Jantarro," he said at last, "what we got is your body on the floor smack in the middle of her place, the front door is unlocked and a lot of frozen food is melting in the kitchen. That's it. That's all we got."

I started to object, but he put up a hand to stop me. "Don't for God's sake ask about prints. You know better than that. Marks on the back door lock? Lots of them. Covered with scratches. Nobody saw anything, nobody heard anything." He undid the button on his jacket, looked critically at his hand, and did it up again. "We spoke to the doctor," he said to the tips of his fingers, "and he explained some of the things that can happen to a person when he gets a head injury." He waved his small hand to cover all of the unspeakable things that could happen to a person like me. "Now I'm not saying you're making all of this up. I

[145]

don't have to say that. But there's no way in the world I'm going to lean on this Demeny just on your say-so. Hell, I wouldn't pull a veteran scumbag in on your say-so right now, even if you swore you saw him rape sixteen kids. You're an invalid, Jantarro. And for me that means you're just not valid."

I hadn't figured on this. It made my guts feel hollow, and for a moment I caught myself believing that I had hallucinated the whole thing. If I could lose a day, I could invent one just as easily. "But you'll talk to him. You don't have to lean on him, but you'll talk to him. Ask about his guns, right? Ask him how he got the lump on the back of his head, right? Ask him if his nuts are sore. Talk to *his* doctor, for Christ's sake, and find out when he came in complaining about sore balls and a split skull. And you're going to check out the molding in the hall to look for blood and hair from Demeny. You're going to do that, right, Bench?" He looked at me expressionlessly.

It was Antonini's turn again. This time he didn't bother with his notebook. "Why were you talking to Rose Morrow?"

"Get stuffed."

"What was the lead you were looking for?"

"Get stuffed."

"What was the connection between Demeny and Helene Georg?"

I didn't bother to say anything.

"Between Demeny and Rose Morrow?"

"Okay," said Bench, and Antonini smiled at me. He knew what was coming. "You're in my way, Jantarro," said Bench. "Now most of the time I couldn't care less, but on this one you're a pain in the ass and I want you out of the road. I'm placing you under arrest for illegal entry into the Morrow premises. When you get released from here, you'll be released into our custody." He ran a hand across the top of his head and then worked the back of his neck with it. There was a curious expression on his face as if he were embarrassed about something, and his eyes refused to meet mine. "Your belongings have been catalogued and put in safekeeping," he said in a bored voice that didn't fit with his face. "You'll get a receipt for them. And that includes your... your prosthesis." He turned and went to the door, pausing there to look at me from a distance, his lips pressed until they disappeared. Finally he said, "I'm not putting a guard on you. I don't need to. I'll just pick you up off the street if you're not here when your time comes. There's no point, Jantarro. It's over for you."

It wasn't as if I had any choice. Not so long as my brain could still work past the pain that shrouded it. The cops obviously weren't going to take Demeny seriously, so it was my job to do it. I gave a second to considering whether I would rather wind up in jail or in a jar, and it was then I realized that I didn't really have any choice. After that it was merely a matter of how.

I needed an arm. There was one at the apartment in the bedroom closet, wrapped in an old pillowcase and stuffed into a cardboard flower box. It didn't have any fancy motors or switches—just a hook at the end of its polished wooden joints and a crude system of internal pulleys. It had been my training arm, and it would have to do. The only problem was, I couldn't go and get it.

I also needed a place to sleep and eat. There were a few possibilities. Glenda's place would be empty and I had the key. The only trouble with that was that it was no secret that Glenda and I went together, and Bench would be there fifteen minutes after he missed me. It would take him longer to get to JoJo's, but he'd make it there too. Besides, I had some repair work to do with JoJo that couldn't be done while I was going after Demeny. I considered a hotel. It would take Bench days to check them all, and if I got somebody else to check in for me, they might never find me. Of course, they could grab me when I made a move on Demeny, but that was one of life's little hazards which couldn't be avoided except by running away. And the whole point was to run toward Demeny, not in the other direction.

Lois, I decided. She'd take me in. And be good company, too. I needed to check with her anyway about the Gorton woman. And JoJo would bring me my arm. That much I could ask him and that much he'd do for me, I was sure. I reached for the phone beside the bed but stopped and wondered if it was tapped. If I had been Bench, I'd have tapped it. But then, I had a slightly better opinion of myself than he did. If he hadn't paid any attention to what I'd told him, why should he care what I said on the phone? As far as he was concerned, I was a nut case, and even he had better things to do than to listen in on the conversations of crazies. So I called JoJo and asked him to visit me with a box of flowers.

It wasn't until Levine stuck his head around the door at suppertime that I remembered my clothes and my gun. I had managed to spend a lot of time worrying about my arm and some company for me—but not a thought for the essentials. That upset me more than losing a day. "I see that we won," Levine said. He seemed happy about it.

"Yeah," I said glumly. I was struggling with the fact that my brain wasn't working at the detective business. "Come here," I muttered, and I crooked a finger at him. He lifted his eyebrows and did as he was told.

"You've lost two nurses," I told him.

"Two women have been killed, yes."

"And the cops...well"—I made a face—"you've seen them."

"They're the police," he said. "They do a job."

"I know them better. They do a half-assed job."

"Not like you, huh?"

"I've got one case," I said, feeling my jaw muscles tighten for no reason I was aware of. "I care."

Levine looked at me steadily for a minute. "I believe you believe that," he said.

[148]

"No games, doc."

"Games? Look who's talking." He began to laugh. "You want to know if I'll squeal on you if you walk out of here, only you can't bring yourself to ask me straight out, so you fish around and try to make me tell you you've got to get back in the saddle for the good of the world—or at least my little acre of it."

"That was the first part of it, yes."

"That's better." He raised an eyebrow this time. "What's the second part?"

"Can you find me some clothes that fit?"

He smiled. "I don't know anyone with a large enough hat size."

"I could jam into one of yours, I bet."

"Don't need one," he said. "Never rains on me."

JoJo showed up with the flower box just as Levine came back with a pile of clothing. "Dr. Levine, JoJo Polifemi." I took the box from JoJo.

"Sam," said Levine, extending his hand.

JoJo took it. "Hi." JoJo cocked his head in my direction and asked Levine, "He going to live?"

"Doubt it," said Levine, not smiling for once. JoJo glared at me accusingly and grunted. I had the hook-arm belted on and was wriggling into a pair of faded jeans.

"It's life," I said as I dragged a lumberjack shirt up the wooden arm. I flailed around behind my back for the other armhole. "Fatal every time."

"That it, then?" asked JoJo.

For fun I tried to button the cuff on the good arm with the hook. I almost got it. "If you're in a hurry," I told him. "But I kind of thought we might go for a walk together." He grunted again and just about vibrated with the tension of trying not to help. The shoes were loafers and I used the hook as a shoehorn. Works like a charm. "There," I said, admiring myself in the long mirror on the bathroom door. "What the well-dressed intern won't be wearing tonight.

Thank him for me, will you?" Levine nodded. "JoJo," I said, "do you think you could do up this cuff?" I held my hand out for a good five seconds before he reached for the shirt and the button.

Levine was watching all of this with open interest. "I won't say 'take care of him,'" Levine told JoJo. "I can see it wouldn't do any good. You have my sympathies... and my understanding." To me Levine shook his head.

At the door I heard Levine say, "Oh," behind me. I turned. He was holding a strip of paper. "I forgot," he said. "This is yours. It came from your pants pocket. They cut away your clothing in emergency and when the police asked me to get the pieces for them, I found this with the bits. It didn't look like the kind of thing the police would need... or miss. I gather it belongs to you."

It was the piece of paper with my name on it from Rose Morrow's apartment. I was going to tell him it was nothing I'd need either, but instead I said, "Thanks, it's a memento." I stuck it in my jeans. "A lady's favor to remind me of why I play with dragons." Levine groaned and shook his head.

I turned and started out the door. "Come on," I said to JoJo. "First thing we've got to do is buy some aspirin."

JoJo DRIFTED AWAY at Yonge Street. The night was almost hot, a freakish night for November, and the strip was crawling with kids in search of pleasurable excess, a forlorn hope if ever I saw one. But JoJo was battle hardened and went to show them the way. We had had a bit of a talk, desultory and oblique, describing our friendship by the things we avoided, the silences that shadowed what we said. Part of me was glad to see him go, but I was looking when he turned around after fifty paces to grin at me and give me the finger.

Lois didn't grin and she was far too polite to give me the finger. She just looked tight and not at all pleased to see me. "I'm busy," she told me in a low voice, her body blocking the narrow opening in the doorway.

"You look great," I said. She softened a trace. "Working?" I asked.

"No," she said, louder than she meant to. "You've got to go. Come back tomorrow. I'll talk to you tomorrow." She was closing the door, disappearing inside.

"Is there a problem?" came a mellow, smooth voice from behind her; and then an arm snaked along her shoulders. The door opened wider and the arm grew into a man—fifty, or thereabouts, blue pinstripe suit, red suspenders over a monogrammed shirt, a silk tie with small red polka dots, and a face that belonged in an ad for monogrammed shirts and pinstriped suits. He had a neat part in his hair, and each silvery strand lay parallel to the next just the way it should. Lois leaned away from his grasp a little, but he pulled her in tight, all protective and masculine.

"No problem," I said with a smile.

"No, no problem," Lois echoed.

The man looked at us brightly, first one and then the other, and said, "Well, now that's settled, perhaps you'll come in and have a drink."

Lois looked distinctly unhappy. "I don't think—" she began, but he cut her off by pulling her back from the door and opening it wider for me at the same time. I was badly embarrassed. It had been stupid of me not to have thought Lois would be busy. That I was in such a state that I could have ignored the possibility made me even more upset.

I backed off. "Thanks," I said. "Maybe some other time. Sorry, Lois. You folks go ahead and . . . and go ahead."

"I insist," said the male model with grim intensity. "Any friend of Lois is of interest to me." The color was rising in Lois's cheeks and she got that ramrod stiff bearing she gets when she has been insulted. The fiancé, I thought. The hot marriage prospect. I thought I knew what his game was, and it would be my pleasure to spoil it for him. I went in and closed the door behind me.

Lois had retreated to the other side of the room and was staring out of the window at the lights of the city. Her back was as cold and as stiff as an icicle, and probably just about as brittle. It was none of my business if her man was behaving like a jerk, I told myself. Who appointed me to straighten him out?

"Drink?" he said. "There's beer," he added as his eyes traipsed up and down my checked shirt and jeans.

I brought my hook hand out where he could see it. "Scotch," I told him. "No ice, no water."

"Something for you, dear?" he asked Lois, his eyes on my hand. She didn't say anything. He splashed some Chivas into a tumbler and brought it back to me. "I'm Alan Turner," he said, handing me the glass.

"Jantarro." I took a sip and put the glass down on the coffee table.

He smiled a secret smile. "Just like that?" he said. "No first name to soften the blow? Or is that your first name?"

I spoke to Lois's back. "I'm sorry I barged in, Lois." How sorry could I have been when I kept doing it?

"You and Lois been friends for some time, then?" Turner was back at the bar pouring vodka over the shrunken icecubes in his glass.

"I'm going," I said to Lois.

"I have some information for you," she announced to the window.

"Buddies from way back?" asked the marriage prospect. "Or did you get your days screwed up?"

The drink on the coffee table peered up at me. I decided to leave it. "Call me at the King Eddie," I said. "Under the name of . . . Scott. John Scott."

"See, it's Thursday." Alan Turner with his beautiful pinstripe suit and his red suspenders and his monogrammed shirt and his perfectly tied silk tie was breathing vodka on me. I noticed his face was puffier than I had first imagined, puffier and dusty white, like a ball of pizza dough. "Thursdays are my day. You'd have to book through me if you wanted Thursday. It seems a little rigid, I know, but these kinds of things are at the heart of civilization, like lining up

[153]

for buses." I told myself he probably wanted me to hit him, and because he wanted it I wouldn't do it. I felt sorry for Lois, for myself, and oddly enough for him too.

Her voice was light and very high, buoyed by hope but carefully beyond it. I tried to be natural, a little bored, a little apologetic for calling so late, but presumptuous nonetheless. The way one of his business associates might have been. But I knew as soon as she said, "Hello," that Frank Demeny had gone. She offered to take a message.

"That's all right, Mrs. Demeny. It'll keep till morning. I'll probably see him on the site."

"Yes!" She sank into hope like an exhausted swimmer.

"But, hey—"

"—yes?"

"—Jimmy might be able to help me."

"No!" Her son was all she had, and no one was going to get at him. "He doesn't know anything—I mean, his father handles the business end of things and Jimmy isn't here—he's just a student—"

I pretended I hadn't heard her. "We met on the site a couple of days ago and he was there when Frank and I were talking about the grade of trim for the plenums and the shafts." I didn't have the faintest idea of what I was saying and I hoped she was one of those wives who have no interest in their husbands' business. "My problem is that I can't remember whether we fixed on B-2 or B-4, and I've got to put the order in as soon as possible. I was kind of hoping to get the telex out tonight. I thought Jimmy might—"

There was a confusion of noises from the other end. She was crying. The receiver was banged against something a couple of times, and then a hand covered it. Through the muffling I heard her say her son's name in a voice that contained all the world's despair.

Jimmy shouted into my ear: "Who is this? What do you want? You leave my mother alone, you hear me? You hear me?" He slammed the receiver down.

I lay back on the big hotel bed and placed the phone beside me. The real Jantarro would have been out there in a flash, working on Jimmy, leaning on the distraught mother, prying into the absent husband's desk. The real Jantarro would have moved relentlessly, forcing the play until someone made a mistake. The real Jantarro was indestructible, a tin toy that bounced off walls and kept on coming no matter how many obstacles were placed in its way. This Jantarro could barely stay awake, and he was having a hard time imagining why anyone would want to make more misery for what was left of the Demenys.

I heaved the phone up on to my chest and forced my eyes open. Room service agreed to bring me a glorified hamburger and a bottle of beer. I let them talk me into french fries. The phone stayed on my shirt front, rising into my view and sinking again with each breath. Finally I sighed and rolled the nagging instrument back on to the bed where I could get at it. The numbers I needed came into my mind as easily as if they had been waiting, and reluctantly I used them one by one. The Crown was a strike out and so was the pizza place on St. Clair. But I got a hit at the Cafe Salerno. The guy asked me my name and told me to wait. In the background I could hear the roar of the espresso machine and the clatter of crockery. I could have sworn the song on the juke box was Volare. No wonder my happy heart sings, your love has given it wings.

"How's the boy?" There was a strain in Groper's voice that tightened me up from my balls to my chest.

"Tell you the truth, Gropes, a little worse for the wear."

"Geez, Cagey, I'm sorry to hear that. Maybe you need a good night's rest. Some castor oil. My mom always said castor oil was good. It cleans you out, you know?"

I knew. Groper felt about his digestive tract the way some people feel about their rose gardens. He has an untutored notion of esthetics. "Yeah," I told him, "maybe."

"Or a holiday, Cagey. Florida's good now. Lie on the beach, look at the girls." There was a pleading sound in his voice that plucked at my tightness and made it vibrate unpleasantly.

"What's the news, Gropes?" I needed to know the worst.

"I was in the Everglades once. They got this boat from a movie and it takes you up this river. Crocodiles and all that stuff. You wouldn't believe."

I was almost doubled up with the tension. I knew I had put my feet into a mess the mob had created. That much was clear from the way Groper danced around the issue. But I had to hear it in so many words. I had to hear Groper tell me that Benny the Fat had said that guy with a small birthmark on his face had told him that Demeny was theirs and that the whole Georg thing was so far off limits that I could only get out if I ran like a son of a bitch and didn't look back.

"And this Spanish moss stuff. It looks fake, you know? Hangs down from the trees—"

"Groper!"

There was a moment's silence in which I heard the juke box tell me that we'd leave all confusion and all disillusion behind. "Sorry, Cagey. What did you want to know?"

What did I want to know. I tried to keep the anxiety out of my voice. I spoke deliberately and calmly. "What does Gumball know about Harriet Gorton?" No sense in coming at it head on.

"Harriet Gorton?"

"The woman I asked you about, Gropes."

"Oh, the whore." He pronounced it "hooer."

"That's right, Gropes."

"Nothing."

"What do you mean, nothing?"

"He never heard of her." There was no false note in his voice now. He was telling me the truth.

"So she isn't one of...one of...He never heard of her. Really?"

"That's right, Cage. I'm sorry." He was sorry. I was confused. "What about this guy Demeny, then?"

[156]

"Him neither, Cage. Nobody has ever heard of him."
There was the lie. I could almost hear the voice that had schooled Groper in that sentence: "Tell him nobody has ever heard of him. Repeat it. 'Nobody has ever heard of him.' Say it again."

Buy why? I almost hung up on him without saying good-bye. And when I did put the phone down, I couldn't figure it out. Why would they want me to think that Demeny was not one of theirs? There had to be some sense to it, but whatever it was my banged-up brain couldn't come up with it. Big butterflies thrashed around in my stomach. No wonder my happy heart sings.

It was pitch black in the room when the door banged open, and if I'd had a gun I would have killed her. As it was I grabbed at the sheet under the pillow like a madman, came up empty-handed, and then hit the floor on the side of the bed away from the door. I guess I thought that they'd never find me under the bed.

But Lois found me with no trouble at all. She simply turned on the light, closed the door with the finesse of a dock worker, and calmly walked to where I was struggling to sit up on the carpet. Then she proceeded to kick me. I was too astonished to prevent her from getting in three good ones before I grabbed her ankle and held on for dear life. The strange thing was that neither of us spoke at all. The whole drama was a dumb show until I toppled her and she erupted in a violent scream of rage. I closed my eyes and leaned back against the side of the bed, letting the noise rip through my brain like a chain saw, too stupefied to be even bewildered. Only when she started to sob did I let my consciousness peep out hesitantly to try to find out what was happening.

"You're mad at me," was my first conclusion. She kept on sobbing, her green silk dress slipping further and further off her shoulders with each heave of her chest. She made no attempt to wipe at the stream of tears and mascara, and it broke into little tributaries as it sought out all her wrinkles. I wanted to comfort her, but I knew enough to understand that I couldn't give her any comfort. So I backed away carefully across the bed and went to the bathroom for an inspection of my bruises and a glass of water.

She was still sitting on the floor crying when I came back out. I turned off the main light and put on the small one on my side of the bed. I got into the bed and covered myself, staring up at the ceiling as I listened to her grief. Under the harsh glare of the fluorescent light in the bathroom I had seen a whole lot of things in myself that I had missed before—forgotten. I felt guilty and remorseful. But most of all I felt desperately clumsy and stupid. At one point I said, "I'm sorry." But I don't think she heard me. I thought about how I led my life, how I might have killed her, how I might be killing myself. I thought about all the foolish, stubborn things I did, and I tried to make up reasons for doing them. I came up with too many for me to be able to believe any of them.

She had stopped crying before I noticed it. She didn't look at me on her way to the bathroom. I heard the toilet flush and the water running. Then there was nothing for a while, and just as I was beginning to worry, she came out naked. She paused at the foot of the bed and cocked a hip, drawing her knees apart. A hand slid across her thigh until it found her crotch, and then it moved deliberately up and down over her pubis. Her eyes were vacant behind a thin, watery glaze.

"I'm sorry," I told her again. "I'll talk to him. Make him understand. You'll see." She said nothing. Her jaw began to go slack and the motion of her hand increased, going faster and harder. Her head was back now, her mouth wide open, and the muscles in her neck were cording. Her whole body shook with the agitation of her hand. I tried to look away, but my eyes stole back to her, and I felt my throat thicken and my penis come erect. She was crouched like an athlete in some desperate competition with herself, heaving breath and barking with the effort. When she came, I nearly came with her.

Shakily, she unbent her knees, and although she hid it quickly, there was surprise in her face. What had begun as a show of contempt ended as a private act, a call on something in herself that answered. She stood trembling for a moment and then with simple dignity lay down on the bed beside me. She drew the covers over her shoulders.

We lay beside each other embedded in a jumble of possibilities, tangled histories cut open to reveal raw strands of life. I felt the need to live by deliberate acts, to weave the strands into the garments we would wear tomorrow, and I wasn't sure I knew how.

Suddenly she flung herself on me and gripped me fiercely in her arms. "Hold me, hold me tight," she whispered urgently.

"I can't," I said softly. "You've pinned my only arm."

Laughter bubbled out of her and she freed me.

SHE WAS CRYING again when I awoke, crying quietly, trying not to wake me. Sleepily I reached a hand toward her to comfort her, and she jerked away from my touch as if I'd been going to burn her. Then a moment later she patted me once or twice under the covers in a placatory, absent-minded fashion. I rolled over on my side and lifted myself on my good elbow to look at her. Eventually she said, "It's no good, Kenneth." She was staring at the ceiling, eyes unfocused. She sighed. "I'm a mess."

"I don't look so hot myself," I said.

She shook her head wearily. "No, no. Not that. My life is a mess." I grunted as noncommittally as I could. "So is yours," she said, turning her head briefly to give me a fierce look.

"I guess so."

"Look at you. Running around like a madman looking for your lost arm. As if it matters a damn."

"Hey!" It stung. "I was this way before I lost it."

"Not really. Oh, sure, you were always brash, and you always ran too fast. But look at you now. You're in terrible shape and yet you're still pushing at it. You've gotten stupid, too. Insensitive. You really fucked things up for me last night."

I got out of bed, went to the bathroom and rubbed some of the hotel's complimentary toothpaste over my teeth with a finger. Lois was right. I was thrashing and didn't seem to care who got hurt. I thought about JoJo as I rinsed and spat the minty mess into the sink. But I'd been hurt too. People were trying to kill me, had come close to succeeding. You have to fight back. Otherwise, you might as well give up and die. There wasn't any other way. Was there?

I shuffled back into the bedroom, feeling old, tired and incomplete. "Yeah," I said to Lois. "I really did, didn't I? I'm sorry. I really am."

She was sitting up in bed, idly running her fingers through her hair. "Oh, Kenneth. It's not you." She sounded even more tired than I felt. There was an undertone of resignation, of deadness in her voice that I didn't like. "I'm just so...so damn mad!" She pounded the bedclothes with two tight fists. "At me! I let myself fall for that asshole, even though I knew he was an asshole. He just seemed so smooth, so powerful. All the things that I'm not." She smiled at me brightly and gave a phony laugh. "Hey, listen. When you're drowning, who cares if the guy with the life preserver is an asshole or not."

"Are you drowning, Lois?"

"We all are, honey." She made a disgusted noise and flung off the covers. "Hell, no. All I'm drowning in is self-pity." She went to the dresser and got something out of her bag. Then she strode toward the bathroom, small shoulders back, head high. "I'm going to scrape some of the mud off.

Order breakfast, will you?" The bathroom door closed firmly.

The toilet flushed, the door opened again and she stuck her head out. I could see her reflected half a dozen times in the cluster of mirrors in the dressing alcove. "Kenneth." I looked at her eyes in one of their manifestations. "About last night. Sorry. I didn't need to take it out on you. And about...about...Well, it can't have been very pretty."

I remembered her shocking, deliberate act of abasement. It hadn't been at all pretty; and the part of me that had responded was ashamed again. "Forget it," I said.

"Oh, I don't think so. That wouldn't be the right thing to do. I think it's something I should remember." All of her mirrored eyes moved somewhere private for a moment. Then she returned to me with a smile. "On the dresser," she said. "Beside my bag. There's a piece of paper. It's for you. That Gorton woman's address." She smiled again and disappeared behind the door.

One of my banks gave me money on my signature from an account I hoped no one knew about. Some of the money went into the hotel safe against emergencies more dire than this one, and some of it I kept with me for a gun and a set of decent clothing. The rest was taxi fare.

According to Lois's information, Harriet Gorton was now Adrienne O'Reilly. Apparently she herself wasn't hooking any more, but for the last year or so she had been hiring girls from time to time for jobs no one was talking about. The speculation was that she'd linked up with a man and together they were running a modest brothel.

If that was true, it was a strange place for a madam to live. The cab dropped me at a small, ugly, modern brick fourplex all the way out at Lawrence. There was a Texaco station on one corner, a parking lot on another, a twenty-store strip mall on the third featuring a Consumer's Discount as its big draw, and her place on the fourth. The shadow of a cloud crawled over me on its way along the street and I shivered. At any moment the seasons would get back on course and snatch away our illusions; winter would make its rightful presence felt.

The typed card in the mailbox said "O'Reilly" so I pushed the buzzer. Somewhere in the second floor rear a nasty noise would be bringing this case to an end. I leaned on it and waited. A woman of about fifty, in a housecoat of quilted polyester and with her hair up in curlers, came to the other side of the glass door and regarded me with a mixture of suspicion and annoyance. Then she went away. I hit the buzzer one more time. When I couldn't make the housewife reappear I rapped on the door with my hook. This time she came as far as the bottom of the stairs at the back of the small lobby and shouted, "Go away," in heavily accented English.

"Adrienne O'Reilly," I shouted back at her.

She yelled something in a language I didn't understand. And then I heard the word "police." I tried to look as if I weren't already under arrest, smiling and shrugging at her with all the charm of an Amway salesman. She disappeared and so did I.

Over lunch I realized I wanted Demeny. More than I wanted the case to end with the capture of the Gorton woman and the information she would have, I wanted to take Demeny for what he did to Rose Morrow. I considered ways and means. One of the means—or was it a way?—had to be a firearm. In my condition, there was no way I was going to roll about in the mud with him as if I were a twenty-year-old buck. Not again. But the problem was that I couldn't just go out and buy a replacement for my Chiefs Special. They wouldn't even sell me a .22 rifle without identification.

The cashier took my money and gave me the change I needed for the phone. He kept flicking his eyes between my face and my hook so I gave him a rest by slowly scratching my chin with the thing while I asked him where the nearest public phone was. He pointed down the road as if he couldn't trust his larnyx. Maybe I could scare Demeny to death.

I let the phone in Adrienne O'Reilly's place ring twelve times before I hung up with relief. If she wasn't home, there was nothing I could do about it. First I would get Demeny, and *then* I would get her. It was just a matter of priorities. I got Groper at home.

"How's the boy?"

"I wake you up, Gropes?" He sounded groggy.

"Naw. Just having lunch. The peanut butter sticks to your teeth, you know?"

"I heard."

"You okay, Cagey?"

"Sure. Why shouldn't I be?" Lois had been good for me. My hand wasn't shaking very much at all. "How are you doing, Gropes?"

"Good, Cagey, real good. I'm going down to Atlantic City with...I'm going down to Atlantic City to have a holiday, do some gambling. How about that, eh? Supposed to be better than Buffalo." There was a sinking feeling in the pit of my stomach. What the hell did they want with Groper in Atlantic City? He was a lousy forger, and he was about as threatening as a koala bear. He couldn't even carry their bags. I said a quick prayer for him. I just hoped it wasn't one of those things where they needed an expendable body to settle a debt.

"Geez, Gropes, that's great. You take care of yourself. Don't take any wooden nickels." He laughed with delight at that the way he always did. The fact that he passed bad checks made the thought of wooden nickels hilarious for him.

"No wooden chips, neither," he said between guffaws.

When we had calmed down, I said, "Hey, listen, Gropes. I need to get my hands on a piece. What do you suggest?"

"Anything special?" he asked.

"Naw, just something that's going to go bang when I pull the trigger."

"Gimme an hour. See what I can do."

"Where do you want to meet?"

"The Crown. That okay?" I told him that it was and hung up. My hand was still shaking and I looked at it with genuine surprise. I explained to it that they had told me that Demeny was not one of theirs, and that helped. A little.

I took a cab to the King Eddie, got more money—enough to give Groper something to gamble with—and walked to the Crown. Each time I passed a cop, I told myself that Bench could have me whenever he wanted and he obviously didn't want me now, so there was no point in my holing up in a hotel and skulking around to buy a gun when a perfectly good bed and a useful .38 could be found with no trouble at all at my place. But why make it easier for him than it already was, I answered back? Again I had the feeling that I was missing something so big and glaring that everyone else could see it except me. I would have shaken my head a dozen times, but it hurt too much.

I was two Scotches into it when Groper came in. He is tiny. He must be all of four foot ten. That's why he got called Groper. The idea was that you had to grope around to find him. When he and I were in the same cell it was the joke of the jail and the source of a few new obscene ideas. It took him a good five minutes to get to my table, because he had to stop to say hello to half the people in the Crown. They were mostly ex-cons like us, and this was their club, a place where they could go to reminisce about that time in Joyceville or that stretch in Kingston. I liked the place but not the conversation.

Groper slid into the booth with a smile on his face and a little bounce when he hit the seat. There was the usual thirty seconds or so of waiting while he wrestled his legs up underneath himself so he could sit on his shoes. It looks as if it would be really uncomfortable, but it gets Groper a bit nearer the rest of us and he reckons it's worth the pain. I once told him it was probably bad for his circulation and suggested he use a cushion or a phone book. For the next six weeks he carried the Yellow Pages with him everywhere he went, and I was about to buy him a briefcase to put it in when he stopped doing it. He told me some guy had borrowed it to look up a number and had never given it back. He said he couldn't find a store that sold them so he was waiting until the new edition came out. The interesting thing is that nobody ever gave him a hard time about it. But he's used his shoes ever since.

"What'll it be?" I asked him when he stopped squirming.

"What do they drink in Atlantic City?" He smoothed his thin hair down and wiped the hand on his pants.

Without thinking I said, "The same stuff they drink here." He looked so crestfallen that I suggested bourbon. We circled around to business by way of the aunt who'd come to live with him.

Groper shook his head dolefully, whether at the bourbon or at the thought of his aunt I wasn't sure. "That's the one thing," he said.

"The one thing what?" I asked him.

"About going to Atlantic City. I don't like to leave her alone."

I frowned. "Is there something wrong with her?" From the look on his face I thought I'd put my foot on it.

"She's . . . she's a woman," he spluttered.

"Oh," I said with a struggle to hide my amusement. "Sure. That. Well, you'll think of something."

Groper tried to look pleased with the compliment. Then he leaned forward. "I got it," he whispered suddenly in a voice that stuck out far more than a normal tone. But considering the amount of stuff that got dealt in the Crown, I wasn't too worried. "You use a thirty-eight, right?" Again the urgent whisper.

"Right," I said quietly. He looked up, shocked, and put a finger across his lips.

"Couldn't get a thirty-eight, but I got a thirty-two Smith and Wesson." This last burst hissed like a nest of snakes.

"Fine," I whispered back, trying not to smile.

"A whole box of rounds, too."

"Great."

"Later. Outside."

"Right."

Abruptly reverting to his usual voice, he asked, "What else do they drink in Atlantic City?" The bourbon was untouched after his first sip.

I had an inspiration. "Rum and coke," I told him. He smiled and nodded at the propriety of that.

Guns make me nervous, and a gun tucked into my belt makes me scared enough to sweat, even when it's parked at the small of my back and the worst it can do is perforate a cheek. So after I left Groper I walked like a man with a bad case of piles straight to the nearest men's clothing store and bought a golf jacket—the only thing they had that was big enough to fit me comfortably. The gun went into a zippered pocket, where it bulged like the head of a nine iron, so I took the jacket off and hid the thing in as many folds of fabric as I could. Then I bent the wooden arm until the hook was at my shoulder, and I hung the folded jacket on it so it draped down my back. Casual.

I strolled down the street trying to think. The sun tightened the skin on my forehead. The breeze tugged at my curls. And every now and then the Smith and Wesson tap-tapped on my spine. Very casual.

Demeny on the comeback trail, I thought. The blue, track-suited figure danced into my mind, bobbing and weaving, weary to the bone after two knockdowns but refusing to give up. I put him in the ring, blue trunks, a cut over his eyes hardened with styptic, knees wobbling. But I couldn't see his opponent. Oh, there was me, of course, still in the dressing room taping my hands. But there was nobody in the ring. He was shadow boxing. There had to be somebody, because ghosts don't drive you to kill, do they? It wasn't right.

I flinched a little as the pistol at my back knocked on a kidney. Then I had it. Demeny wanted to be a boxer, but he wasn't one. Never would be. The ring, the fight image, it was all wrong. Demeny was a long-distance killer, a sniper, a brave man at a hundred yards or more. Now I saw him in a tree, laid out on a web of branches like a big caterpillar that would never fly. His long gun was pushed out ahead of him, and the only world for him was what he saw in the telescopic sight, a tiny, make-believe world displayed on glass. I peeped at his world and under the cross hairs that told him what was true I saw myself.

I broke out in a sweat and almost ducked. Automatically I looked up, but there was nothing above me except the pigeons busily soiling the cornices of the old city hall.

None of this told me why. I still had no idea why Demeny had killed Rose Morrow. Maybe Helene had confided some suspicions about Demeny to her before he made his move on Georg's wife and son—before he ordered it made, like the long-distance killer that he was—and somehow he had found out. But if that was true, why hadn't she gone to the cops when Helene was taken? Why hadn't she shared those suspicions with me after Helene had been killed? Maybe some of Demeny's rage at the Georgs had extended to Helene's lover. Maybe, maybe. None of this told me why. But it told me where to find him.

20

I WAITED until rush hour. That gave me the cover of the crowd on the sidewalk, so I made it to the hoardings without sticking out at all. It also gave me the cover of dusk. But all that cover didn't make me feel less exposed. The top of my head was as tight as a drum and I imagined it glowed like a neon light. I told myself that if he hit me from that angle I would never know it. I wouldn't even be aware that the light had gone out. Somehow that was no help at all. I even imagined I was being followed, which only goes to show how far gone I was. Demeny was all around me.

I told myself that I could call the cops and let them do it. But they probably wouldn't listen to an invalid like me. If they weren't even going to question Demeny, they wouldn't go hunting for him in the dark. Well, then, I could wait him out; I could park myself here and lay siege to him. Sooner or later, if my hunch was right, he'd have to show himself. But damn it, I wanted him, and I wanted him now. I was tired of waiting, tired of what this case was doing to me. It needed to be over, quick.

The big wire gates were chained together with a chain that was long enough to let a man slip through. I put a hand on it. Someone banged into me and cursed. It was all in my mind, of course. I didn't *know* he was in there. I couldn't know he was perched in the topmost branches of the giant concrete and steel tree he had built himself. If he wasn't in there, there was no danger at all. I ducked under the chain and past the gates.

The site was as still as a graveyard. Even in the fading light I could make out all the machinery and the piles of materials, so I scanned the area and picked a small mountain of gravel as my first stop. Keeping low—as if it mattered—I ran quickly to the gravel and dropped against the side away from the building. I looked up and saw the whole edge of the roof grinning at me like a rictus. If I really wanted cover, I was going to have to pick something that rose from the ground at a much steeper angle. I scurried to the office trailer, twenty yards off.

Nothing happened. I made it to the trailer and lay just under it, out of breath, heart pounding, and only a little disappointed. Since I figured him for the roof, my plan was to go up and get him. It wasn't quite as crazy as it sounded —if I had him figured right. He was a sniper, a long-distance killer, not a hand-to-hand man, and if I could get close enough to him, I could take him. I didn't think he had what it took to kill at close range. I would get up into that roof shack and spot him against the night sky. Then I would stalk him and take him, suddenly, from inches away. His rifle wouldn't do him any good. Anyway, if I did it right, I would always be able to retreat to the elevator, leaving him stranded again.

The tricky part was going to be getting to the foot of the

building unscathed and preferably unseen. I tried to recall whether you could hear the winch motor over the sound of the wind on the roof. I wasn't sure.

When my heart rate had slowed to the point where I couldn't hear the thumping in my ears any longer, I slid out from under the trailer and eased myself to a standing position flat against its safe side. There was a bulldozer and a crane between me and the footings, and these were going to be my waystations. I crouched at the end of the trailer and reconstructed in my mind the place where the bulldozer should be. On your mark, get set. The wind would have to cover the sound of the elevator motor, that's all there was to it. On your mark. Only twenty, maybe thirty feet to the bulldozer. Get set. I couldn't climb the stairs. I didn't even know if there *were* stairs. When did they build the stairs in a skyscraper? At the start, or at the end? All in my mind. On your mark, get set. There was no good reason to believe that he was there. He had probably run off to Brazil. I stood up and leaned back against the safety of the flimsy aluminum, closing my eyes and calming my breathing.

Then I heard it. Through the sound of the traffic beyond the hoardings, over the white noise of the sundown wind, between the knockings of my heart, I heard a steely whang and a whine after it. It might have been an overheated part of some engine contracting as it cooled, it might have been a bolt blown off a high ledge striking a girder on the way down. It might have been. But it wasn't. It was Demeny's way of reaching out to touch his fellow man.

With my head just above ground level I peered around the corner of the trailer to where the bulldozer squatted like a giant carcass. The sun was completely gone now and the sickly yellow glow of the city sky threw all objects into doubt. It was the light for a troubled imagination. Closer to the building itself a line of steel-shaded bulbs swayed from the electrical cord and wiped patches of glare back and forth across the dirt at the whim of the wind. I retreated the essential few feet and got my gun from the zippered pocket, making sure that the safety was off and that there was a round in the chamber. If that really was Demeny up there shooting, my pop gun wouldn't do me a damn bit of good. But it helped against ghosts.

I inched forward, exposing myself.

There were three shots in rapid succession, one creasing the ground in front of the bulldozer and sending up dust, another hitting the machine again and this time sounding as if someone had dropped a sledge hammer, and a third that hit metal beyond the bulldozer creating sparks and that terrifying whine. High above me I thought I heard a trio of tiny cracks, twigs snapping under the weight of someone climbing a tree. By then I was facedown in the dirt, hand and hook under my head so as little as possible would brighten his sights. My gun was under my nose and the smell of oil was nauseating. I waited, spread eagled, for the hammer of Thor to strike.

When nothing happened after what seemed like hours, I decided to move. Forward was the safest way. If I tried to turn around I might take too long to get back to cover. I drew my legs up under me and suddenly lunged for the protection of the big machine.

Only when I was secure against the thick steel treads did I begin to think once more. The shots had gone wide. Could he have been firing blind? But then why fire at all? Did he want to frighten me rather than kill me? If so, he had succeeded. But it didn't make sense from the man who had calmly destroyed Rose Morrow. It was time for a reassessment of the situation.

The element of surprise was gone and with it any chance I had for taking him on the roof. Now it was important to get myself under the best cover available. Then I could wait him out. I peered through the gloom back the way I had come. Against the city lights everything was black shadow. If he was using an infra-red scope, there would be little hope for me that way. I could stay where I was, but I would be cramped as hell in no time; and I could easily miss him if he left while I cowered behind this thing. My best bet was to cover the last few yards to the base of the building, where I would have room to move and still be secure. The angle was simply too steep for him to be able to hit me there unless he leaned over the side and fired straight down.

I squirmed around and lifted my head above the treads and up into the cut in the body for the cab. The roofline of the building was clean so far as I could tell, and for a moment I wondered whether the whole thing had been my imagination. I picked a spot between two puddles of light near the foundation and I ran.

The concrete was warm, filled with the heat of the day that seemed so long ago. My heavy breathing echoed in the hollows of the skeletal ground floor. I started to spook myself, so I moved, hugging the monster, bumping past the concrete pillars that jutted out every fifteen feet or so along the bottom of the building. I could do laps until morning. It would be good for me.

Suddenly I came to the vertical wooden trough that held the elevator. Dust swirled into my eyes, drawn up by the rush of warm air that climbed the face of the tower on its way to the cold night sky. As I wiped my face, I thought of something. If I disabled the elevator, I would trap him completely. He would be mine for the taking in the morning.

I swung out past the boards to find nothing. Of course. He would have climbed the tree and pulled the ladder up after him. The damn cage was at the top. And then I remembered the way Jimmy had played with the wires that were attached to the building somewhere near where I was standing. If I ripped them out, he would be stuck. I felt around in the dark until my hand landed on a tangle of cables. I gave them a pull but they held. My hook slid behind them, and I twisted them as hard as I could; they still held. Then I moved my good hand down a foot, grabbed as many as I could and with both hands I jerked and wrestled them as if they were snakes around my neck.

Suddenly, through the boards I heard a rumbling, the vibration of the elevator coming down. Was Demeny coming down to investigate, or was the cage coming down empty? Either way, it was all right with me. I got out my gun again, and I waited, crouched low and out of sight behind the boards.

When the cage hit bottom, I held my breath. Nothing. I held it some more. Still nothing. Boldly I jumped out and thrust my gun ahead of me. There was nothing inside. I pulled at the door and it came open with a squeal of bent metal hinges. I got in to disconnect the junction box.

"Freeze, asshole." A quiet voice behind me.

I bellowed with fright and started to swing round.

"I said freeze!"

He hit me a glancing blow to the kidney with something hard and small, and I managed to make it to the far corner of the cage, where I cowered in shock. In the gloom I couldn't see him properly, but I knew by the voice it wasn't Demeny.

He moved into the cage with me. "Drop the piece, asshole." I just stared at his shape stupidly. "Drop it." When I understood that I was still holding a gun, I looked down at it for a moment and let it fall to the floor of the cage. He crouched and swept a foot out to kick the gun away from me. Then he grunted and I saw his shoulders drop a bit. "We're going to the top," he said and he chuckled through his nose. "This is your big chance, asshole, to make it to the top. But if you want I'll kill you right here. Makes no never mind to me. So you want it, you just ask for it by moving. Understand what I'm saying? Hey, asshole?"

I could feel the shame burning my face. That and the fear left me stupid, speechless. He didn't seem to care. Grunting once again, he reached behind him and pulled the cage door shut, feeling around until he got the wire in his hand to give it a twist. Then he groped at the cage wall with his left hand, looking for the button to make it go. When he didn't find it, he brought his hands together and put the gun in his left, all the time making sure it was pointed right at me. "I'm ambidextrous, you know?" he said. "Kill with either hand. So don't get any ideas." His right hand now felt along the cage wall, and suddenly we lurched upwards.

I thought of a time when I was a kid and I'd been on a night ride in a ferris wheel, how the wind had made my eyes tear, blurring the colored lights on the ground below. How I'd been so scared that my hands gripped the bar until cramp set in, sending excruciating pain up to my elbows. How I'd started to throw up when the thing stopped with me at the top, and I'd made myself swallow back my own vomit. I remembered thinking I knew what it was like to be dying. The slow, rhythmic bumping of the cage hypnotized me and made me try to go on remembering.

Then it took a lurch and I felt my stomach heave. I started sweating. A point inside me screamed that I should do something, anything. Unwillingly I came into the present. This was mob business and I was part of it. When I had asked about Demeny, some smart son of a bitch had figured I might be useful; I would be the second body the cops would find, the equalizer that would give them an even number of corpses to soothe the official minds. Here was the reason for the lie that Groper had been handed to pass on to me. Let Jantarro get next to him. We'll take them both out. Demeny does Jantarro and Jantarro does Demeny. It'll look good.

They wouldn't have had any trouble keeping track of me. They could have tapped Groper's phone. They could have tagged along with Demeny and waited for me to show up. They could have followed me. I was easy. I was a patsy.

It wasn't hard to slide down the corner of the cage, to sink to the floor in a small pool of jelly. I was so easy a kid could have handled me. That's what the man with the gun must have thought, because he turned his head casually to look out over the city and to show me that one of us, at least, was a man.

I shot a foot out and caught him on the knee, driving his

leg the way it wasn't made to go. He yelled and staggered back onto the cage door, which gave an inch before it was held by the wire loop. His arms reached high into the cage, grabbing at safe air, and the gun went off as his hands clenched. I swung my wooden arm along the floor until the hook bit into his leg, and gripping the fake arm with my good one, I jerked his foot out from under him. Once more his arms went up, and this time he fell on his ass just in front of the door. The whole cage bucked and jumped away from the building, slamming itself back into line half a second later. Something cracked and the man threw himself sideways to get his hands on the floor so he could stand up. I kicked at his gun hand and he pulled it away, but he brought it back to the same spot just as quickly, so I lifted my leg and drove the heel of my shoe into the fist that held the gun. He let go of it and started shouting something I couldn't understand. He gave a funny lurch, screamed and disappeared.

The whole world was wrong. I couldn't get a grip on what was happening. At first I thought the door had sprung open and that he had fallen out, but the wire gate was right there in front of me where it should be. I was losing my balance. My arms flew out and then I dropped through the big hole in the floor.

Someone was hitting my feet. And every now and then he punched me in the stomach. Bang, bang, bang on my shoes. Whack in the guts. Bang, bang, bang. Unkind, I thought. And then it occurred to me I had been crucified. Nails through my shoes, a sword in my side, and one arm stretched to the point of pulling my shoulder off. Suddenly it all stopped except the agonizing pull. I let myself hang, twisting slowly back and forth in the peace.

I looked up to see my torn sleeve flapping against the wood of my arm. My hook hand was curved over the lip of the hole in the bottom of the cage. Gently my mind informed me that if I looked down I would see nothing for forty stories, and then I would see my burial ground. I started crying before I could decide whether I wanted to or not. Without thinking I reached to dry my eyes and the motion made me revolve until I saw the city. Slowly my body was turned away and then back again, less and less each time until I was once more facing the building. A calmness that was flatter than any calmness I had ever known filled me then. With deliberateness I reconstructed what must have happened. I saw the flap of plywood that hovered in front of me, the broken board that had opened under his feet and down which I had slid. I reasoned that it was this that had hit my stomach, and the walls of the chute that had punished my feet.

It felt good to know what was what.

Well, I thought, that just about wraps it up. All that remained was to see whether the leather straps that held my arm to my shoulder would break before the hook slipped from the floor of the cage or the wood under it gave way.

I considered trying to undo the buckles under my shirt.

Somehow I couldn't bring myself to do that.

I cried some more.

There was nothing dramatic about it, no crisis point, no moment of truth. I simply began to work at pulling myself up through the hole. Carefully—I didn't want any more views of the city—I slipped my good arm up the wooden one until I found the flat edge where a wrist would be, and I fastened on to the junction of wood and steel. Then I pulled. I rose easily for the first foot and then I began to tremble as the muscles in my right half tried to go into spasm. I was committed. If I dropped back I might bounce the hook off its perch. So I ignored the protest and gave it more than I had. My head hit the back edge of the hole, near the strip of wood by the door, and I dipped forward and used my skull to lever my head up and through. Then with the edge cutting into the back of my neck, I let my legs walk up the swinging flap of flooring. I was nearly horizontal now and right at the point when I would have to get another purchase on the cage. If I took too much weight off the hook it might slip away and take me with it. But if I didn't find a way of distributing my weight fast, my good arm would simply fail and I'd swing out into oblivion.

I snaked a leg over the side and up onto what remained of the floor. I tensed my thigh muscles, taking some of the weight, and the hook held. Holding my breath, I drove my head tight against the lip and brought my other leg up and in, rolling and arching at the same time. I fell onto the floor and hit the side of the cage.

In fact, I had to tug the hook free of the two-by-six into which it had buried itself. My wooden arm was busted at the elbow, and when I got shakily to my feet it flapped loosely against my side. I stood there for a moment wondering whether I should push the button and go down. The thought of falling, even slowly, was too much for me. I reached across the nothingness, undid the wire, and then stepped into the hut.

On the roof I could see the stars. "Demeny!" I shouted into the wind. A light brighter than the stars flashed at me and then I heard the shot. I ran toward him. Demeny was nothing to me. He was a coward. I had been resurrected.

"Don't come any closer," I heard him scream. A pure fool, I ran on, feeling the good traction of tar under my feet. I wanted this to be over, finished and done with. Another shot, and I corrected course by its light.

He was lying on his back when I found him, his rifle by his side. There was a dark wetness, darker than night, all over his chest, and his eyelids fluttered like a maiden's. "Demeny," I said.

He strained to see me. "It's you," he said finally. "I thought it was..." And he closed his eyes.

"Why, Demeny? Why?"

"Money." He said it like a prayer.

"No. Why did you kill Rose Morrow?"

"Money." Whispered. And then: "For the children."

His eyes sprang open. I could see the starlight caught in their whites. He arched his back and came up into my arms. I let him down slowly, feeling the warm, soft hole he had made in himself.

[178]

AT SEVEN I had to get up to go to the bathroom. And a
couple of hours later the maid came in but I scared her off.
I finally woke up at noon. Every time I came out of sleep I
was dreaming about killing people. In the shower I realized
I should have been more worried about being killed, since
the mob was missing a soldier. I let the water run cold
until the wet hair on my arm practically stood straight up,
and then I got out and punished myself with a stack of the
small hotel towels.

I phoned the desk and asked them to send someone to get
me a new pair of underwear, new socks and a white shirt—
seventeen, thirty-six. The guy didn't say anything except,
"Yes, sir." My tailor kicked a bit, but eventually he promised to fix up something from the rack and have it here by

two. "Ask for John Scott's room," I told him. He sniffed a couple of times. I had to phone him back when I remembered shoes and a tie.

Then I called Glenda at her Florida motel and the switchboard let it ring the regulation ten times. So I phoned her partner, my lawyer, and told her to tell Glenda that I was all right. "No questions," I told her. "No time." I should have mentioned to her that I was under arrest, but there would be time enough for that later on.

When the coffee came, I picked up the newspaper from the hall floor and scanned it idly as I took in caffeine. There was no news of Demeny. I hadn't really expected it, because the paper goes to bed too early. I toyed with the idea of turning on the TV to see what the all-news channel had to say about it, but my heart wasn't in it. While I waited for my clothes I let the bridge column explain a dummy reverse to me, something I thought I already understood pretty well. South won again, as usual.

My tailor was kind enough to send me the tie already knotted for my neck. The suit was okay, even if it was a blue that I wouldn't have chosen. The hotel quite correctly had picked black socks and three pairs of boxer shorts in different sizes. The biggest ones fit but they felt funny. I laid the jacket out on the bed and put the shirt inside it, stuffing the left shirtsleeves into the sleeve of the suit because I wasn't wearing an arm. The wooden one was ready for the fireplace. Then I wrestled myself into the combo and tucked the ends of the empty sleeves into the pocket of the jacket, smoothing the material out as flat and as neat as I could. I examined myself in the mirror and decided I was ready.

My hand didn't tremble as I made the call to Benny the Fat. Benito Fazzalari pretends to be an accountant, with an office, secretaries, clients—the whole bit. I guess he does make a few thousand a year that way. But the simple fact is that he's a bag man for the mob. He works between here and Albany and sometimes Miami too. When I was green I

[180]

did a job for him—a private thing, he had told me, that required delicacy and tact. And I suppose part of him actually believed that, because he was as convincing as any man I've ever met. He seemed to be genuinely surprised when I pointed out to him halfway through the job that if I took it any further it might seriously prejudice my nonexistent relations with one of the top drug dealers in town, and along with that my life. We worked it out, but he would have been just as happy if we hadn't. Three-hundred pounds of duplicity is six-hundred pounds of trouble.

"Cagey," he purred, "how wonderful to hear from you."

"You, too, Benny."

"How can I help? Too late for taxes. A business problem, perhaps."

"A matter of debt," I told him.

"Ah, yes. How—Cagey, may I put you on hold for a moment? Another line. It will only be a second." A click and I was listening to a woman complaining about her husband in some faint electronic world of disembodied conversations. It was no use, she wouldn't take any more. Then there was a distant fanfare of tinny beeps. "Cagey? I'm terribly sorry. Now, where were we? Oh yes, I was going to say how distressing for you, but how fortunate for me, because it gives me a chance to repay your kind efforts on my behalf. A debt for a debt, you might say. Now, what... what can you tell me?"

I was reluctant to play his game, but it was fairly likely his line was tapped and I didn't want to hand the feds anything that they might be able to use against me. "I was approached by a man who was trying to collect for his employers. I persuaded him not to bother me anymore, but I'd like to open up negotiations with his bosses to see if I can clear up the misunderstanding. I'd like you to set up the meeting. Do you think you could do that, Benny?"

"Oh, I think so. I think so. And if you don't mind my saying so, Cagey, I think that is a very sensible way to approach the matter."

"I don't mind," I said.

He chuckled and then became brisk, businesslike. "Now, do you have a place in mind?"

"It doesn't matter to me."

"I see. Yes. Well, then. What time did you have in mind?"

"Tonight. You fix it. I'll call you this afternoon."

"Yes. Well, you're being most...accommodating, I must say. Rather...well, rather unlike you, if you know what I mean."

"Relax, Benny. Nothing up my sleeve. And I've only got one of them."

"I'll see what I can do."

"I'm sure you will."

She opened a moment after I knocked. I watched her eyes widen slowly as it dawned on her who I was, and then she slammed the door hard—on my new shoe. I hit the door once with my shoulder, sending her tottering back into the apartment. Quietly I stepped inside and shut the door behind me. My gun was out and I waved her to the couch.

She'd done a good job of changing her appearance. I probably wouldn't have recognized her on the street. All the flash and brass was gone and in its place was competence straining for appeal. She wore glasses, a beige blouse and a calf-length brown wool skirt. Her short hair was dyed red, and you would have said she should use more makeup. Her fingernails were unpainted and bitten.

"What is this?" she asked in a dry voice. "What do you want? I've got nothing. Nothing to steal. Look. Go ahead, look." She was trying to act frightened but it didn't work because resignation kept leaking through. "I'll scream," she said, raising her voice. I just kept looking at her, letting her see the gun, and finally she averted her eyes and sank heavily on to the couch.

From where I was I could see into the kitchen and the bathroom, but the bedroom door was partly closed. I remembered her blond friend and his surprise entrance.

"Come here," I told her. She got up and walked over to me, stopping an arm's length away. "Turn around." She hesitated. "Turn around," I repeated in the same colorless tone. She did and I put the muzzle of the gun at the back of her neck.

"Are you going to kill me?"

"Move." I prodded her forward. "To the bedroom door."

"Oh," she said, and she went carefully down the little hall.

I put my foot against the door and pushed it open slowly. It hit the wall with a little thud. I couldn't see anything that wasn't furniture. I made her go into the room, and stepping back from her I said, "Move the bed."

"Oh, come on," she said. I kept quiet and after a second or two she began to push on the footboard. The bed slid away on the parquet floor and the bogey man wasn't underneath.

He wasn't in the closet either, or on the balcony.

For a while I just sat and looked at her. There was so much I wanted to know that I didn't know where to begin, and yet there was nothing she could tell me that would make me understand. An eternity of questioning silence seemed to be the proper thing. Two women and a retarded man for what? Money? And Demeny and the poor creep in a broken pile at the bottom of an unfinished building. And maybe me too, if I couldn't talk the mob out of it tonight. I tried to get a hold on what it was that bothered me about this. I've seen lives traded for money before. Slowly at fifty a trick or twenty a hit. Or fast as a breath for a couple of bucks. I thought I understood that there were things I would never really understand. "Are you going to kill me?" she had asked. Was I? Is that what I was leading myself up to? Why would I do that? For two women and a retarded man?

"Tell me," I said.

I must have moved the gun, because she was looking right at it. "Tell you what?" The words came out hesitantly.

[183]

"Why. That will do for a start."

"I'm not saying anything." She hugged herself tight.

"Look, lady, you've got it wrong. It's the cops that have to respect your rights, not me. With me you don't have any rights at all. I'm the guy you tried to kill, remember?"

She hunched her shoulders and drew her head in. "Go on," she said, "do it. Get it over with."

Fuck it, Jantarro, I told myself. It's over. Let it go. Are you really going to beat on her until she tells you something you won't understand? Or are you going to kill her in case she holds up a mirror and you recognize yourself? I let out a lungful of air and allowed the muzzle of the gun to drop.

"Bring me the telephone," I told her. She shrugged and got the phone. I gave her the number to dial, and then I took the receiver from her and tucked it between my left ear and my shoulder. She went back to the couch and watched the gun some more.

They found Bench for me, in a squad car by the sound of his voice over the wire. He listened to my offer and eventually said yes. We both knew he had to. He would drop the charges against me in return for the woman. He'd done that kind of thing many times before. And I? Would I drop the case now?

It wasn't just that the blond bully was still out there somewhere. They'd scoop him up easily enough now that they had the woman. It was the lack of understanding that was eating at me.

While I waited for Bench I looked at her and thought of all the unfinished business in the world, all the loose ends and the unanswered questions. Who knows why Uncle Harry drinks? Who knows what became of the kid up the block who used to date Suzie? Who knows why they split up? Other people seemed to be able to handle it fine. Why couldn't I?

As Bench took her away, I asked her once more. "Why?" She said nothing.

• • •

"Benito you know, of course. And this here's my cousin Nino. He's a lawyer. Sometimes it's good to have a person around good with words. Uses his head. Me, I think from here." Giovanni Carpeneto grabbed his vest somewhere between his chest and his stomach. Nino made his mouth smile. And Benny distributed his bland gaze evenly among the three of us. "You"—Carpeneto grabbed at air between us—"you come alone. You good with your head and your guts, eh?" He made a sound that might have been a laugh or a cough. "Okay, Benito. You can go. We take care of this privately." Benny got to his feet. Carpeneto reached across the small cafe table and placed his wrinkled hand over mine. "Unless you want he should stay," he said to me. "A friend for you?" I didn't say anything, and he smacked the back of my hand lightly. "Good! Us together." Benny left without looking at me.

We were in the back room of a small bakery out in an industrial district, and half a dozen tables that during the day would hold sausage sandwiches and plates of veal with deep-fried zucchini now supported upturned white iron chairs. It felt lonely, out-of-business. When Benny had disappeared through the bead curtain that separated the restaurant part from the front, Carpeneto leaned back and tugged at the points of his vest. He looked tired. "Okay," he said, as if calling himself to order, "you wanted this meeting. You got the floor."

I told him about Demeny and enough about my case for him to understand why I had become interested in Demeny in the first place. I explained how I had guessed that Demeny's money had been their money and how I had checked with Groper to make sure I wasn't stepping on their toes. Then I told him how it had worked last night and why he had lost a soldier. "Somebody thought it was a piece of luck that I stumbled into your business," I told him, "and it was—a piece of bad luck." His eyes darted over to Nino. Bad luck, Nino, I thought. "That's the way it happened," I said. "And now I want to know where I stand." Through it all I managed to keep my hand flat on the table, my voice even and low, and my feet firmly planted on the floor.

"You want some wine?" he asked when I stopped.

"Sure," I said. He looked at Nino again, and the lawyer got up slowly and went into the kitchen.

"I hear you say it was...like an accident...this...this death. You don't have the blame. Eh?" He spread out his hands.

"That's right," I said.

He seemed to lose his place, to withdraw into himself to consult some memory the way an old man will. Nino came back with two glasses and a bottle without a label. Carpeneto and I sipped, and then he looked at me expectantly. I pursed my lips and nodded slowly. "Yeah?" he asked.

"Good," I said. "Mellow, like purple sunshine."

He laughed with pleasure like a kid. "You not just telling me this?"

"Mr. Carpeneto, would I do that?"

He laughed again. "I make it myself," he said.

"No kidding?"

"No kidding."

Nino cleared his throat impatiently and rattled off a string of Italian. Carpeneto regarded him as if he had farted at a wedding. "Okay, then, I'll say it in English," Nino continued unperturbed. "This man here has made a widow out of Teresa. There are four children who don't have a father because of him. Moreover, he interfered with our business. We owe him nothing. There must be a sanction or we lose respect. That's how it is, and you know it."

Carpeneto poured himself another glass of wine. "Moreover," he said to himself. He lifted his head and looked at me with nothing in his eyes. "My cousin is right what he says. You are nothing to us. I like that you come to us. I like that you drink with us. You are brave." He raised his hands off the table and dropped them gently again. "But brave is only one thing. Not so special." I waited until he paused and then I made myself reach for the wine bottle, grateful that I could pour without hitting the neck against the glass. "I might say, 'Cut off his arm,' but—." Carpeneto shrugged. "Better to kill you, I think, than no arms at all. I might say, 'Break his legs,' but not for this. For stealing, maybe, but not for this."

I put the wineglass down and slowly got up. "That's it, Jantarro?" Nino asked with a trace of amusement. "No argument? No protestation?"

"What shall I say?" I asked him. "That I didn't interfere in your business? That you tried to use me? That I didn't kill your man? That he dropped through a hole in the earth because Demeny wasn't a good builder? You know that already. You guys are just pissed off because Demeny dumped your money in that hole and now your profit and loss statement won't look so good. Should I beg or plead? You might get a kick out of that, Nino, but I don't think Mr. Carpeneto would.

"I made a mistake, Mr. Carpeneto." He lifted his eyebrows. "I came to find out where I stood, just to know. It's a weakness I have, needing to know. But the mistake was that I knew all along. I stand the same place now that I did yesterday or a month ago. Who knows if a hole is going to open up under that place? Who knows if some bolt of lightning is going to hit that place? I stand wherever my feet happen to be, and there's nothing you or anyone else can do about that. So I've wasted your time, Mr. Carpeneto, and I apologize for that. Thank you for the wine."

"You are welcome," the old man said. "You have no advice for me, what I should do?"

"No advice," I said. "You don't need it. You know already. You've just forgotten." At the bead curtain I stopped and turned back. "A favor, though."

"A favor?"

"Yes. I would appreciate it. Groper. Treat him well. He's a friend."

"Why would I do a favor for you?"

"I don't know," I told him. "Maybe nobody does."

[187]

22

GEORG'S LAWYER, Norman Postitch, picked me up at ten the next morning and we drove out to our client's house for the last meeting. It was raining again, and the whole world was warm and wet, the way it had been in my dream. Only then the water was the color of blood and I was a fish living in it. It's funny being a fish. You don't miss having arms at all. And as for the blood all around you, you just take it in gill measures and let it out again, passing through your world the way it passes through you.

"You ever eat carp?" I asked Postitch. The wipers were going tickety-thwack, and the tires hissed on the wet pavement. The rain noises made me think of when I was a kid, sleeping in the back of my parents' car on long trips.

"C-c-carp? Th-th-the fish?"

"I wondered what it tasted like."

He sent me a quick look to see if I was having him on, and his sad clown's mouth twitched at the corners, ready to make a smile if it turned out that the joke was going to be on him. "Odd, you sh-should ask. I had it at Georg's. He eats it every Christm-m-mas Eve. Old German tradition. Boils it whole. It t-t-turns blue. It's hard to s-s-say wh-what it t-t-tasted like. You eat it w-w-with horseradish s-s-sauce. M-maybe like d-d-d-dirt." He took a hand off the wheel to wipe a mixture of sweat and rainwater from his forehead. His shiny curls sparkled unnaturally with beads of water that clung like tiny decorations. "Carp is a bottom feeder," he announced fluidly.

I hadn't gone down to police headquarters to get my arm, so my left sleeve was tucked into my pocket. Georg noticed it right away. "You are not hurt, I trust," he said as he ushered us into his big, empty house. "Not further, I mean."

"Not further," I assured him.

"You were hit in the head. Am I right? You see, truly I am recovered. I remember everything. Merweiss says I may live forever. I accuse him of hating me."

"My head is fine."

"Good, good. Come, sit. *Renate, Kaffee und einen Tropfen Schnapps, bitte.*" Renate Ebers was going to protest, but she scurried away, tugging at her dress. If you're going to live forever, what harm can a little coffee and liquor do? I was surprised at the change in Georg. Flesh was creeping onto the bones, sculpting a different man, a more evidently prosperous one. Where before I had seen him as a water animal, sleek and streamlined, I now thought he resembled a house cat—perhaps a Siamese, for there was still the narrowness around the eyes and a glint in them that made me wary. He wore a sweater—one that buttoned down the front, and he looked less lost than he had in his stiff jackets, more domestic.

"Norman tells me that because of you the police now

have the woman who took my wife and Hugo." The conversational tone startled me.

"That's right," I said. "It's only a matter of time before they find the man who worked with her."

"The one who..."

"Well, we know he was the one who attacked me in the garage, and he probably was the one who killed them. Your wife and child."

He read the disapproval in my face and his eyes looked hurt. "This has been an ordeal for you, Mr. Jantarro."

"I tend to take things personally."

"Yes. Perhaps that is why you are so successful."

"Perhaps."

We sipped coffee and a colorless liquid that burned like napalm. The big window was fogged at the sides, framing the garden with hazy uncertainty, and in the center I could see bare trees standing still and suffering the rain.

"Some of them are beginning to bud." Georg nodded in the direction of my gaze.

"What?"

"The trees. They are beginning to bud and it is only November. The poor things think that spring is here. This is a funny time."

"The money," I said. "I haven't found any of the money. Maybe the cops will, when they pick up the man. I don't know."

"The money does not matter."

Postitch said, "I think Mr. Georg may be able to deduct it somehow." We both turned to him. "For t-t-taxes, you know."

"Yes," said Georg.

"It isn't over," I said. My head was buzzing and I felt a little dizzy. "This thing isn't finished yet."

"Well," said Georg, "there is the matter of this man. But you, yourself, said that the police will find him. After all, they have the woman. It seems sensible to leave it to them. Don't you agree?"

"Norman," I said, "here's a dollar." I held out the bill and he took it hesitantly, holding it by the edge.

"Are you all right?" asked Georg.

"Norman is a lawyer and now I have retained him—for advice I may need."

"Oh," said Postitch, "I see." He folded the bill in quarters and put it in his pocket. "This way," he said to Georg, "I c-c-can't testify against him." He thought for a second. "But Mr. G-G-G-Georg is not a lawyer." It was the first time I had heard him have trouble with his client's name.

"I don't think Mr. Georg will testify against me," I said.

"What is this all about?" Georg was a little petulant.

"Have you heard about the death of Frank Demeny?"

"Yes. Renate read it to me from the paper yesterday evening." He was very still and he spoke quickly.

"I was there when he died."

"Do you mean you . . ."

"No. The account in the papers is accurate as far as it goes. But I was there. I was there because he was the one behind this whole mess. He killed another nurse, Rose Morrow, a woman who worked with your wife."

Georg gave me a flash of annoyance. "But then it is surely over. If, as you say, Demeny was the monster behind this, then it is over because he is dead. I am not interested in how he died."

"He killed himself."

"Coward."

"Indeed. But it doesn't fit. There's something missing."

"Motive?" asked Postitch, who had drawn closer and was taking a real interest in all of this. I was probably his first criminal case. "Money. Th-that c-c-could be th-the m-m-motive."

"That and revenge," said Georg heavily. "He was a thief and a covetous man. I exposed him so."

"Money and revenge do fit," I admitted, "but there are things that bother me." The drink had done strange things to my head and I could see my objections as plainly as if

[191]

they were solid objects in the room with us. I had a harder time putting them into words. "Rose Morrow," I said, feeling my way. "Why did he kill Rose Morrow?"

Postitch was trying to think, and Georg didn't seem interested in my problem. "He was a crazy man," said Georg dismissively. "He probably tried to force his attentions on this Morrow and when she rejected him, he became enraged against her."

"*Crime passionnel,*" said Postitch suddenly. And then a moment later, "But that doesn't f-f-fit w-w-with th-the—"

"Carefully planned kidnapping. No, it doesn't. Or at least not so nicely as I'd like. And how did Demeny run into her? Through your wife?" I looked at Georg.

"It does not matter," he said firmly. "I am sorry about the Morrow woman. But I did not hire you to find out why she was killed. I hired you to find out who kidnapped and killed my family. And that you have done. I am grateful and want an end to it."

"And Demeny said, 'for the children.' When I asked him why, he said, 'for the children.'" I looked at Georg. "What was that all about? He has one kid, a young man. Who are the children?"

"For the last time, Mr. Jantarro, I do not care." His color was up and he had set his expression carefully. "You are finished with this assignment. Norman will pay you whatever your fee is."

I got to my feet. "When I wanted to quit because you were a Nazi, you were hell-bent on getting me to stay on the job. Now, with all the loose ends, you want me to quit. It's not the money, is it? Neither of us cares that much about money. There's something else, isn't there?"

Georg was staring out the window. "Drive him home, Norman. Drive him and pay him. But act no further for him if you wish to keep me as a client. Is that clear?"

Postitch looked upset. "It's all right," I told him, "I never take advice anyway."

When we got to my apartment house Postitch pulled up

and turned off the engine. "What will...you do?" He was making an effort to get it right.

"I don't know. I haven't decided yet," I told him. "Any ideas?"

He bumped a hand along the steering wheel. "Do...you think...G-G-Georg is a N-N-Nazi?"

"Maybe he was. I'm not sure. I'm not even sure it matters any more."

"Send me your bill, okay?"

"Sure."

I got out and walked to the door. He called after me. "Jantarro." He had the window down, and I went back a few paces. "I'm Jewish," he said. I nodded and he rolled up the window.

BAGATELLE. Something negligible, unpretentious. A trifle. Beethoven wrote one for the piano that lasts eight seconds the way that Stephen Bishop plays it. I lay on the couch and thought about how that great, roaring bear of a man could fashion such delicate, perfect jewels as the Bagatelles —the same man who would abruptly end a bout of improvisation by banging down the lid of the piano and bellowing with laughter. On and on they came, brief lives as full of character as any lived by men and women, serious, questioning, humorous, and self-contradictory. Each unfolded with its own integrity, each fulfilled itself, natural and spontaneous.

Together they made a community. Not an army or a nation, the way that a symphony does. But a small community where each individual could be heard and appreciated in relation to all the others. It was this smallness of scale that I needed, and as I listened I let myself believe that I could become one of the bagatelles.

I wouldn't push it, I promised myself. I'd let it unfold for once. I would simply have my existence and meet whatever came along. What I did could make no difference to what had already happened. To think otherwise would be to live my life backwards.

Simple themes, stately chords revolved in my mind. Demeny's blood was on my hands again. Georg's family, ash in the rain. Rose Morrow danced her dance once more before my sorry eyes. And I wondered. What would Harriett Gorton tell us after a few days in jail? Jail.

Without warning I heard the wheezing of the fat guard, the one who smelled rancid and had slippery hands. "Hold him still, hold him still," the fat one had kept saying. He was on my legs like all the weight in the world. The other one kneed me in the face and then smashed it down on the granite steps. They were wet, cool and very old, I remembered thinking.

"He's a big one." I was unable to struggle any longer. My shame was overwhelming me like a mountainous wave.

"Won't have no trouble finding it then."

"Jesus, keep him steady till I'm on."

"The fuck you think I'm doing?"

"Holy shit, he hit me. The sucker hit me."

"I got it. I got it."

"Look at him go. Ride 'em cowboy!"

"Hey, come back here with that!"

"Hurt him, Willie. Hurt him bad!"

"I got it. It's going to go. It's going to go. I broke it, man. I broke it. Can you fucking believe that? I broke it."

"They're freesias."

"Yes, I know." John Scott plucked at the blanket over his knees, adjusting it to satisfy some precise need that only he could feel. "They were your mother's favorite. She liked the heavy scent."

"I brought you these as well." I set the pile of books on the desk he had rigged up in the corner of the hospital room. "I don't know what you read. If you don't like them, tell me and I'll exchange them for what you want."

"I read anything," he said. He wheeled closer and grabbed at the topmost book. It was a new biography of Eric Blair—George Orwell—who had also fought in Spain. He grunted and flung it on the bed. The next was a recent history of the Communist party in America, and after a page or two it joined Blair on the bed. The final three he poked at, bending sideways to read their titles off the spines. On top was a reprint of Goethe's study of plants, with decent reproductions of his drawings; in the middle was Burton's *Anatomy of Melancholy*; and on the bottom was *The Cloud of Unknowing*, Progoff's modernization.

"Which pile is which?" I asked him.

"The new stuff I'll read tonight. The old stuff I'll reread slowly. Thanks."

There was an awkward silence as we each accepted the presence of the other and wondered what there was between us. "It was raining the last time too," I said.

"I didn't notice." He rubbed at his face. "You look like shit, boy."

"Yeah, I don't feel so hot."

"Are you in a jam?"

"Not really."

"Troubles detecting, or whatever it is you do?"

"I just finished a case," I said.

"Postpartum depression?"

"That's probably it."

He traced a pattern in the tartan on the blanket. "Nobody can help you, you know. Even your father, if he were alive, couldn't help you. I'm not saying that people can't help each other. They can and they do. But you're looking for something that nobody else has got, so it's not in their power to give it to you. And you've got to face the possibility that you'll live your life without what it is you want."

"Time," I said.

"How's that?"

"Time. The arrow of time. It only goes one way, from the past to the future, and it keeps hitting you in the back."

"Hell, no. Time goes both ways. Everything is rushing into the past faster than you can see. And into the future at the same pace. If the future has any meaning at all, you're moving into it. You, scratching your nose, that's the way you have of going a little distance into the future. And yet even as you scratched your nose you were making history, you were entering the past."

I laughed. "A nose for the future and a nose for the past. Two of me?"

"Why not?"

"Twins."

"Or mirrors, facing each other. Augustine's image for despair." He brought his hands together suddenly. "You like this metaphysical nonsense?"

"Sometimes it beats the physical nonsense."

"Go on," he said, "get out of here. Go do something."

He had the Blair biography in his hands and he was already reading when I got to the door.

There wasn't a bell so I pounded on the door and Dumbrowski answered in his underclothes. He stepped back when he saw the bottle, letting me in to his grubby room. He was already drunk. "I know you," he said. "You I know."

I unscrewed the cap and put the bottle down beside his dirty glass. An old radio was playing old music. I turned it off and looked for a place to sit. There was a pile of newspapers in one corner of the room that reached up to the ceiling, all of them yellowed and torn at the edges, and next to it there was a wooden chair. As I went to get it he said, "I wouldn't do that. Oh, no. That holds the world up. It is the great turtle on whose back we all depend. It is the testudinarious carapace from which we reach heaven. 'Testudinarious' means mottled with red, yellow, and black, as in the shell of a tortoise and the flags of our past. From 'testudo', a screen formed by overlapping shields of Roman soldiers, and at base the simple tortoise shell. Whence..." He flapped his hand and moved to fill his glass.

"Try saying 'testudinarious' after a few drinks. I dare you. Only a newspaper man could do that. Only a newspaper man would want to." He lifted the full glass to me and drank most of it.

"It's the flags that interest me," I said. I found another wooden chair and put it across the table from him. I wanted something between us.

"Mem-or-a-bil-i-a," he said. "Em ee em oh are..."

"The flags and the men who waved them."

"I remember you!" He pointed at me with the hand that held his glass and slopped some of the liquor out of it. "The chess player," he said before licking his hand.

"No games now," I said.

"Always games. Have to play."

"Tell me more about Fritz Georg."

"*Elsässer*," he said. "You know what Hitler said about the Alsatians?"

"I know. You told me. Now tell me about Georg."

He emptied more of the bottle into his glass and made a careful attempt to sit without spilling any. His yellow skin bulged out from under his T-shirt in great rolls that nauseated me. His stick legs looked oddly pathetic by contrast. "Georg," he said. "Well, now." He drank and closed his eyes.

"Wake up," I barked.

Slowly he raised his eyelids. "I *am* awake," he said. "Georg, he was small beer. Came with the Jews expelled from the Alsace in nineteen-forty, into Vichy. Only three thousand. He was part of the SEC, I guess. The *Sections d'Enquête et Contrôle.* The anti-Jewish police, you know? They couldn't do anything, really. Just push people around. Small beer, as I say. But when the Germans occupied all of France, he got transferred to Paris, made part of the regular police. Then he could do things. Made a lot of money. How he got it out, I don't know. Doesn't seem fair, really. I mean, there I was on the goddamn Eastern front eating snow and Russian bullets and I never even got my pay." He leaned forward for another drink and belched.

"One day of glory, he had. One day. I'm risking my life and he's pushing Jews around. One day."

"Tell me about it," I said.

"Sure you want to hear? Better have a drink. Always better with a drink."

"Tell me."

He closed his eyes again and set the glass against his chest. "Nineteen-forty-two, a big operation planned for July, middle of the month, fifteenth, sixteenth, seventeenth —in there. The word came from Berlin. Round up the Jews. They wanted twenty, maybe thirty thousand Jews scooped up in two days. *Vent printanier,* they called it. Spring Wind. The word got out. Some sympathetic police gave it to an underground Jewish newspaper. Some Jews ran or hid. Some killed themselves. And the Paris police got some of the rest. The cops herded the ones that couldn't get away in to the Velodrome d'Hiver. Seven thousand Jews in a place that shouldn't hold more than a thousand people for a sports event. Most of them were kids. Five days they were there. It got rough. Then they got shipped out to Drancy. It was a half-finished apartment complex near Paris—no water, no windows, no johns. It got rougher. From Drancy the trains went to Auschwitz. End of the line. Fritz Georg played a small role in making *Vent printanier* the modest success it was."

"How do you know?" I whispered.

Dumbrowski was drinking. "He told me," he said into his glass.

I couldn't understand. I didn't want to understand. "Why?" I heard myself say.

"Why did he do it? Why did he tell me? Why am I telling you? Why are you asking me?" He started to pour and then took the bottle by the neck and drank. "Because we are all of us shits. That is the reason, mister chessman. Any time you get asked why, it's a safe bet the right answer has to do with the essential excrementory nature of man. I have a coliform view of the world, mister chessman. I was a party member"—he lurched to his feet—"and a soldier. A fresh turd in uniform, a bolus in battle." He saluted with the bottle still in his hand, draining the last of the liquor down his neck and side.

This time I phoned her first. She sounded distracted. I could come over if I wanted.

She was wearing a sweat suit with a rolled cloth headband, no makeup on her face, and she had her hands in a bucket of water. The whole place smelled like pine oil. She told me where the Scotch was. She didn't want anything, but kept on cleaning and cleaning.

"Lois," I said after a bit, "what are you doing?"

"Seven maids with seven mops sweeping for half a year."

"Huh? Oh, *Alice in Wonderland*, right?"

She was standing on the arms of a chair swiping vigorously with a gray rag at the molding above the kitchen door. "Wrong. *Through the Looking Glass*," she said between grunts. She got down carefully, examined the rag, tut-tutted and knelt to rinse it in the bucket. "The Walrus asked the Carpenter if he supposed they could get it clear—the sand, that is." She wrung it out viciously and shuffled on her knees to attack the floor under the radiator beside her.

"What did he say?" I asked.

[200]

"Kenneth. You are illiterate. The Carpenter told the Walrus that there wasn't the ghost of a chance in hell."

"Oh," I said.

She stopped scrubbing and sat on the floor, facing me, arms wrapped around her drawn-up knees. I looked at my Scotch and I looked at her. She smiled kindly. "What's up?" So I told her about Demeny and about Gorton. I told her about Georg and my feeling unfinished. She listened by watching my eyes, and when I stopped she said, "So you're not finished yet."

"Trouble is, I can't see where to go with it."

"Home," she said.

"Huh?"

"Kenneth, honey, you are a dear but I've got work to do. You have to go home."

I nodded slowly. "I just thought you'd like to know," I said. "What happened."

"I'm grateful."

"But now go home?"

This time she nodded and I left.

24

THE NEXT MORNING I did what I usually do when a case is over. I hung around and waited for the phone to ring with another case. There was a string of junk on the answering machine, small stuff that I wouldn't want, by the sound of it. What I needed was a good one, an absorbing one, a case intriguing enough to take my mind off the raw ends of the Georg case.

I made out a bill to send to Postitch and then I put it in a drawer. If Dumbrowski had been telling the truth, I didn't want Georg's money—at least not yet. Maybe when things had healed over I would reconsider sending him the bill. I could always give the money to charity, I thought. And then I wondered about whether charities cared about tainted money. Even if time flowed in two directions, as John Scott had said, money couldn't do that; it could never buy back the lives that had been lost. If time is money, then Dr. Subtilis was wrong.

I went around and around in airy circles while I waited for something to happen. I thought about Georg's change in attitude. Less than a week before he had been pressuring me to stay on the case, and yesterday when I pushed him he threw me off it. Both times I had raised the Nazi point. First he didn't care and then he did. What had happened in the meantime? An old man's senile whim? Demeny's death? Was it that simple? Demeny's death had given him the satisfaction he was after and now he was finished with it. Or had he pushed me so that I would pin it on someone to take the heat off him? JoJo had said that the cops thought he was a Nazi; they had considered the possibility that he'd done it. But Demeny wasn't just someone I had picked out of a hat; he was the real thing. He blew away Rose Morrow. He had to be connected with the Georg killings. Otherwise it made no sense at all. And that left me where I started, ready to go around the circle one more time.

Then the phone rang. But it was only a guy from the cop shop telling me to come and get my stuff. At least it gave me something to do. The sun was out and it was still warm. That wouldn't last forever. So I walked the mile and a half from my place to the station, making an effort to smile at people and feel good about the weather.

I signed for it and opened the big plastic bag right there. I threw away the rags that were once a good suit of clothes and I pocketed everything else except my arm. As I counted the money, I remembered the cash I had left in the King Eddie's safe, and I decided to walk the two miles to fetch that. But first I stripped off my shirt and strapped on my plastic arm. The cop behind the property counter tried not to be too obvious about watching, but his eyes never left me for more than a second. I could see him touching his left hand as I put my jacket back on. Make him feel good all day.

At the King Eddie the manager proudly handed me a brown paper parcel after I had got my money out of the safe. In it were the clothes that Levine had given me, all neatly washed and pressed. The rip in the sleeve of the golf jacket had been mended, and pinned to the jeans was a hotel envelope with John Scott's name on it. In it was the piece of paper I had taken from Rose Morrow's apartment. Someone had unfolded it, and now next to my name I saw a list of women's names, maybe twenty of them. I smelled her perfume, unsure whether I was remembering or picking it up off the paper she once had touched. It hadn't just been me that she'd kept under the statue of the child; there had been a crowd of us there, back to back, unaware of how close we were. But why? I walked home thinking about her and the names of the women. Were they friends? Lovers? People she had meant me to talk to? Could it be that Rose Morrow had given me the new case I was looking for?

I poked around the freezer and found a chicken breast which I threw in the microwave. I was going to make a sauce for it, but at the last minute I decided that ketchup would do. The fridge door stood open for the five minutes it took me to realize that white wine and ketchup didn't go together, and I took a beer instead. I shivered as the motor kicked in. With the phone book on the table beside me, I pawed at the chicken and considered the list of women's names. There were twenty-five of them. The first name was Nancy Hobart. I scanned the others and couldn't find any order. Ann Montgomery followed Nancy; Eileen Grau followed her. Ann Timms, Bronwyn Butcher, Alicia Young, Darleen Klein, no rhyme, no reason.

Finding out where women live is no easy task. The phone book is useless. It's four or five to one, initials to names; and the names are men's names with the rare exception. You have to figure that women would feel freer to use their initials than their names, but even so, most of the letters would stand for their men rather than themselves. But there are lists prepared for advertisers and I knew a man who had one. I would phone him and have him trace the names. In the meanwhile I checked the rest of the women's names in the phone book just in case. The one before the last was Bettina Dehnka and there was only one Dehnka in the book, which made it seem like something worth trying.

"It's dane-ka," she said, "like the people from Denmark. Only that's not where we're from." The screen door was propped open on her hip, and she was smiling at me with that bright kindergarten-teacher smile that reveals infinite patience in the cause of instruction. From the house came the sound of a baby crying, and she replaced the smile with a concerned expression. "You'd better come in," she said, after checking my feet. "It's time for her afternoon bottle." She held the door for me, paused to let me wipe my shoes, and then gave me a little push into the living room. "We won't be a moment," she said.

The room was blue—the broadloom, the walls, the furniture, and even the two prints that hung over the couch. Elevator music insinuated itself into the air from some source I couldn't find. A book on something called 'parent effectiveness training' lay open on one of the easy chairs. I sat on the other one—carefully—and crossed my legs. Mr. and Mrs. Dehnka and baby Dehnka smiled down at me from a photograph on the mantlepiece. I smiled back and crossed my legs the other way.

"Ah, there you are." She came in carrying a pudgy infant who was sucking greedily on a bottle. "We get so many different pronunciations, you know. Donkey, dinka, denka." She sat on the couch and adjusted the baby and its bottle. "Now, what can I do for you?"

"My name is Jantarro," I said distinctly, and she nodded as if I'd got it right. "I'm a private investigator."

"Oh, dear," she said, dabbing at the baby's chin where milk had dribbled out. Then she smiled at me encouragingly.

"I'm investigating the deaths of two nurses from St. Albans Hospital, Helene Georg and Rose Morrow."

"Yes?"

"Did you know either of them?"

"No, I don't think so." She withdrew the bottle from the baby's mouth, checked the level of milk, and then hoisted the kid upright and over a shoulder, patting it on the back. That done, she returned to me with an expectant look.

I frowned. "That's curious, because I found your name on a list given to me by Rose Morrow's family. It came from her apartment. Have you been in a hospital recently or had any contact with nurses outside a hospital? In a club or association, say?"

"I don't use hospitals. Alexandra was born at home, weren't you, sweetie?" She screwed up her face in concentration. "You see, Mr. Jantarro"—she waited a fraction of a second to see if she'd remembered correctly—"you see, we feel that hospitals are sources of infection. In fact, most illness is, well, you could say, psychogenic—that is, brought about by the improper management of the stresses that modern life imposes. We're great believers in the power of mind over matter. Not that we're Christian Scientists or anything like that. We're Presbyterians, in fact. Although, I must say, there's probably a lot to whatever it is that they teach. It's just that, well, Carl's family has always been Presbyterian. A lot of people around here are." The baby burped and she looked to see if anything liquid had come up with the gas.

"Perhaps you met Miss Morrow in a completely different context, then."

She gave it some thought. "I doubt it. I know everybody I know. I mean, I can't think of anyone whose name I don't know who would put me on a list. Although it's possible."

"I have a photograph of Helene Georg and a newspaper

picture of Rose Morrow. Would you take a look?" I got up and gave her the pictures. The baby started to bounce and she put them down on the couch beside her. Then she shook her head at me.

"Sorry," she said. "I don't know them. I don't know *any* black people."

I put the pictures back in my pocket and took out the list. "Could I read you the rest of the names to see if anything rings a bell?"

"If it won't take very long," she said. "I'm afraid Alexandra's been naughty." She was holding the child almost at arm's length. I read her the list and she shook her head at each name. "Isn't that funny," she said, getting to her feet.

"You're the only Bettina Dehnka in town?" I asked.

"Oh, yes. I'd know any other Dehnka's."

"Might Mr. Dehnka have known either of the women?"

"Oh, no. We both know the same people."

JoJo stacked his french fries into a tower while he thought. I'd told him about what had happened since he'd brought my arm to the hospital and how I was planning to run down the list of names. His black eyes had watched my face closely as I talked, jumping all over my features, looking for whatever it is that he sees in people. When I finished, his broad face was expressionless, and his hands took up the motion from his eyes, darting here and there to arrange the food into shapes more to his liking. The tower of french fries was a good eight inches high by the time he spoke. "This Carpeneto thing, it's pretty serious. What are you going to do about it?"

"What's to do?" I didn't want to talk about that. I wanted to talk about the list, about the Georg case. "I can't run. I don't want to run." I shrugged. "He'll do whatever he'll do."

He looked up from his project, damned if he was going to show his worry but letting it leak through all the same. "Your funeral."

"My funeral." I felt my insides go light and bounce around. "Make me a good gravestone," I said as casually as I could.

"Don't do work on commission."

"An old piece, then. The big one with the cutouts on an angle. You were going to call it 'stairway to heaven' anyway."

"Arnie," he said, considering whether to pull the key french fry from the bottom of his tower.

"The cop?"

"Yeah."

"What about him?" I was still defensive about that whole thing and I must have showed it in my voice, because he leaned back in his seat and spread his shoulders slowly, displaying himself for my benefit.

"He's been back. He likes me." He rubbed a hand up the muscles of his arm. "Hell, he loves it."

"Good."

"Good for you, too."

"How's that?"

"He keeps telling me all sorts of stuff about the Georg investigation. He thinks it turns me on, I guess. Ever since the time—"

"—Yeah."

"Most of it's junk. This cop thinks this, that cop thinks that. Bottom line is they're stuck. The Gorton piece clammed up tight on them. They had a lottery to see who got to go to work on her, but Bench found out about it and there's a couple of guys working out in the 'burbs now."

"Nothing on her blond friend?"

"The one who took you in the garage?"

"Yeah, him."

"Arnie hasn't mentioned him. I guess he's still out there. Maybe that's why Gorton is keeping quiet. Figures he'll off her if she talks."

"Easy enough."

"I guess." He looked at my arm, the fake one. We both

knew that jail is the least safe place in the world. "That help you?" He pulled the tower down and ate one of the fries.

"Sort of. Not really. I still feel unfinished about it."

JoJo dumped some ketchup on his plate and began making patterns in it with his finger. "What's the problem?" he asked. "Demeny needs money and he likes the idea of getting it from Georg. Maybe he also wants a bang at his wife. He gets a hold of the Gorton woman and she ropes in a couple of other guys. They wait until the signs are right and bingo, everybody gets what he wants until you come along. Seems pretty tight to me."

"Except for three things. One, why take Hugo? Two, why kill Rose Morrow? Three, what's the list of names all about?"

JoJo stuck his finger in his mouth and sucked off the ketchup. "Hugo? Maybe he got in the way at the last moment. Maybe it was easier to let him come along for the ride. He could have been the bait for the woman. It could work a whole lot of ways." I wasn't buying it. It *could* have happened that way, but the rest of the thing had been so carefully planned that it didn't make sense to take the son as well as the wife.

"And Rose?"

"Blackmail," JoJo said. "She figured out what had happened and tried to put the squeeze on Demeny. So he killed her." He saw my face. "Okay, okay. How the hell do I know? You have any better ideas?"

"No," I said, "and that's what bugs me. That list, what about the list?"

"Jesus, Cagey, some things just don't make sense."

We ate for a while in silence. The corned beef sandwich was cold and the coffee was lukewarm. And I didn't want to admit it even to myself, but my head hurt. It wasn't as bad as it had been. It was just a dull ache, as if something heavy was riding around in my brainpan.

"Glenda back yet?" asked JoJo as we split the check.

"Still in sunny Florida."

"I don't know what you see in that woman." He was smiling.

"Long periods of nothing. Maybe that's what I like."

"What you need is a couple of days to relax. I've finished a piece and I'm going to take some time off. What say we go up to my uncle's place, hang out, maybe even go swimming if the weather keeps up? Do you good, you know."

"Thanks, JoJo. Some other time."

"Come on back to the studio. Smoke up a little."

I hesitated. "Okay. Only beer for me. I'm working."

25

BEFORE NOON the next morning I had a list with addresses for all of the women. There were two possibles for Nancy Hobart and for Ann Montgomery, three for Joan Murray, and just one for all the rest. I decided not to phone first. I wanted to look at them, and if they weren't home I'd only have wasted cab fare. I was going to play it straight, the way I had with Bettina Dehnka, at least until I had an idea how I might get better results. Taking all the names with only one address, I spent about half an hour with a map figuring out the best route, then I swallowed some aspirins and hailed a cab.

We fixed on fifty bucks up front for the first couple of hours, and by the time we got rolling, the aspirins were working, I was feeling good and the cabbie was humming to himself. I had that sense of expectancy that puts bubbles in my blood, that makes me feel my skin and like it.

At Darleen Klein's house the door was opened by a man who smelled of booze and expensive male perfume. He was wearing a bright yellow terrycloth bathrobe that had some sort of animal prancing beside a lapel like a character from the DT's. He hadn't shaved or bothered to comb his fashionably cut hair. "My name is Jantarro," I told him. "I'd like to speak to Darleen Klein."

"She's out back," he said, and shut the door.

"Out back" proved to be a marble-tiled deck sheltered by tall, well-manicured cedars. A fountain in the shape of a fish spewed a stream of water into a pool. Darleen was lying on a lounge chair in a bathing suit, a beach towel over her legs and her head set in one of those solar reflectors. She was twenty pounds overweight and the reflector caught her between the double chins. Her thin, black hair was plastered to her scalp with sweat that ran down over her broad features in shiny tracks. The top to her suit was on the marble beside her, and as her chest rose and fell her breasts swayed in and out. I backed up a few paces to the shelter of the side of the house, and then I called her name.

"Heard you the first time," she called back. "Come on in. The water's fine."

She was leaning forward, pretending to have difficulty capturing her breasts in the skimpy top. "My name's Jantarro. I'd like to talk to you for a couple of minutes if you don't mind. Your husband said you were back here."

"Do me up, honey. Then we'll see." She swung her legs off the lounger and presented me with the loose ties of her top.

"Sorry," I said, "I'm not too good at that sort of thing."

"Well, you can just fuck off, then, mister." She rapidly did up the ends and stood up to confront me, hands on hips and a flush on the points of her cheeks. Then she saw the plastic hand I was holding in front of me. "Jesus," she said, and her eyes got big. "I never saw one of those. You poor

[212]

baby." She looked up at my face with a prurient expression that I recognized. "Can I touch it?"

"I'm a private investigator," I said.

"It's private enough back here. Don't worry about Harold." She straddled the lounge chair, making a sour face at the back wall of the house. "The drink rotted off his nuts a long time ago. He doesn't even like to watch." She pushed out her lips. "Come," she said, patting the spot in front of where she was sitting. "Let's investigate."

"Mrs. Klein—"

"—Darleen."

"I'm investigating the death of two nurses from St. Albans. Helene Georg and Rose Morrow. Did you know either of them?" I handed her the pictures.

She took them and gave them a brief look, then put them down on the other side of the lounge chair. "What if I did?"

"Are you saying you knew them?"

I was still standing and she looked at me with narrowed eyes. "You're a real big guy," she said. "I like big guys. What do you say? There's enough here for you." She cupped her breasts and let them fall. I didn't know what to say. Or rather, I knew what I wanted to say but I didn't know how to say it without losing her completely. She had grabbed my plastic hand and was rubbing it with hers.

"I can't," I said.

"What do you mean you can't? We can go inside, if that's your problem."

"I can't," I said again, and I gestured vaguely in the direction of the prosthesis she was holding. "You know," I said. "The injury."

"Sweet Jesus," she shrieked, and she let go of my hand as if it were hot. Her eyes were fastened on my crotch. "You're kidding," she said.

"You get used to it."

"Not me. Not me never."

"So do me a favor. Tell me about those women." I pointed at the pictures on the marble.

"You look all right," she said. "Did they...you know, make a...you know?"

"The nurses, Darleen."

She was lost in a strange world. "What? Oh, yeah. Never saw the black one. But the other, she was there... when I had my baby." Her eyes started to narrow.

"Your baby?"

"Yeah, my baby. Say, what is this, anyway?"

"Mrs. Georg was your nurse."

"You'd better go," she said, pulling the towel around her shoulders. "Harold!" she called. "Haar-oold!"

"Please, Mrs. Klein. It's important."

She got clumsily to her feet and held the towel together. "Go on," she said with a slightly hysterical edge. "Beat it. You give me the creeps. Get out of here."

There was no one home at Alicia Young's address or at Cynthia Carver's either. The cabbie and I had lunch—coffee for me, and burger, large fries and a chocolate shake for him—and we talked about the weather and the economy. He seemed to think they were related. We settled on another fifty, and he was mine for the rest of the day. The first thing I had to understand, he told me as we headed for Ann Timms, was that it was no accident that you could have depressions in the atmosphere *and* in business.

We had worked our way down to Rosedale and the big houses of old money. The one that my paper said belonged to the Timms family was a lovely Georgian copy, three stories of perfectly proportioned windows and freshly painted white trim. I heard the sound of a piano as I got to the door and it stopped when I rang the bell. A young woman of about twenty-five answered the door. She was dressed in black, and her light brown hair was pulled back into a bun. Her features were small, almost delicate, and they were gathered a little too closely together on her face, making her look old-fashioned, Victorian.

I explained who I was and what I wanted. "You'd better come in," she said.

She led me into a dark room that was set up as a music room. A grand piano stood in the middle and a semicircle of chairs was under the window, each with a music stand in front of it. On a long oak table piles of scores threatened to slide into one another. "That was you playing the Chopin," I said.

"None other," she said with a little bow of her head.

"It was nice."

"Thank you. Do you play? Oh, no, I see that you don't. How clumsy of me. Please excuse me." She spoke in spurts, not hurried but pausing after a few words as if she had run out of energy. "Although, you know there is music, piano music written for one-handed people. I can't remember the name right now. I seem to recall it was a woman. She wrote it for her father. Or was it her husband? He was a concert pianist who had lost a hand in an accident." She stopped and put thin fingers over her mouth. "I've only made it worse, haven't I? I shall stop talking right now."

"That's all right," I told her. "I don't mind."

"You said something about nurses."

"I'm investigating the deaths of Helene Georg and Rose Morrow. I wonder if you knew them." Once more I took out the pictures and gave them to a woman on the list, but this time, when I saw her reaction, I knew I had found a woman who could explain it to me. She went a bright pink and turned her head abruptly away, as if the sight of the nurses offended her.

"You say they are dead?"

"Murdered in fact."

"Oh, my God." Both hands were at her mouth now and the pictures slid off her lap onto the floor.

"What is it, Mrs. Timms?" She kept her hands over her mouth and shook her head. I waited until the reaction had lessened and her hands fluttered down into her lap. "It's important, Mrs. Timms. I need to know how you met these women, what they mean to you."

She was trying hard not to cry, squeezing the muscles

around her eyes, holding in the tears that welled up inside. "What an evil thing," she said at last. Her head was still averted and I barely heard her. "I feel an evil...an evil... thread running through..." She sliced her fingertips up and down her stomach with a spastic, febrile motion.

"The murderers are dead themselves, Mrs. Timms. Dead or caught. There's no reason to be afraid. I'm only trying to discover why the nurses were killed."

Suddenly she was composed. Only her shining eyes betrayed the intensity of her feeling a moment earlier. "Oh, but you are quite wrong. The murderer is not dead. The murderer cannot die, and it is a mistake to think it can. The killer lives on in all of us." She smiled at me sweetly. "Didn't you know?"

I felt cold inside, disappointed and a little afraid of the strange woman in front of me. "How did you meet these women, Mrs. Timms?"

"I'm afraid I can't tell you that. It's far too personal."

"I see," was all I could say.

"I'm sure that you don't see, but it's kind of you to accept my decision."

In desperation I said, "Is there anything you'd like to say to the others?"

"The others?"

"Yes, the others on the list."

"I'm sorry, I'm not following you. What list?"

"The list of...women like you."

"There is such a list?" She was more fascinated than upset.

"Rose Morrow kept one."

"Goodness me, what a complicated thing this turned out to be." She sent a hand to her forehead and brushed at strands of hair that weren't there. "I don't know what you know, and you don't know what I know. Or is that just my mind playing tricks again. That's always the worst part, you know. The absolute inability to be certain." She sat with her back straight and her hands splayed in the air in

[216]

front of her, as if at any moment she might begin the Chopin piece again. "I know what you're trying to do to me," she said slowly, listening to herself, testing the words. "But it's all right. You are a good man." She put her hands calmly in her lap and looked straight at me. "I feel that about you. And I must trust someone. It's simply that I can't...I can't..."

She was so obviously in distress that I didn't have the heart to push her any more. There were others on the list. There was time. "Don't worry, Mrs. Timms. I'm sorry to have upset you. I'll go."

"Tell them to be proud," she said quickly. "The other women. Tell them I believe it is worth whatever it cost."

And then I understood. At that moment I knew how the list had been composed. I had no way to explain this rush of understanding. It simply came. And then a hundred questions grew in my mind where only one had been before. "What is his name?" I asked her.

"She. Her name is Ione. Isn't that a lovely name. Shall I tell you about her?"

"Yes, Mrs. Timms, I'd like that very much."

"It's Miss Timms, you know." She said it coyly, shyly. "But first I'll play for you."

Two pieces of a puzzle. Two parts that together should make a whole. I cupped my palms and imagined that one part lay in each, one on the rough, lined, elastic skin that sweated and pulsed and felt, and the other on the smooth, shiny, man-made polymer that we call a modern miracle. I brought them together and saw how they almost fit, rise and declivity, hollow and swelling. I wanted a clasp that was tighter.

I remembered the bodies of Hugo and Helene and the way they joined inextricably. And I shuddered. Perhaps if the whole had to be sewn together with Ann Timms's thread of evil, I would leave them separate. I pulled my hands apart. No. This thing was going to fit.

[217]

26

"Don't you take a break for lunch?" I caught Liz Brook at the nursing station on the pediatric ward. She was buried in a mound of battered aluminum clipboards and making furious notes with a well-chewed pencil.

"What, and ruin this waistline?" She put down the chart she was working on and stuck the pencil in her hair. "How are you, big boy?" she said.

I wagged a hand and said, "So so."

"I know what you mean." She reached for a cigarette and then remembered where she was, sticking it back in the pack. "I shouldn't be talking to you."

"Why's that?"

"You're the angel of death, I reckon. Or I am, and you're only my bird dog."

"It wasn't either of us, Liz. He would have killed her anyway."

"Yeah. I know that. I think." She sighed and grabbed the pack of cigarettes. "Come on," she said, getting up. "I've got ten minutes. You can buy me a sandwich in the lounge."

We talked about Rose Morrow and drank machine coffee from styrofoam cups. She chain-smoked and pecked at her chopped-egg sandwich as she told me what a good nurse Rose had been. I talked about her beauty and her dignity, and about the day she was killed. And then we were quiet together, letting the chatter of the other nurses fall on our retreat like the rain on the roof at night.

"You didn't come here to grieve," she said finally.

"No," I admitted, "I'm not ready to let go yet."

"Nothing dies for you, does it?"

"Not if I can help it."

"That should be my line." She butted her cigarette in the dregs of her coffee and it made a hissing sound. "You would have made a good pathologist."

"I want to know about Helene Georg's work history— here at St. Albans."

She frowned, trying to make the connection. "Well, she was here, in pediatrics for the last six months or so. Under me."

"And before that?"

"She moved around a lot. It's common. Some nurses fix on a practice and stay with it, others like to move around. Change is as good as a rest. That sort of thing."

"Where, Liz? Where exactly?"

"Well, I'm not sure—exactly. I'd have to check."

"Then check. It's important."

"Why, Jantarro? I need to know why before I feed you any more stuff."

"You won't trust me on this?"

"Should I?"

"There aren't going to be any more killings, if that's what

you're worried about." If I was right, there wouldn't be. And I thought I was right. I thought. Reluctantly, I showed her the list of names and sketched out for her my idea. She didn't like it. I could tell from the way her face shut down.

"You want me to do it now?"

"Could you?"

She was getting to her feet. Slowly. "This is it, though," she said.

"Promise."

"Bullshit," she said, leaving me there.

I got another coffee from the machine and flipped through the pages of *Health* magazine and *Cosmopolitan*. But mostly I tried to reassure myself that I was right. After Ann Timms it had been easier, because I knew how to play it, knew what questions to ask and how to get the answers. Three more women had been willing to talk and that was enough—more than enough to make sure about what had been going on. Now I needed to know who had been involved.

Liz was gone a long time and I started to worry that she had decided against helping me. I was on the point of going back to the ward when she came through the door, a grim expression on her face. "Something's wrong, Jantarro," she announced, and she lit a cigarette, fumbling with the Zippo. She took a big drag and spoke through the smoke. "Something's wrong."

I felt my heart sink. "What do you mean?"

She flung herself down into a chair and let her head fall back as far as her neck would take it. Then she brought it forward and groaned as she rolled the tension out of her shoulders. "The records are all fucked up. Both sets. There's a good eighteen months where the stuff on the screen looks like a bagful of scrabble letters. Garbage. I only found out because the girl in registry owes me. I sidled up to her real gentle like, because they get pretty uptight about patient records here." She had her cigarette in her mouth and it jumped around as she spoke.

"You went to patient records?"

"That's where you were going to send me next, wasn't it?"

"What about Helene's work record?"

"Oh, that. It's just what you figured. She worked at the fertility clinic before she came here and neonatal before that, and pediatrics before that. Two years in the clinic. Rose Morrow was there for eighteen months." She stopped and pinched the bridge of her nose. "Get me coffee, will you?" I brought her a cup and she sipped noisily for a minute.

Then she looked into the dark liquid as she continued. "See, when they set up the clinic they wanted the records to be extra secure. You can see how that might be. So they set up a separate data bank for the clinic—passwords, code words, special access numbers and all I don't know what. This girl owes me, like I said, so I remembered a couple of names from that list of yours and I got her to try them out. Well, shit. All around where they should have been was a wasteland. It's like they were at the center of a big explosion. Same thing with the regular hospital records.

"Jesus, Jantarro. They don't even know how it happened. They're keeping this so close to the chest it'll give them cancer. The official secret word is that there was a bad chip. Some gizmo farted when it should have burped. But that wasn't it, Jantarro, was it? This wasn't any computer error, was it?"

27

I NEEDED the blond man. He was the only player left in the game that I could get my hands on. As I sat around that evening with a box of crackers and a jar of peanut butter, I tried to work out where he might be. Brazil came to mind. And every place in the world where a quarter of a million might take you. In which case he was out of my reach.

They say in the bridge columns that if the only way the contract can be made is by assuming that the missing ace is on your right, then that's where the ace is. In this game it meant that he was still here in the city. Gorton seemed to think so too, because she had refused to talk, and the only reason that made any sense was her fear that he would kill her if she did.

But where? To look properly I'd need an army, and since

the cops weren't exactly at my beck and call, finding soldiers would be difficult. Then I had an idea that almost put
me off my hors d'oeuvres. That idea led to another one
which was a little more appetizing. Before I could reason
my way out of it, I grabbed the phone, looked up the
number and dialed.

"Funny you should call, Cagey." Benny the Fat was all
smoothness and warmth. "We were just discussing you,
my friend and I."

"Is that so?" A line of pain sprang up between the back
of my right eyeball and the nape of my neck, a hot wire that
fried all the neurons around it.

"Indeed it is. It seems, Cagey, that there is a dimension
to this...matter that we had not fully appreciated before."

"A dimension?" I was doing really well. Two witty
comebacks in under thirty seconds.

"Yes, Cagey. Perhaps it would be best if...my friend
were to discuss it with you. Or would you rather we talked
first about your business? It's your call, after all."

"I'll talk to your friend. I want his help."

"I see. Will you hold the line?"

"Mr. Jantarro? You remember me?"

"I remember you." Carpeneto.

"You got a list, I understand."

"A list?" The list of women? How could he have known
that, I wondered?

"Yeah. If you don't mind, I'd like to have it."

"Can I ask why?"

"You're not Italian, right? I mean, Jantarro could be an
Italian name but you're not."

"No, I'm not Italian. Is that important?"

"What kind of name is that? Spanish?"

"It's Basque. What does it matter?"

I heard him ask Benny, Basque? Basque? His voice
drifted back to the mouthpiece. *Che?...Ah, si...basco...*
"So you are *basco*, eh?" I didn't say anything. "You know
about families?"

[223]

"I know about families."

"Well, some people in my"—he asked Benny something and got an answer—"my extended family got involved with bad business, wrong business. That list, well, it could be embarrassing to them and then it would be embarrassing to me."

Bad business. Wrong business. I thought of the list of names. Which ones had they been? Could the old criminal have sentimental spots of morality? "I'll make you a deal," I said. I had called for a favor but now I had something to bargain with. "There's a man I want. He's tied up with the whole business. And I have an idea where he might be. Your people might have the precise information that could help me locate him. If you can find out where he is, you can have the list."

"Talk to Benito." He paused for a moment. "You find him, you... finish him?"

"I'll put him out of business." I knew what he wanted, but the deal was made in euphemisms that gave me room to move.

"Okay." He coughed a couple of times. Then he said the words I longed to hear. "We're even now."

The call came the following day just after three in the morning. It had been fairly easy. Benny had all the records on Demeny's properties and among them had been three warehouses in town. Two of them were rented and the third, the empty one, was staring me in the face. It was a squat, brown-painted brick structure that in the dark seemed full of sullen menace. Benny couldn't be sure but his people thought they had seen a light inside earlier in the evening. And once, when they had been tailing Demeny, he had lost them not too far from here. I shivered in the cold and crossed the street.

It wasn't a bad deal. Carpeneto got his list with the embarrassing names on it and I got to clean up the last of the mess. Benny had given me the obvious instructions about not copying the list, and we both knew that if a copy in Rose Morrow's handwriting showed up in public I was in more trouble than I could handle. The copy in my bank box, of course, was an insurance policy. Moreover, as Nino would say, if there was a killing tonight, it would be me and not Carpeneto's people who would have to face death or Bench. It wasn't a perfect deal. Things could go wrong from both sides. But it wasn't bad.

As I squeezed into the narrow passage that ran beside the warehouse, I saw that the building next door had a couple of plastic pink flamingoes in the front window. Someone had pasted moustaches onto their beaks. Artists had been moving into the warehouse district. The sight of the birds made me want to go home. If he was there now, I reasoned, he'd be there in the morning. And in the morning there would be light, traffic, people around. Life, instead of brown brick and plastic flamingoes.

I checked all the windows on the side. They were covered with steel mesh, just like the ones in the front. Further toward the back I ran into a pile of soft, smelly garbage. Small, furtive noises traveled away in the dark. I felt the corner of the building and turned.

At the back I risked a light, a thin pencil beam, crawling carefully up to the brickwork and along. One of the mesh cages had come loose and hung at the side of a basement window, a failed protector. I shut off the light before it hit glass, hunkered down beside the window and gave it some thought. If he was in the room on the other side of the window and if I went in that way, he could take me out and be back asleep inside of thirty seconds. But if he was in there and I used the light, he might see it and run.

I turned off the flashlight, put it right up against the glass as quietly as I could, clamped my fake hand on it, and with my good hand free, worked my gun out of its holster. I pushed the switch with the barrel of the gun. The beam shot through an empty room and came to a weak stop against a peeling brick wall. I worked it around. There was no one in the room.

Using tape and more patience than I thought I had, I cut my way through the glass and dropped into the room. For maybe five minutes I stood perfectly still, listening for something other than the pounding of my own blood. Then carrying the flashlight in the plastic hand and the gun in the good one, I started on my search of the building.

Ten rooms in the basement, five on each side of the hall. And ten jolts of adrenaline before I knew that apart from a damp mound of old cardboard boxes I was alone. Once I thought I heard music, but as I listened it went away. It was probably some kid driving by with his radio on too loud.

There was a brand-new metal fire door at the top of the stairs to the ground floor, and I pressed my nose against the tiny pane of reinforced glass, looking for a sign of my blond quarry. All I could see was the same thick darkness on the other side that I had just struggled through below. The handle turned noiselessly and the door swung easily on its hinges. I went through and to my right, feeling my way along the wall with the back of my gun hand.

Someone began to sing. I thought my heart had stopped forever. I would have shouted with fright if I hadn't been using all my air just to keep living. It was a high, keening sound coming from the room to the left of the stairs. And then I made out a melody. Rock-a-bye baby...on a tree top. It continued raggedly with no care for tune, the same nasal whine. When the bough breaks the cradle will fall. I turned and crept reluctantly toward the singer.

AND DOWN will come baby, cradle and all.

I crouched in the hall outside the dark room, rocking slightly on my heels and waiting for the song to continue. But there was only silence. I considered how I should do this. It could have been the blond man singing. Then again it could have been anybody. A kid stoned out of his mind. A drunk who had crawled in here somehow. I'd have to know before I used the gun. It felt cold and heavy in my hand, and I imagined I smelled the oil on it.

Light. I had to have light. The little flashlight wouldn't be much help now. It might take too long for me to see what I was dealing with. In each room I had investigated in the basement there had been a light switch just inside the door to the left. If the power was on, if there was a bulb in the socket, if the rooms up here were arranged the same way, if, if, if. What choice did I have? I had come this far. Was I going to slink downstairs and run away?

I stood up, pressed myself to the wall, face against the mildewed plaster, and inched forward until I felt the molding at the edge of the doorway. A creaking noise floated out of the room. I parked the gun in my fake hand, snaked the good one around the door frame and stroked the inside wall. The switch crawled into my hand. No more caution.

I flipped the switch and stepped into the floodlit room, grabbing my gun from my plastic hand. The blond man in the rocking chair blinked and blinked and said, "Oh, God." He had a blanket wrapped around him, and under that, on his lap, there was a large doll whose head peeped out, staring at me from under his chin. Against the far wall of the room there was a row of small cots with brightly colored mobiles hanging over them. The doll began to scream like a klaxon. There was a .45 automatic on the table beside the man, and I swept it to the floor with my left hand. I couldn't see the Magnum. The doll kept screaming like a machine going on and off and I saw it was a woman he was holding. Her head would dip down when she made the siren noise and jerk up again when she took in air. I still couldn't see the Magnum, and I was afraid it was with him under the blanket, ready to disembowel me from its hiding place.

I may have shouted something. The screams unnerved me. The man threw down the blanket and then reached for it again, his hands flapping like a spastic's. The woman was in his way and he tossed her off his lap to the floor. I shouted again. His arms flew high up into the air. He looked scared. The woman stopped screaming and scuttled to a corner where she curled herself up into a tight ball.

I backed around the room, keeping the gun pointed at him and kicking at things to see if the Magnum was covered. I felt like someone doing the dance of death, and I wasn't leading. There was a pile of dirty bedding over in one corner. I swiped at it savagely and on my third lunge the big gun skidded across the floorboards and banged up against the wall. My relief was so great that I started to shake and sweat.

The blond was letting his arms drop. "Do you a deal, man," he said. "Whatever you want. Money, man. Lots of it."

"On the floor," I yelled at him. "Get down on the floor."

"Aw, man."

"Do it!" My gun went off. In the small room the force of the explosion was intense. It rammed my head like a pile-driver and my ears sang with every sound at once. Both of us looked down at the scar on the floor that the bullet had made, an inch or two from his feet. He gave a little sigh and slowly came forward, first on to his knees and then on to his hands as well, sliding down like a reluctant convert to Islam. He started to make whimpering noises.

I sidled over to the pile of bedding, watching him intently all the while. I don't know what I expected him to be able to do from his position, but I wasn't going to take any chances at all. His eyes followed me, milky-blue marbles rolling on the floor. With my foot I began to kick things off the bed and into view in front of me. I was looking for a shirt, a belt—anything I could use to tie his hands. My mind was already worrying about how I was going to be able to do that with only one good hand, and I realized I might have to shoot or club him into unconsciousness.

"Don't hurt me," he was saying. "I'm just a kid. I'll be good. You'll see. Don't hurt me, please. Mama, mama. He's going to hurt me." Let him babble, I thought. My footwork had found nothing useful, and I decided I'd have to use my own belt. I brought my hands together at my waist and started the tricky business of teasing open the buckle while keeping the gun on him at the same time. "Help me, mama," he was whining. Some guys turn into mush when they're not in control.

[229]

I saw him start to rise. "Hey!" I yelled, and my gun shot out to arm's length.

"Hey yourself, man. Don't look now but little mama's come to baby's rescue. I'd let it fall, if I was you." I glanced where his eyes were pointing. The woman had the Magnum and was waving it unsteadily in my direction. I darted my eyes back to him and then back to the woman again. She was old, wrinkled like an apple doll. Something horrible had crept into my consciousness. Helene Georg. This doll figure, this old woman, the one he had been singing to was Helene Georg. I felt unreal, suspended outside the tableau instead of a figurine in it.

"Helene?" I asked with wonder.

"It's a stand-off, man. You kill me, she'll kill you for sure."

"Put it down, Helene," I said. "It's all over now." There wasn't a whole lot of conviction in my voice. She glided past me in a trance until she was standing next to him. He took the Magnum from her.

He held out his hand to me. "Give it here." I let him take my gun. He laughed and slashed at the side of my head with the muzzle. I fell to the floor and tried to stay afloat.

29

HE USED my own belt to tie my ankles together, and with the loose end he snared my good arm and drew it behind me toward my feet until I was bent in half. I was too groggy to resist. Then he put his heel on my left hand and bore down until it cracked. While this was going on Helene knelt beside me, cooing and murmuring nonsense as if I was a baby. She began to sing softly to me in German. With part of my mind I wondered why he hadn't killed me. The rest of me told me to mind my own business.

"Welcome to the nursery," he said. He had gone back to the rocking chair and now sat slumped in it, chin on his chest, looking at me with a faint smile on his mouth. "I call it the factory, but Helene doesn't like that, do you, babe?" He laughed and put his gun on the table next to him. "No, she doesn't like that at all. But hey, so what? I'm out of the business. I'm out of the whole business of giving a shit about what other people want." He stretched and scrubbed at his face.

"Turn him around so I can see him better," he said to Helene. "Turn him around, woman!" She pushed me until my face was pointing in his direction. Then perversely he got up suddenly and walked behind me. I felt my skin shrink. "I'm kind of bummed out," I heard him say. "These four o'clock feedings are really bumming me out, know what I mean?" He laughed. He was rustling through some stuff on the floor.

When he came back into my field of vision he had a plastic pill bottle in his hand. He shook it at me like a rattle. "Want some? A little meth. Do you up brown, man. Well, okay. Mind if I...?" He snapped the top off and shook out a few pills into the palm of his hand. Helene stopped singing and looked over to him. "Aw, no, mama. You *know* you shouldn't. You love it too much. You can't have what you like. That wouldn't be right." And he laughed again, still holding the pills in his palm.

"Please." It was the first word I had heard her say in English. She inched forward along the floor. "Please, Jack. I need them." Her voice was low, throaty.

"What would Frankie boy say? Frankie boy doesn't approve. And we wouldn't want to upset Frankie boy, would we? Hmmn?"

Demeny? Did he think Demeny was still alive? It could be, if he had been holed up here ever since the kidnapping. I hadn't seen a radio in the room, or a newspaper for that matter.

She was halfway to him now, groveling. "I don't like Frank. I like Jackie. Jackie takes care of me. Please, Jackie, please. I'm so tired." Her tone was that of a little girl.

"Well, mama, what can I say?" He winked at me over her head and deliberately put two pills into his mouth, one after the other. "Ummm good!" He looked at her. "I guess a couple won't hurt." He clenched the remaining pills in a

fist and held up a finger. "But first, got to pay the piper."
He pointed down at his crotch.

She scrabbled quickly across the remaining distance between them, clawed at the zip in his pants and then bent
hungrily between his legs. He winked at me once more,
and I closed my eyes. I tried to remember how in jail you
can ignore what you don't want to know about, how you
can cleave your life into cells and shut the doors on all but
the one you inhabit in the moment. I tried but I couldn't
really recall.

When he was finished he opened his fist and put the pills
in her mouth for her. She sighed and crawled off to the
bedding. "Should try it, man," he said to me with a grin.
"Only things that make waiting worthwhile." He took a
couple more himself.

"See, that's what we're doing. We're waiting. Because
I'm not going to lose it all by being in a hurry. I'm good at
waiting. Takes patience. Got to have patience." He was
feeling the meth, chopping his thoughts and spitting them
out in broken bits. "Look at me. I was an orderly, man.
Can you believe it? A fucking orderly. And now, now I'm
rolling in it. Megabucks. More on the way."

The rocking chair tipped back and forth faster and faster.
"Wait. See your chance. Pow! You jump on it. And wait
some more. That's nature's way. The big cats. All
crouched down now, waiting for Frank. Pow! Hey, Frank.
You want the lady? I want the money. *All* the money.
Pow! Old deal is off, new deal is on. I mean, why? I took
all the fucking risks. I made all the fucking decisions. Why
should he get half? Pow!"

He seemed to remember my existence. "Got any kids,
man? I don't figure you for kids. Me neither. But"—he
held up a hand—"but...they are the most precious thing
on earth." He giggled. "Valuable."

"How many?" My voice was hoarse. It sounded strange,
as if it didn't belong in the room. "How many did you
sell?"

He pretended to look surprised. "Hey, baby. Smart.

[233]

Thirty, maybe. Ten, fifteen grand a pop. Could have been more, could have been really big. All you need's a few whores. Bit of the good juice. Mix well. Don't even have any inventory costs. Not really. Yeah, could have been real big. But. But. You gotta have the right management. The right management. Not like crazy Frank. I'm done with him, man. I tell you? Done. Over. Finito. And crazy mama, here. Got to get me a better madam, a better PR person. She do give a good blow job, though. Think I'll keep her around. Got kind of stuck on her this last little while. Treats me real good. Should see her when she's all dolled up. She's something, man."

"What went wrong?" I had one thing to try, and I had to keep him talking while I worked it up in my head. "Sounds like a sweet deal to me."

"Aw, man. It was sweet. It surely was. Feature it. Here I am, an orderly. I'm tripping down the halls, pushing gurneys loaded with meat, wiping up puke, humping ugly old folks in and out of bed. Great job, man. Pow! I see little mama, here, helping herself to a dead baby. Can you believe it? A dead baby. Now, I say to myself, Jackie boy, what's a fine-looking broad like that want with a dead baby? I mean, there ain't a whole lot of things you can use them for. No, but there she is tippy-toeing out of the morgue with a dead baby wrapped up in a towel. Bam! I'm on her trail. Up we go. Up to the nursery. Mama nurse looks this way, mama nurse looks that way. No one but me, and I'm hard to see. Whip! Into the nursery and out again. It's the old switcheroo. Now a live baby I can see. Some folks like them. Not me. But some folks do. And I see where she's coming from, with the dead baby and all."

"How does Demeny fit in?" I heard Helene behind me making sharp mewing sounds and hiccupping. I imagined the speed working in her, making her restless.

"Yeah. How does he? That asshole. Standing me up. Been days now. But he'll be here. I got the woman. Think about it. I mean what kind of a cross can he pull? I got

[234]

her. See, that's how it was. I follow her, 'cause I'm on to something. I brace her with it. In the parking lot. She's high as a kite. Should have known then that she'd flip on me. Hops in her Merc and I follow her to Frank. Big pow-wow. Seems mama likes babies. Can't keep her hands off them. The model we got is not the first one off the production line. No, it's number two. She's gaga over babies, Frank is gaga over her, and me, I'm the man with the plan. They sold the first one, see? And now here's number two, like it was meant to be.

"Only we can't keep letting her play the switcheroo. Too risky, yessir. So Jackie boy—that's me—comes up with the plan. Let's. Make. Babies. Frank loves it. Oh, he does. Money. That's why. And it gives him a thrill to feed her with what she wants. Only he has to handle her, 'cause she's not all there. Keep those babies coming in, so she doesn't worry too much about the babies going out. Get her pumped up, she was good. Really was. But you know, she started to come apart at the end there. Flake right out.

"But that's cool, because—pow!—I'm right there with plan B."

"The kidnapping." It was coming around to where I hoped I could use it.

"Yup. The kidnapping." He looked at me carefully. "Should have killed you way back then, you know? But look how good it worked out. Now it's you and Demeny. Bang, bang. When he shows up. When he brings me his share of the money. Bang, bang. Always good to have a body in reserve." Now I knew what was planned for me. It had been tried once before.

"The way you killed Helene's real child." I said it loudly.

"Huh?"

"Hugo, remember him?" I punched his name.

"The dummy. What're you going to do, man? He was here when Plan B went down. Useful, though. She's dead, man, as far as everybody knows. Neat, huh? One real, one wrong. Hand is quicker than the eye."

[235]

Helene was near me, I could tell. I was sure I could feel her heat on my back. "Jack didn't kill Hugo," she said.

He looked up at her, startled. "Hey, mama. Ready for another hit? I'm ready."

She wandered into view, clutching a ragdoll to her breasts with folded arms and rocking jerkily from the waist, a mother with a difficult child. "You said you wouldn't kill Hugo." She looked down at me. "Hugo is safe. It's best for him not to be involved. I'm going to join him soon. Isn't that right, Jack?"

"He killed him," I said to the pinpoints of her eyes. "He killed him and poured gasoline into his body and burned him to a crisp." I wrenched my gaze around to him. "Smart plan, Jackie. Plan C. It really worked."

"Sure," he told me uncertainly. Then to Helene he said, "Piss off. I'm busy." He looked back and forth between us, getting angry. "I don't know!" he shouted. "How am I supposed to know? I always have to know everything."

"Hugo's body was mutilated," I said, "but not so badly that we couldn't tell who it was. I saw him. Dumped on railroad tracks. In the arms of a strange woman."

He got to his feet. "Shut up!" he shouted at me.

Helene stood over me. "Oh, Hugo," she said.

"You shut up too!"

"Poor Hugo."

"It's gonna work out! More money. More than I ever dreamed of!" He came toward her menacingly, as if he could force her to believe what he was saying.

"You lied to me about Hugo." In her voice was all the sadness in the world. And I saw that he would kill her too. I had wanted her angry, filled with rage, killing mad. But instead I had stolen from her the last treasured hope. She was empty, a hollow woman.

And then I saw, nursing at her breast, the Magnum. Squat and ugly beside the doll, it offered its black mouth to her, hungry beyond all possibility of feeding. "Hugo," she said to the blond man. And then she shot his head off.

[236]

30

"YOU might have trusted me." The asters in his garden were all dead, their petals dried and drooping from listless stems. The sun was hiding and a cold wind blew unhampered across the big lawn. I put my good hand in my pocket to keep it warm.

"I trusted you would find her." Georg had insisted we walk. We were in the middle of nowhere, headed vaguely in the direction of the bare maple tree.

"With the truth, old man, with the truth."

"That," he said simply, as if it were a small thing that had slipped his mind.

"Yes, that." He stopped to catch his breath and to poke at the ground with his stick. His skin had gone a sweaty gray, like putty, when I had told him about my early morning encounter with Helene and the blond man. His features all had slackened, and it seemed to me that his new-found health was wasting away even as I watched. The light in his eyes no longer glinted. It was only a small, fading glow, and I found myself able to imagine liking him.

"This Levine," he said. "He is...good? He will take care of her?" He had screwed up his face to look at me, anxiety pulling on his flesh like a puppet master.

I thought of how when I had brought Helene to him this morning Levine had said nothing, how he had listened with his eyes closed while I told him all that I knew, and how afterwards he had held out his hand to her, patient, gentle, still silent, until at last she had touched his fingers. Only then had he smiled. "Yes," I said to Georg. "Yes, he is good."

The tip of his stick traced a line in the grass and came to rest against his foot. "I love her, Mr. Jantarro." A gust of wind tore at him and drew water from his eyes. I shuddered in the cold and turned up my collar. The horror of that morning was still on me too tightly for his love to be a warming thought.

"Then why didn't you tell me what you knew?"

"I had to protect her." He hesitated and tried to shrug his brittle shoulders. "I have always...had to protect her."

"From herself?"

"In a way. That is true in a way. But she is not to blame. You must understand that she is not to blame. She has not the power to live as you or I, with reason, with restraint... with hope." He spoke in a rush of dry clicks and whispers, a late autumn breeze catching dead leaves and sticks. He plucked at my sleeve. "I must tell you."

"Now," I said. "When it is too late."

"It was always too late. Always and ever."

"Surely not."

"Her name was Helene Sohn," he whispered. "A Jew. She was born a Jew. In the Alsace. So you see, it was always too late. They swept her out into France. The Nazis swept them all out. She was a little girl, a girl of ten years old. Her hair in braids, I remember. Do you not think it was too late? Was there something she should have done?"

Abruptly he set off walking, head down against the wind, body lurching as he struggled to stay upright. I walked on his left, my good arm ready to catch him if he stumbled. Slowly he understood there was no place to run to; he shortened his steps, staggered a bit and came to a halt panting. When he spoke again, his voice was louder. "Our families knew each other. I was a grown man, a shopkeeper then. I hid in trees behind the station, watching as they put the Jews on the train. People from my village. People I knew. Not friends, and that was part of it. But all the same, people I knew. France will take them, I thought. We had been a part of France for all her life. She will be safe there, I thought. She and all the others. She will be safe." He was out of breath, his tiny chest heaving so hard that he swayed. I reached out to steady him, but he jerked his arm out of my way. He squared his shoulders and lifted his head. He was testifying, I realized, saying now what should have been said before.

"Afterwards," he called to the emptiness, "afterwards we were told what had happened. When they brought Helene back to my village—her village—we were told. She was the only one who came back. The only one who...who survived. Vichy didn't want them. Wrong class of Jew. Foreigners. Not really French. Many, many reasons. Many, many lives. She and her family were put into a camp from which they escaped—were allowed to escape. And they ran, hiding, eating roots, eating dirt. They were caught, of course, and because they had refused to stay in the camp they became criminal Jews. It was intended. They were taken to Paris and held there. It was intended."

He wiped at his brow and examined his hand as if it belonged to someone else. Beads of sweat stood out on his face, and what his hand didn't find was taken as I watched by the wind.

"Come inside," I said.

He brought his hands together. "Their release was arranged. It was. Some friendly police were willing to take bribes from underground Jewish organizations. They were to be free again, free to run and hide." He looked at me for a long moment. "One week later—one week!—all the Jews in Paris were rounded up and imprisoned in the Velodrome d'Hiver. Children too. Many, many children. Helene was one of these."

"*Vent printanier,*" I said. Spring wind.

"Yes," he hissed. "The Germans culled her out at Drancy, their pen for the Jews from Paris. She didn't die there. So many did. Children who didn't know their own names, who had little dog tags of wood around their necks with names cut into them. No one to care for them, no one to teach them...to kiss them. Helene. She was so... beautiful that they...took her for themselves. Took her for themselves and...used her." He held his stick at arm's length and beat at the air. It flew from his grasp and he kept striking out with his hands. I went to him and put my arm around his shoulders. He tried to shrug me off but I wouldn't let him. He began to sob.

"She was then twelve. When they let her go, when they were finished, their seed was in her. They took her soul. Their seed. My son. My only son." I folded him into me like a little boy and he cried and cried.

It started to snow, small flecks of ice at first, then quickly big, soft crystals. For a moment we stood together and shivered in the swirl of winter's coming, and then I led him into the house.

Renate Ebers wanted to put him to bed, but he fought her and so she relented and wrapped him in a blanket. He sat in his chair and watched the snow through his window on the garden. "You see," he said at one point, speaking softly into the silence, "she was unable to have more children." He blinked at me and turned away. "How white it is," he said. "How quickly it covers the earth." We drank Renate's tea, and when the whiteness became too much, we talked again.

"HE LIED," I said to JoJo.

"You sound surprised. Get many clients who don't?" He took a pull on his beer and licked the foam off his upper lip.

"Yeah, well, he lied about being a Nazi. You don't meet too many people who do that."

"I bet you could find a bunch who'd be willing to lie now about what they were then. You believe him?"

He was right, of course. I had no proof one way or the other. But something in my guts made me believe him, made me want to believe him—which is almost the same thing. "I guess I do," I said.

He floated the beer glass around on the wet patch on the table top and smiled at me. "Then you and him are both crazy. I mean, who in his right mind would want to pretend he was a Nazi?"

"It was Helene," I explained. "When she was brought back to the village, she was full of the party line. I guess she identified completely with her captors."

JoJo grunted. "That's easy to understand. A little kid, for God's sake."

"Well, it made life pretty much impossible for her, and she didn't have the sense or the ability to keep her head down. They shaved her hair off, they spat on her, called her every name in the book. Georg got so he couldn't stand it, as if the whole thing were starting all over again. I guess he was carrying a large burden of guilt about not having done anything in the first place. So he tried to talk to her, to get her to see what had happened to her and what was going to happen if she didn't cool out. Then he fell in love with her."

"Dum-da-dum-dum," said JoJo to the tune of the old Dragnet theme, shaking his head in mock disapproval.

"Look who's talking. You fall in love more often than... than..."

"More often than you do."

"Yeah. Well, he finally gave up trying to convert her and hit on the idea of going along with the thing, pretending to have been a Nazi. She ate it up, kept pressing him for details. The only stuff he really knew was what he had learned about her experiences, so he fed that back to her. Spring wind, the whole thing. After that, she would do pretty much what he told her. But she would brag about him to certain people they met, people she thought would approve. Made her feel protected, I guess. Married to a big-shot Nazi. That's why he told Dumbrowski."

JoJo pursed his lips. "Could be," he said thoughtfully. "I once told a guy I was straight so I could get him to hit on me with missionary zeal."

"It was probably a good thing for her. Maybe stopped her from going crazier than she did. It affirmed her actual experience."

"Levine talk."

[242]

"He's quite a guy. He had most of it figured out already —that something like this had happened to her—but he says that there may be some chance she can stay this side of complete withdrawal."

"Bench charge her?"

"No. He agrees that she wasn't in control of anything. They just manipulated her like a puppet. It was all this Avery guy, Jackie boy."

"Your blond man."

"The same."

"And Demeny, right?"

"Georg too, in his way. See, she stole a kid way back in the Alsace, before they came. After Hugo was born she discovered that he was retarded and that she couldn't have any more kids, and I guess it blew away the last of the props. So she just went out and took a kid. She was clumsy and she got found out, of course. But Georg smoothed things over. Misunderstanding. No harm meant. Quite the opposite, in fact. And, oh, here's a wad of money just to show that we really do care about the little tyke. That sort of thing, I suppose.

"Georg reined her in after that. Talked adoption, but she wouldn't hear of it. Got her trained as a nurse so she could deal with kids all the time. Then when it looked like it was coming apart again, he moved here. It worked for a bit. But then she snatched another kid right off the street. It was when Demeny was building their house and going ape over her. He saw her with the kid and she told him what she had done. She didn't see anything wrong with it, I guess. He freaked. He told her he'd take the kid back somehow, only he got this idea to give it to this mob friend of his who had been turned down for adoption. Certain favors were returned. At least, that's the way I figure it. Anyway, Georg learned about the baby and Demeny's involvement and he hit the roof."

"So that's what his fuss with Demeny was all about."

"He didn't steal stuff from the site, and Georg didn't lay

any charges. That's why the cops didn't have anything on him. Georg did come close to ruining him, though. But he couldn't press too hard because his own wife was involved. And so far she'd been lucky. The investigation never came anywhere near her."

JoJo swallowed the last of his beer and held up the empty bottle to signal for another. He scratched his head. "So why didn't he tell you all this when he hired you?"

"He says he never connected the baby stealing with the kidnapping."

"Bullshit."

"I don't know. He was geared up to see danger coming from one particular direction, and when it came from another he was taken by surprise. He's an old man, don't forget. And in a way he was right. Avery was an opportunist. He took Helene and Hugo as a second best, once the baby-selling business was wound up."

"Why did they stop it?"

"Couple of things, I guess. Rose Morrow had probably figured out what was going on. She had even made up a list of customers. According to the Gorton woman, Rose was brought in on the pretext that the whole thing was an underground, hassle-free maternity clinic for poor women. She helped out with the deliveries and basic health care. But I think she knew pretty much what was happening from the first. She was no dummy. She hung in there for Helene is my guess. And then there was Helene herself. At first Demeny and Avery sold to a couple more people in the mob. But they soon realized that Helene was a much better deal. She could get information from the fertility clinic about women who couldn't get pregnant or who didn't meet their guidelines. Then she would approach them with an offer. What with her being a nurse and a classy lady, it gave it all a veneer of respectability. But she started to come apart and they couldn't use her any more. Demeny didn't want to go back to using his mob connections, not

[244]

with the way things were going with his finances lately. So that was the end of the business. Then the kidnapping."

"Then you."

"Yes," I said, "then me." And a lot of death. I swirled the ice around in my empty Scotch glass.

JoJo pointed at it. "Another?"

"Six," I said. Avery, Demeny, Rose, Hugo, the unknown woman who had died in place of Helene, and some mobster with a wife named Teresa.

JoJo raised a dark eyebrow.

"We take our time, you help me—we can manage." I held up my empty glass.

I STOOD in the airport lounge straining to see the flying monsters feel their way with radar to the ground. You could hear them as they made their last approach, like thunder in the snow clouds. Then suddenly they were there, impossibly big and very vulnerable, moving far too slowly in the struggle to come home. I tensed at each abrupt appearance and exulted when the thrusters reversed and rattled the windows. Glenda was in the belly of one of these behemoths, but no one seemed to be able to tell me which one or when it would do its dance out there.

I reread the postcard from Lois. "I got away. The weather will be fine. Sometimes I will wish you were here. Always I will wish you safe." On the front there was a picture of one of those kids who jump off the cliffs in Acapulco for the amusement of tourists. His little body was arrow straight, poised halfway between the rock and the water, in the middle of nowhere. I let the card fall into the litter bin.

A short waiter in a red vest offered to bring me a drink. I thanked him but told him no. He hovered at my elbow for a minute, looking at the whipped snow with me. "It's okay," he said. "They do it all the time." He smiled at me and went back to work.

I thought about the list sitting in my safe deposit box. Benny the Fat had called to tell me how satisfied Carpeneto was. When he had finished telling me that Groper's trip to Atlantic City had been canceled, I hung up on him. I could have taken the list to Bench, but what good would it have done? Would the children's lives have been better? I had no way of knowing. Chances were that they would grow up to be just like everyone else, no matter what anybody did. Like you, Jantarro, I told myself, and like all the people reflected in the big, dark window in front of me.

Harriet Gorton was going to plead to attempted extortion. Bench figured she'd get three years, and be out in one. He had said he didn't like it any better than I did. But what could he do? He was only a cop. It didn't seem right, and yet at the same time it didn't seem to make much difference.

It was always this way with me. I couldn't let go easily, even when it was the end. The faces kept turning up in my mind's eye, the possibilities kept rearranging themselves, the past stayed fluid and I kept swimming in it. A 747 tiptoed to earth with a roar of triumph, and I shook myself. I looked once more at my reflection. Here I was, by myself, as I had been before Helene Georg. Two low-slung trucks raced by, right through my image, red lights flashing. They slithered under the flurries like sharks and sped out to the tarmac.

And before that there had been Glenda. I looked at my

watch. It was time to check with the airline once more. The waiter smiled reassuringly at me on my way out of the lounge. Home again, I thought.

I saw her before she saw me. She was walking briskly down the covered ramp with the other passengers, her head bent, watching her footing or maybe just beat. Her oval face was tanned, and against her white blouse it looked like the face of life itself. Her black hair bounced lightly as she stepped. It was good, very good to see her.

Her head came up and she saw me. She grinned. I took the bag she was carrying. "Hi," she said, and she put her hand up to touch my face.

"Did you win?" I asked her.

"You look tired. Around the eyes."

"Welcome home."

"You've been letting it get to you. I can tell." She slapped my cheek gently a couple of times.

I had to put the bag down to hold her right.